THE SPIDER'S WEB

THE SPIDER'S WEB

MARGARET COEL

THORNDIKE
CHIVERS

This Large Print edition is published by Thorndike Press, Waterville, Maine, USA and by AudioGO Ltd, Bath, England.

Thorndike Press, a part of Gale, Cengage Learning.

The text of this Large Print edition is unabridged.
Other aspects of the book may vary from the original edition.
Set in 16 pt. Plantin.

LIBRARY OF CONGRESS CATALOGING-IN-PUBLICATION DATA

Coel, Margaret, 1937–
    The spider's web / by Margaret Coel.
      p. cm. — (Thorndike Press large print core)
    "A Wind River mystery."
    ISBN-13: 978-1-4104-3331-2
    ISBN-10: 1-4104-3331-5
    1. O'Malley, John (Fictitious character)—Fiction. 2. Holden, Vicky (Fictitious character)—Fiction. 3. Fiancées—Crimes against—Fiction. 4. Serial murderers—Fiction. 5. Wind River Indian Reservation (Wyo.)—Fiction. 6. Arapaho Indians—Fiction. 7. Large type books. I. Title.
PS3553.O347S555 2011
813'.54—dc22   2010042437

BRITISH LIBRARY CATALOGUING-IN-PUBLICATION DATA AVAILABLE

Published in 2011 in the U.S. by arrangement with The Berkley Publishing Group, a member of Penguin Group (USA) Inc.
Published in 2011 in the U.K. by arrangement with the author.

U.K. Hardcover: 978 1 445 83620 1 (Chivers Large Print)
U.K. Softcover: 978 1 445 83621 8 (Camden Large Print)

Printed in the United States of America
1 2 3 4 5 6 7 15 14 13 12 11

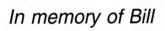

In memory of Bill

ACKNOWLEDGMENTS

I would like to thank Virginia Sutter, Ph.D., and Jim Sutter for generously advising me on the Arapaho Sun Dance. Merle Hass, director, Sky People Higher Education, was gracious and hospitable as always in making me welcome on the Wind River Reservation. Fred Walker in Boulder took the time to talk to me about various weapons and suggest the type that different characters would be likely to use. My nephew John Dix read over the baseball scenes and made helpful suggestions on what Father John should do and say. Father Tony Short, S.J., was kind enough to share some of his experiences as former pastor of St. Stephen's Mission on the Wind River Reservation. My friends Karen Gilleland, Beverly Carrigan, Sheila Carrigan, and Carl Schneider read the manuscript in various stages and offered wonderful and insightful comments, as did my husband, George,

7

always my first reader. And the late Bishop Bernard Sullivan, S.J., one of my first writing teachers, a wise and gentle man whose memory inspired the character of Bishop Harry Coughlin. My agent, Richard Henshaw, and my editor, Tom Colgan, were, as always, most helpful and encouraging.

Niatha: The Arapaho word for spider, a creature capable of mysterious things.

Also the word for white person.

1

A washed-out sky spread over the reservation, and darkness was coming on fast. The humps of the Wind River range loomed like dark smudges on the horizon. Ahead, the asphalt road crawled over the rises that passed for hills on the plains. Every now and then the truck's engine gave a raspy cough, as if it might spit out the dust churning beneath the wheels. The taste of dust drifted through the open windows.

Roseanne Birdwoman shifted her gaze between the two men in the front seat. Lionel Lookingglass, bent over the steering wheel, stiff black hair bristling from the ponytail that trailed down his white tee shirt past the knobs of his spine. Dwayne Hawk, riding shotgun, black hair cut short above the missing piece of his left ear. Gray lines of sweat ran around the thick neck of his red shirt. Outsiders, both of them. Showed up on the rez about a year ago. They were talking to each other now. Grunting noises lost in the wind, punctuated by nods and Dwayne's fist thumping the dashboard, nothing she needed to know about. The sour smells of beer and sweat cut through the dust.

She adjusted her legs in the cramped backseat and looked out at the brown plains rolling past. God, what had possessed her to come with these losers? She could have said no thanks, when the white truck skidded into the yard, barely missing the wood stoop. "Party time, Roseanne," Lionel had yelled. "Over at Berta's place. Get your ass out here."

Why had she gone outside? They would have driven off and forgotten about her. They would have found some other girl. But she had been so lonely. Sitting around the house when she wasn't dragging herself to work, listening for the phone to ring over the drunken rants of Aunt Martha or the loud snoring noises when she finally collapsed. Sometimes Roseanne would think the phone had rung. She would pick it up, her heart pounding, hoping it was Ned. But there would be only a buzzing noise. She had loneliness to thank for the fact she was now on her way to a stupid, drunken party.

The truck took a sharp right turn that sent

the rear end into a skid. Roseanne crashed against the door, aware of metal biting into her ribs. They were on a side road that had faded into a dirt washboard. The lights of Arapahoe twinkled in the dusk ahead.

"What are you doing?" She gripped the front seat and pulled herself forward.

Dwayne turned halfway around and gave her a raised-eyebrow look. "Don't you wanna see Ned?"

"You didn't say we were picking up Ned."

"He's back on the rez, ain't he? Time he got out and enjoyed himself." Dwayne was looking at her out of slanted eyes. "You still got the hots for him," he said.

"Shut up."

"She don't like getting dumped for no white girl," Lionel said. He was laughing under his breath. "No white girl's gonna take your man. We're gonna get him for you."

"Maybe the white girl don't wanna let him go," Dwayne said.

"We're gonna find out." Lionel curled even farther over the steering wheel. The truck bounced and skidded over the hard earth before the tires settled back into the tracks.

Then they were in Arapahoe, white frame houses and propane tanks passing outside, towels and sheets and blue jeans blowing on outdoor lines. Trucks and cars littered the dirt yards. She spotted a crumpled two-wheel bike with the seat jutting sideways. Another turn, and Lionel hit the brake. They slid to a stop a few inches from the corner of a yellowish, sun-bleached house. Lionel laid on the horn and stuck his head out the window. "Come on, Ned!"

Roseanne felt as if the wind had sucked all the air out of the cab. The dry, dusty smells of the plains mixed with the sour odor of beer made her stomach turn over. She thrust her head out the opened window away from the house and tried to lean into the wind that washed across her face. Lionel was still shouting, and now Dwayne had joined in, shouting and beating a fist on the passenger door that sent the truck into a rocking motion.

"He's not here," Roseanne heard herself say. "Let's go. I need a drink."

"Truck's here," Lionel said.

Roseanne pulled her head inside and looked at the house, the black truck parked next to it, the left reflector smashed, the bumper dented. The images spun like a whirlwind: last April, a cold evening, part rain, part snow, and snow banked along the roads, and the roads silvery with ice. They stopped at the convenience store at Ethete. Ned maneuvered the truck into a U-turn and backed toward the gas pumps. They'd had a couple of beers, and there was the hard bump and the squeal of metal against metal. Roseanne threw out both hands to brace herself against the dashboard.

"Sonofabitch!" Ned had slammed out of the truck and walked back. She had expected him to get back in, gun the engine, and squeal the hell out of there before somebody came running out of the store, but the next thing she knew, he was filling the tank. The sounds and smells of rushing gasoline drifted through the cab.

Ned had left for Jackson Hole not long afterward. "Construction projects going on there," he'd told her, "and they need electricians. I got a job right in the town of Jackson." She had nodded, trying to take it in through the dread building inside her because this was the end, she knew. He'd said he would send for her as soon as he got a place. Maybe they'd get married. Had he really said that, or had she imagined it? Heard what she wanted to hear? She couldn't remember now.

The truth was, Ned had wanted to go away for some time. Nothing had been going right, not the electrician's job in Lander, not his plans to save the down payment on a ranch. That was his dream, a ranch. He had to get back on track, or he was gonna choke to death, he said. She felt the same way, with the dead-end job stocking shelves at Walmart. So his going would be the chance for both of them, only he hadn't sent for her. When he came back a couple of weeks ago, she had gotten her hopes up again. They would be together, things would go on as before.

Then the white girl showed up.

"I'm gonna get him." Lionel opened the door, kicked it back, and jumped out. He was drunk, pushing himself off the hood and staggering toward the house, finally lurching for the railing and pulling himself up the wooden steps. Dwayne got out and staggered after him.

"Why don't we just get the hell outta here," Roseanne shouted. Then she pushed herself into the seat again and tried to ignore the tiny spark of hope firing inside her. Maybe the white girl had left. It made sense. She couldn't have felt at home in the house where Ned grew up, where his grandfather died. All those memories everywhere she turned. Arapahoe. Arapahoe. Ned might come to the party after all, but he would take his own truck. She would run over and jump in beside him. They could talk, put things back the way they used to be.

Lionel was shouting and pounding on the screened door that jumped and banged against the frame. The whole neighborhood was probably watching. Then Dwayne yanked open the door and pushed against the inside door. They fell into the house, bumping and clawing at each other. "Where the hell are you, Ned?" Lionel shouted.

"She's not gonna let him come," Roseanne said out loud. The sound of her own voice gave her a jolt of surprise. She realized that, for a while, she had let herself believe that the white girl was gone. But the truth had come roaring back. She was still inside with Ned.

Roseanne turned away from the house and stared out her window. The wind mowed down the tufts of wild grass that sprouted in the dirt yards. Her mouth had gone dry. She could have followed Ned, she was thinking. Nothing had stopped her from moving to Jackson Hole, finding another dead-end job, but Ned had promised to send for her. There was something important in that.

The screened door banged open. Lionel came out first, Dwayne pushing against him and both of them stumbling down the steps and plunging for the truck. Lionel turned the ignition as he slid behind the wheel. He gunned the motor and the truck jumped backward with Dwayne still righting himself on the passenger seat, struggling to pull the door shut. Then they pulled a U-turn and shot out onto the road.

"What's going on?" Roseanne leaned forward. "What happened in there?"

"We gotta get outta here," Lionel said. She could see the speedometer needle jiggling at fifty miles an hour as he sped down the bumpy dirt road. He took a sharp turn that flung the truck across a dirt yard, then wheeled out onto another hard-packed road, the truck rocking and dust ballooning along the sides.

"Tell me!" She pounded a fist into Lionel's shoulder. "Ned. What about Ned? Is he okay?"

"He's dead," Dwayne said, looking sideways at her.

She flung out her fist and connected with the hard curve of Dwayne's jaw. He flinched and rolled his head against the door frame. "Jesus," he said. "Take it easy."

"What do you mean?" She grabbed a fistful of Dwayne's shirt. "Tell me," she shouted.

"He's dead, Roseanne." This from Lionel,

gripping the steering wheel, peering down the ribbon of asphalt coming at them at eighty miles an hour. "Somebody tore up the place."

"He can't be dead," Roseanne said. "We have to go back. We have to help him."

"Don't you get it? There's no helping him. We gotta get away."

She was shivering with the tremors that had started in her legs and moved into her stomach and chest, and were now shooting into her arms. "Why?" someone said. It was the little voice she'd had as a child.

"Somebody shot him," Lionel said. "He's on the bed, got a hole the size of a baseball in his chest. White girl's dead, too, over in the corner."

Roseanne fumbled in her jeans pocket for her cell. "We have to call 911. They can help him."

She felt the hard edge of Dwayne's hand cut against her arm. The cell bounced across the floor. "We don't have nothing to do with this. The fed finds out we were at the house, what'd'ya think's gonna happen? Lionel and me ain't going back to prison, got it?"

"You sure the white girl's dead?" Lionel looked over at the man in the passenger seat.

"She was dead."

"Maybe I seen her move a little."

"You didn't see nothing."

"We've gotta get help." Roseanne leaned down and ran her hand over the scraped floor, groping for the phone. She wrapped her fingers around the warm plastic and flipped open the top.

"Shut that cell," Dwayne said. "You know what's good for you."

Roseanne did as he said. She was shaking so hard, the cell slid out of her hand and thudded back onto the floor. Her mind was blank now, a big, vacant space that Ned Windsong had once filled.

"We never went to the house." Dwayne leaned back, ropy forearm hanging over the seat, fist clenched. "You got that? Anybody asks, that's what you say. Long as we stick together, we're okay. There wasn't nobody around. Even if somebody seen us, they can't prove nothing. It'll be our word against theirs. You open your mouth, and you're gonna be like Ned."

Roseanne could feel herself nodding like a robot. The sobs had started, rising in her throat like hard rocks that she could neither swallow nor spit out. Dwayne was a blurred face in the background moving under water. What was before her was the image of Ned Windsong and a hole as big as a baseball in his dear chest.

2

The instant the truck topped the rise, Roseanne saw the lights flickering in the cottonwoods ahead. The booming noise grew louder, like the rumble of a train in the night. It was dark now, a few stars flickering in the black sky. She huddled in the backseat, afraid she would be sick. Ned might still be alive and she could do nothing — nothing — to help him. She could feel some part of herself already slipping away.

Lionel must have been standing on the gas pedal because they flew down the road. Then a sharp turn, and they bounced across the borrow ditch and the rutted earth and skidded to a stop halfway between the trucks parked in the trees and the blocklike house with blue siding. Shadowy figures darted around the vehicles, in and out of the streaks of light from the campfires. Sparks danced in the air like fireflies. A thumping, undulating wall of noise from a

CD player fell over the truck the instant Lionel cut off the ignition.

Nobody moved. Then Dwayne turned around, lights striping his face. "We come straight here from your place. Got it?"

Roseanne managed a nod. She was still pressing her palm against her mouth, fingers digging into her cheeks. Lionel pushed on the door handle and kicked the door open. She managed to open the back door and follow him outside, stomach churning, acid eating at the insides of her throat. A skinny guy with black braids and floppy arms lunged out of the shadows as Dwayne came around the hood.

"Where's Ned?" His voice boomed over the rift of drums. She recognized him the instant he stepped into a shaft of light. Mervin Oldman, Berta's nephew. He looked up to Ned. He had begged him not to move to Jackson Hole. Then he had gotten Berta to try to talk him out of it. "They'll eat you alive," Berta had told him. "Rich folks'll invite you to their big houses and show you off like some kind of artifact they stole outta a museum. Their own pet Indian. They'll piss you off pretty bad."

Ned had laughed. "I'm gonna be wiring the big houses, so nobody's gonna piss me off."

"Ain't he here?" Lionel said. Roseanne spun about and watched the lies creep like shadows across his face. The sour-breath smells of whiskey and beer wafted over her. "Had to wait on Roseanne here to get herself together. Figured Ned and his white girlfriend was already here."

"Haven't seen 'em yet." Mervin shrugged his thin shoulders and headed back into the trees.

Roseanne leaned against the side of the truck to get her balance, then started toward the house. She felt the hard pressure of Dwayne's hand on her arm, yanking her backward. "Where you think you're going?"

"I'm going to the bathroom." Roseanne tried to pull herself free, but his fingers were like a tourniquet compressing the muscles and bones in her arm. "Do I get your permission or do I pee on your boots?"

He gave her a shove at that. She felt the knobs of her spine hit the hard surface of the truck, and for an instant she thought her legs would give way. She pushed herself off the truck and started for the house as fast as she dared, aware of the crunch of sage and dried grass under her sneakers. The image of Ned floated ahead in the darkness.

She stumbled through the front door and

into a living room lit by a white rectangle of TV light. Shadowy bodies lay sprawled over the sofa and chairs and curled on the linoleum floor. The sound of grunts and snores mingled with the close smells of beer and whiskey and ketchup and stale food. The music outside sounded muffled and far away.

"Hey, Roseanne." A hand rose up and swiped at her as she picked her way through the prone bodies. "Wanna beer?"

She kept going. The kitchen was wedged in a corner between the dining area and the back door. An appliance light flooded the stove and spilled across the counter to the sink where a large, square-shaped woman was running water over a yellow plate, swiping at it with a brush.

"Berta?" Roseanne could hear the relief in her own voice. She had been hoping Berta would be here. Sometimes she left when Mervin threw a party and pretended the party wasn't going on. Mervin was her brother's boy, but he was her own now, she always said, ever since a drunk had run down her own boy in Riverton, and he was just thirteen, starting to live. Mervin had been about eleven, and from then on, he could do pretty much whatever he wanted, as far as Berta was concerned, just so long as he stayed alive.

Berta swung around, surprise flashing in her dark eyes. She was in her forties, with long black hair streaked with gray, caught in back by a beaded comb. A few strands spilled about her face. "Party too much for you?" she said, her eyes settling down.

"Something's happened." Roseanne glanced toward the living room, half-expecting Lionel or Dwayne to show up. The shaking started again, and she clasped her hands together to keep them from flying away.

"Yeah? What?" Berta threw her own look in the direction of the living room. "One of them jerks come on to you? They're all drunk." Disgust flared in her eyes, and she blinked it back. "I told Mervin, this is the last party. Trouble is, he'll just find a party somewheres else. Least I can keep an eye on him here."

"It's not that," Roseanne said. Keeping her voice low, she told about going to Ned's house. "Lionel and Dwayne came running outside. They said Ned was dead."

"Dead!"

"It can't be true." She was crying now, the words choking out of her. "They said he was shot in the chest. He might still be alive. He could be . . ."

"You call 911?"

"They wouldn't let me."

"What?"

"They don't want to get involved. They think the fed will try to pin it on them."

"Ned the only one there?"

Roseanne peered at the woman through the moisture in her eyes. Berta knew about the white girl; everybody knew. "The girl's there," she said. "Lionel said maybe she was moving."

"My God! We gotta report this." Berta grabbed a towel and began drying her hands.

"They'll kill me if they find out I called the police."

"Go on back to the party," Berta said. "Make sure they see you." She tossed the towel onto the counter, walked over to the phone, and lifted it off the hook.

Father John pressed down on the brake pedal and steered the old Toyota pickup toward the flashing red, blue, and yellow lights. He could see the dark uniforms of the Wind River Police milling about the vehicles parked in front of a small, blocklike house. Lights flared in the windows and the opened door. A couple of officers bumped into each other in the doorway.

He switched off the motor and got out. Nobody seemed to notice another pickup in the swirl of colored lights. The night was hot, as if all the heat of the day had compressed against the earth. The black sky was filled with stars. It was the first Tuesday in July, the Moon when the Buffalo Bellow, in the Arapaho Way of naming time. It could have been peaceful here. He wondered if that was ever the case.

Another murder on the reservation. How many murders had he been called out on in the ten years he had been at St. Francis Mission? More than he could count, and all the calls the same: "Sorry to bother you, Father. We got another dead body. I'm sure the family would appreciate . . ."

And he would go. John Aloysius O'Malley, Jesuit priest, Irishman from Boston, pastor of a mission church on the Wind River Reservation. Boston was so long ago — another life teaching American history in a Jesuit prep school and drinking himself senseless on the weekends — that he seldom thought about it. This was home now. The call from the dispatcher at the Wind River Police had come thirty minutes ago. A dead body in a house in Arapahoe. No positive ID, but the house was in the name of Ella Windsong. Father John's heart had gone into overdrive. The last he'd heard, Ned Windsong, Ella's nephew, had been staying at the house.

He realized he had been hoping there was some mistake, but this was the same house he had come to last year to anoint Ella's father, Albert, before he died. The Windsong family had been parishioners at St. Francis Mission longer than he had been here. He had known Ned since he was a kid, brown face and big teeth, playing first base on the Eagles baseball team. Ned had moved to Jackson Hole for a while, but then he'd come home. He'd stopped by the mission twice, something on his mind each time, Father John thought, but when he tried to ask, Ned had shrugged away the question. He was going to go into the Sun Dance, he said. Donald Little Robe, one of the elders, would sponsor him, be his spiritual grandfather, teach him the prayers and the rituals and help him catch up to the other dancers who had been preparing for most of the year. "I wanna get back to myself," Ned had told him.

"There you are, John." Ted Gianelli, the local FBI agent, emerged out of the shadows and colored lights. "Coroner's about to bag the body. You want to say a prayer first?"

Father John fell in beside the fed through

the tunnel of official vehicles — white Jeep, coroner's van, three or four white police cars with BIA Police on the sides. Homicide was a federal case, he knew, but the rez police would assist Gianelli in gathering evidence. "You have a positive ID?" he said.

"Not official." Gianelli was six foot two, a couple inches shorter than Father John, but there was bulk to the man — barrel-chested, thick-necked, and dark hair going to gray. Twenty-five years ago he had been tackling ballcarriers for the New England Patriots. He still looked as if he could stop a grizzly bear.

He stopped and Father John felt the pressure of a mitt-sized hand on his arm. "Girlfriend says it's Ned Windsong. Somebody shot him in the chest. We found the casing; looks like a .380 caliber. No weapon anywhere. I'm sorry, John. I know you knew the guy."

Father John nodded. The colored lights flashed in the blackness, the lights in the house glowed in the windows — a nightmare, he thought, something unreal and unholy.

"You sure you want to see him?"

"Yeah," Father John said. He took a moment before following Gianelli into the house, across the living room, and down a short hallway. The house had been ransacked — drawers pulled open, chairs tossed about, cushions and pillows and clothes scattered on the floor. Police officers and technicians and a man in a yellow jacket carrying a camera parted as they approached.

A couple of other technicians and a gray-haired man that Father John recognized as the Fremont County coroner huddled over the bed. The coroner looked around, then they all stepped back, and Father John walked over. Ned was in the middle, sheets and blankets bunched around his body. Eyes open, the frozen stare of a corpse; mouth half-open and rounded in surprise or, Father John thought, the beginning of a shout. Part of his plaid shirt looked sucked into the blood-crusted hole in his chest.

Father John leaned in close. Making the sign of the cross in the air over the young man's forehead, his mouth, his heart, he prayed out loud: "May God have mercy on your soul, Ned. May he take you to himself and show you his promise of everlasting life."

The room had gone quiet for a moment, then someone said, "Amen." There were small sounds of footsteps shuffling behind him. Father John stayed at the bedside, praying silently, a part of his mind screaming: This cannot be. Ned Windsong, full of life, stopping by the mission, two weeks ago? Then again last week? "How are the Eagles doing? Need an assistant coach?"

Father John had told him that he was welcome to help coach any time. But Ned hadn't come back.

It wasn't long afterward that the white girl had arrived.

"You said you talked to his girlfriend." Father John stepped back and looked at Gianelli.

The fed gave a short nod. "Ambulance took the girl to Riverton Memorial. She was roughed up pretty bad. Said two guys burst in here shouting for the money Ned owed them. Hit her a couple of times when she tried to get in the way. Pushed Ned into the bedroom and shot him. We found her on the floor in a fetal position." He nodded toward the empty space between the dresser and a chair.

"She called you?"

"No." Gianelli took a second before he went on. "She might've been unconscious. It was an anonymous call. Let's get outta here." He took hold of Father John's arm and steered him through the door and back down the hall into the living room. "Marcy

Morrison's her name," he said. "White girl, twenty-two, about five foot seven, blonde. Pretty enough. You ever heard of her?"

"Yeah, I've heard of her," Father John said. He could see the dark red pickup slowing through the tunnel of cottonwoods that led into the mission grounds and pulling around Circle Drive. Oklahoma plates. And the girl with blonde hair climbing out from behind the steering wheel. The white tee shirt that stopped above the top of her blue jeans, the three inches of exposed pink skin. "She came to the mission two weeks ago looking for Ned. Said he was her fiancé."

"Fiancé? And she didn't know where to find him?" Gianelli kept his eyes steady.

"Some misunderstanding," Father John said. "I told her I'd make inquiries, but she didn't come back." Father John took a moment. "She told me her name. She seemed to think I should know who she was."

"Do you?"

"No," he said.

3

Father John followed the red taillights ahead. Every once in a while a gust of wind pitched the old pickup off course. The night was silver in the moonlight, and black windows gaped in the houses set back from Plunkett Road. "You want to notify the family?" Gianelli had said. There was no one to notify except Ella, Ned's aunt. She had raised him from the age of two, after his mother died and his father took off for Denver or Oklahoma. Ned was a teenager when he heard that his father had been killed in a car wreck in Texas.

Officer Henders, an Arapaho who looked about twenty-five, had offered to come along, and Father John was grateful. It was the hardest part of his job, knocking on doors in the middle of the night, bearing unbearable news. One minute, everything the same for the family, and in the next minute, everything changed forever.

He followed the police car into a right turn across the borrow ditch and around the sagebrush that dotted the dirt yard. The image of Ned Windsong stretched on the bed, a hole in his chest, alternated with an image of the wide, trusting face of Ella. He had seen her two weeks ago when he'd stopped by Ned's house to tell him about Marcy Morrison. Ned wasn't home, so he had driven over to Ella's.

"Fiancé?" she had said, turning one ear toward him, as if she hadn't heard correctly. She had let out a peal of laughter. "So that's why he's been acting so weird. Gonna marry a white girl? Well, that's okay with me, long as it's okay with him. I'm gonna have a talk with that boy," she had said. "No sense in keeping secrets."

The house had looked normal then, gray siding, greenish roof, Ella's pickup nosed against the front stoop, a white propane tank anchoring the clothesline on the left side. Now the house looked desolate, like a vacant dwelling adrift on the silvery plains. Father John parked next to the police car and headed for the stoop, Officer Henders's boots scuffing the dirt behind him. He knocked on the door and wondered how many of these calls the young man waiting at the foot of the steps had made; it never got easier, he wanted to say.

The door opened a few inches. Ella peered around the edge, shadows playing over her face. Her black hair was sleep-mussed; the hem of her white robe snaked past the door. She was still in her forties, but she looked older, worn down. He saw the picture that she was seeing: the priest and the police-man, the solemn looks plastered on their faces, and everything about them, he was sure, screaming the news. He watched the puzzlement in her eyes give way to under-standing. She flung the door open wide. "No!" she screamed. She started back-pedaling across the living room, crashing against a lamp that thudded onto the floor, glancing off the back of a chair, until she was pressed up against the far wall. "No! No! No!"

Father John stepped inside, the officer behind him. He found a light switch on the wall that turned on a lamp next to the sofa. A dim circle of light fell over the rug in the middle of the room. "I'm sorry, Ella," he said. "We have very bad news."

But she knew that already, doubled over now, both hands clasped against her mouth. "Oh, God, no," she said, the words garbled in grief. "Not Ned. Tell me it's not Ned."

Father John walked over and placed an

arm around her shoulder. She was dead weight, leaning against him, her slippers skimming the surface of the rug as he led her to the sofa. She dropped onto the cushion, as if she had fallen from the ceiling. He sat down beside her and slipped his arm around her again, aware of Officer Henders standing just inside the door, gripping his cap against his stomach. "I'm sorry," Father John said again. "Ned was shot tonight."

She snapped her head sideways and looked at him. Hope flickered in her eyes.

"He's dead," Father John said.

She dropped her face into both hands and seemed to pull inward, gathering herself around a new reality. The house was quiet. He could hear the in and out of the officer's breath a few feet away, the faint creaking of boards and plaster in the night. "How did it happen," Ella said.

Father John told her that he was shot inside the house. "His fiancée said —"

"The white girl." Ella gave him another sideways look, than leaned into the back cushion. Her hands curled in her lap, small and red against the white robe.

"Two men burst into the house, shot Ned, and attacked the girl."

"She call the police?"

"The girl was unconscious," Officer Henders said. "Ambulance took her to Riverton Memorial. An anonymous call came in, and we're checking the phone records."

"Out of nowhere, two men bust through the front door and kill him?" Ella lifted both hands, then let them drop back into her lap. "Ned never hurt anybody. He came home to pledge the Sun Dance. He was working hard, learning the prayers and ritual, running and fasting, making himself strong. Those two men" — she brought her lips together in a thin line — "they took his life from him. They took everything. They should die themselves."

Father John took her hands into his. "Can we call someone?" he said.

"Call Ned." She was sobbing, great expulsions of breath that shook her body. "Ned looks after me. Ned comes when I need something."

Father John let the grief play out a moment. He could feel the pulse throbbing in her hands. Finally she said, "Marie and Jerry. My sister and her husband. Jerry looked after Ned, hired him and his buddies on the ranch, seen they stayed out of trouble. Call Marie and Jerry." She lifted a hand in the direction of the kitchen. "Number's on the pad by the phone."

"I'll make the call." Officer Henders crossed the living room in three steps and vanished through an arched doorway, as if he welcomed something to do. A column of light burst out of the kitchen and swept the shadows into the edges of the living room. There were beeping sounds as he tapped out the number, then the officer's voice, a muffled drone, low and serious.

"It's gonna be hard on 'em." Ella turned toward him. Her eyes were wide and reddened, tears beading in the corners. "They treated Ned like he was their own. Jerry's gonna want to know who did this. You know Jerry?"

Father John shook his head. He had met Marie a number of times when she came to the mission with Ella. Sodality luncheon or carry-in dinner. Once he had come across them wandering through the exhibits at the Arapaho Museum. Marie and Jerry Adams were ranchers, he remembered Ella saying. Owned a spread south of Lander. "Marry a white man and get yourself a big ranch." She had thrown her head back and laughed.

"I'll tell her you're on the way," the officer said. There was the click of the receiver dropped into the cradle. Out of the corner of his eye, Father John saw the officer walk past and resume his station at the front door. "Your sister and her husband should be here in about thirty minutes," he said.

"If Jerry finds the bastards that killed Ned," Ella said, "he'll wanna kill 'em."

Jerry Adams filled the doorway. Six foot tall with thick, rounded shoulders shoved inside a plaid shirt, a shaved head, prominent, red-veined nose and veiled eyes that surveyed everyone in the living room as Marie ran to the sofa and plopped down on the armrest next to her sister. Father John guessed the couple had made some phone calls, because the news had gone out on the moccasin telegraph. Ten minutes after Officer Henders had hung up, Janice and Lou Whiteman from down the road knocked on the door and traipsed inside, a shocked, half-awake look about them, Janice still in bedroom slippers, Lou tucking the tails of his shirt inside his belt. Then other neighbors and friends had flowed through the door, filling up the living room, bustling about the kitchen. The smells of fresh coffee drifted past the arched doorway. Officer Henders had left, and now it was just people gathered in grief, with Ella and her sister folded together, whispering and emitting little sobs, and people taking turns hovering over them, patting Ella's shoulders.

How many nights had he sat with the grieving in the years he had been at St. Francis Mission? Hardly the path he had laid out for himself all those years ago when he used to think about the future, as if the future were a physical object he could shape and control. He would be a professor, teaching American history in a New England college, close to his family in Boston, but not too close. A cottage on a quiet lane, a nice wife, and two or three kids. He hadn't seen himself as a priest. And yet it didn't just happen. At some point, he had understood there was something else for him. A ridiculous idea, the priesthood. He had fought it for years. Surely there was a mistake, the calling meant for someone else. But the understanding had remained. And finally he had accepted.

Here I am, Lord. He always liked Isaiah. *Send me.*

Jerry Adams shouldered his way past a group of people and planted himself in front of Ella. Father John got to his feet and waited while the man leaned over close and set both hands on the woman's shoulders. "You don't have to worry." He had a deep bass voice that seemed to rumble around his chest. "We're gonna take care of you. See you got everything you need, just like

Ned would've done. He was a good boy."

Ella nodded. She reached around and clasped one of the man's hands and held on for a moment, biting at her lower lip, blinking up at him through tear-bleared eyes. "I don't know who could've done it," she said.

"Don't you worry about that, either," he said. "Whoever done it is gonna pay, and that's a promise." He straightened up and turned to Father John. "You the mission priest?"

Father John gave his name and shook the man's hand. It was like placing his own hand inside a baseball mitt.

"I heard Ned used to come around and talk to you, that right?"

"Not so much lately," Father John said.

"I guess he had other things on his mind. You seen the body?"

Father John nodded.

"Ned ever talk about somebody wanting to kill him?"

Father John was quiet a moment. Jerry Adams had deep-set black eyes that bored into him, waiting for the answer. Father John looked away. He had sensed something off-balance in Ned after he got back from Jackson Hole, but he had never imagined it might be this — that someone wanted to kill him.

41

He locked eyes again with the man. "Ned was looking toward the future. He had pledged the Sun Dance."

Jerry Adams waved a hand between them. "Foolhardy thing, I told him. Takes a good year to prepare. He was cutting it short. You gonna run a marathon, you don't cut the training short, not if you want to cross the finish line. Three days and nights those dancers have to fast. Don't take any liquids, not even water. Have to learn all the ritual and prayers. I tried to tell him it wasn't for him, but Ned was stubborn." He threw a glance around the room, and fixed his gaze on two young men. "You seen any of Ned's friends yet?"

"Who do you mean?"

The man shrugged. "Guys he hung with before he went off to Jackson Hole? Lionel Lookingglass, Dwayne Hawk. Used to have an Arapaho girlfriend, Roseanne somebody."

"Roseanne Birdwoman," Ella said. "Always thought he was gonna marry her."

"I heard he planned to marry the girl he met in Jackson Hole," Father John said. Then he told Adams that the girl had been in the house. Two men had burst in, struck her, and killed Ned. They had ransacked the house.

Adams looked away. He slid his jaw sideways and kept his eyes on two elders settling themselves on straight-back chairs that someone had brought from the kitchen. A blue vein pulsed in the center of his forehead. Finally he looked back. "She can identify them?"

"Possibly," Father John said.

"What you say her name is?"

He hadn't said, Father John realized. "Ned didn't tell you about her?"

"Marcy Morrison," Ella said. She took a moment to blow into a wad of tissues. "Must've had his reasons for not telling folks about her."

"Where's she now?" Adams asked.

"Riverton hospital," Father John said. He watched the man for a couple of seconds — he'd met men like this before, sure of themselves, in control. He added, "The police have her under protection."

4

Dawn traced the eastern horizon when Father John parked adjacent to the portico with the lighted sign overhead that said Emergency in red letters. An ambulance stood under the portico, the rear doors hanging open. He caught a glimpse of the gurney and an array of small steel cabinets as he walked past. He let himself through the double-glass doors. Behind the counter on the right, a dark-haired woman with rimless glasses and narrow shoulders sat hunched over a computer screen. "Help you?" she said without looking up.

He was about to give his name when she jumped to her feet. "Oh, Father," she said. "Sorry I didn't realize it was you." She shot a glance toward the glass doors, and he looked around, half-expecting to see someone else coming in. The sky was getting lighter. The asphalt in the parking lot sparkled like diamonds. Except for a few vehicles, the lot was empty. "Don't get a lot of visitors this time of morning," she said. "You here about Marcy Morrison?"

Father John turned back. "How is she?"

"I'll get the nurse." The woman leaned over, picked up the phone, and pressed a key. "Father O'Malley's here," she said. She replaced the phone and gave him a sympathetic smile. "You knew the young man that got killed?"

He nodded. He had to blink at the contrasting images in front of his eyes: Ned, striding across the field in the middle of Circle Drive, waving and calling, "Hey, Father." Ned, lifeless on the blood-soaked bed.

The metal door on the far side of the entry swung open, and a woman in green scrubs, with sandy-colored hair, walked over. She was about thirty, he guessed, but something in her eyes made her seem older. "I'm Jan Peters," she said. She kept her hands at her sides. "I've been looking after Marcy Morrison."

"How is she?"

"Traumatized." She shook her head. "Fiancé murdered in front of her eyes. She has some bruises where she was struck, but fortunately her injuries are minor. No sexual assault." She drew in her lower lip and took a moment. "The two men were probably in a hurry to get away. She was lucky."

"May I see her?"

"Well," she said, lifting her eyes to the ceiling. "No visitors, except for family, as long as the killers are on the loose. There's an officer outside her door. But I'm sure we can make an exception for you, Father. The poor girl doesn't have any family in the area."

She swung around and headed toward the door she had come through. Father John followed her down a wide corridor paved with gray vinyl and lit with the white light of fluorescent ceiling bulbs. She wore foamy shoes that made a squishy noise on the vinyl. They turned past the plaque on the wall that said Rooms 100–110. Seated outside a closed door was a blue-uniformed police officer. He got to his feet as they approached.

"All right if Father O'Malley sees her?" the nurse said.

"Family only," the officer said. He gave a sideways nod toward the door. "You gotta be the next best thing."

The nurse ushered Father John into a room not much larger than a cubicle, like a thousand other hospital rooms he had visited: beige curtains pushed against the wall on either side of the narrow bed, plastic tubes and bottles dangling from a metal stand. Curled away from the door, a plastic tube jutting from the needle taped to her arm and a white sheet pulled to her shoulders, was Marcy Morrison.

There were things about the girl that Father John couldn't reconcile. She had seemed brittle and cocky and self-assured and a little spoiled the day she had driven into the mission. And something about her story not straight. Looking for her fiancé, a man who hadn't thought to mention that she existed and hadn't told her where he was.

She stirred and looked over one shoulder. Reddish-black bruises circled her eyes, and a long red bruise ran across one cheek. There was a flash of recognition in her eyes. "You heard what happened?" she said. Gone were the snap and bravado. Her voice was as thin as a child's.

"Yes," Father John said. "I'm very sorry, Marcy."

"He really loved me." She squinted at something across the room, some image she might have wanted to bring into focus. "We set our wedding date. July twenty-second. After the Sun Dance."

"Are there any family or friends you

would like me to call?"

"Daddy says he's gonna come." She turned her head and closed her eyes. "That'll be a first," she said, her voice muffled in the pillow.

Father John glanced at the nurse standing at the foot of the bed. "We called her father. He's coming from Oklahoma."

"I wanna go home." The girl's eyes sprung open. "They say I can't go anywhere. I gotta hang around and wait 'til they catch those two guys. I don't wanna stay here. I never want to see the rez again." She made a little motion, as if she wanted to sit up, then flopped back. "They're keeping me against my will," she said. "Tell 'em they can't do that. I have rights, you know."

"Listen." Father John tried for a soothing tone. "They could arrest the two men tonight. They'll want you to identify them, then you'll be able to go home."

"What if they don't get them tonight? What about tomorrow, or next week, or next month? Am I supposed to hang around with some guard watching me?"

"If you like, I can speak with the fed." Where would she stay, Father John was thinking. A motel in Riverton or Lander, someplace on the reservation? Whoever had killed Ned could come after her. "There's a guesthouse at the mission," he said. There were always parishioners coming and going. The minute a couple of strangers showed up, someone would spot them. "You could stay there until the men are arrested."

She stared at him wide-eyed, gratitude and incredulity moving in her expression. "Daddy'll get my pickup at Ned's place," she said, choking a little. "Soon's he gets here."

"The doctor will have to release her," the nurse said. "And there's the orders from the fed, and the guard . . ." She nodded at the door.

"I'll speak with the fed," he told her.

The fiery red sun lifted off the eastern horizon and the sky was streaked in reds, oranges, and pinks when Father John turned past the billboard that said St. Francis Mission and plunged through the shadows of the cottonwoods that lined the road. Tiredness dragged at his muscles. He could grab an hour or two of sleep before he started the day, he was thinking. Gianelli was probably doing the same; he would have spent most of the night at Ned's house. Homicide cases were often solved in the first hours, Father John had heard him say many times, when evidence was either collected or lost.

He would call the fed as soon as he got into the office.

He wasn't sure when he had first spotted the truck — a white Ford in the red-hued morning. Maybe out on Seventeen-Mile Road, several car-lengths behind. Or maybe the truck had been in the oncoming lane. Staring past the lower edge of the visor, he had missed it. But now it was diving through the shadows close behind, and he could make out the dark faces of two men, cowboy hats bobbing in the windshield. They looked young, in their twenties, most likely Arapaho. He kept an eye on the rearview mirror. They could be anybody. Any of dozens of young Indian men on the rez. Daily Mass wasn't scheduled for another hour. They hadn't come for Mass.

Father John turned left onto Circle Drive and drove toward the administration building. The residence was on the right, but there was no sense in bringing the visitors to the residence. Whatever they wanted, they could talk in his office. But the truck made a sharp turn and sped around the other side of the drive. The left side of the bed was damaged.

He pressed on the brake pedal, stopped in the gravel, and jumped out. The truck made another sharp right into the fields alongside the residence and kept going, bouncing across the baseball diamond that he and a group of kids had cleared that first summer at St. Francis, when he had decided to start a Little League baseball team. He knew baseball; he had pitched at Boston College. He could coach the team and keep the thirst away, he'd thought. He'd been wrong about that. Now he watched the pickup careening around the bases, churning up the field. Great swoops of brown dust rose about the tires.

He got back behind the steering wheel, rammed the gear into reverse, then forward, and went after the white truck, aware of the bed shimmying, the chain on the tailgate banging. He bounced along the dirt road that ran next to the outfield, parked close to what was left of third base and got out. The truck ripped across home plate and headed for first, rocking on the chassis, trailing clouds of dust.

"Hey!" Father John shouted, waving both arms. "Get out of here!"

The truck had swung left, and he realized it was turning toward him. He jumped toward the pickup, yanked open the door, and got inside. He rammed the gear into reverse and bounced backward as the truck sped past. The windows were down, and the driver banged a fist on the door. Then the truck ground to a stop, pulled a U-turn, and headed for him again.

In forward now, Father John floored the gas pedal and drove for home base. The old pickup balked and squealed over the dry earth. In the rearview mirror, the white truck was bending into another U-turn. Father John cut between the bleachers and home base and out onto the back road that connected the mission to Rendezvous Road. He could feel his heart pounding, the red heat of anger moving into his face. He skid to a stop, made another U-turn, and headed back to the mission. He could see the spire of the church swaying through the cotton-wood branches. They would not drive him away!

The diamond was on the right, the white truck carving a circle in the middle. Then it stopped, and Father John saw the rock fly out of the passenger window and land a few feet away. The truck started up again and sped toward the road he had taken. Then it spun left onto Rendezvous Road, black exhaust floating through the dust clouds.

Father John got out and walked across the diamond. The rock was the size of a base-ball, and clasped to it with a rubber band was a piece of paper. He picked it up and pulled out the paper.

Smeared across the middle in thick black marker were the words *Stay out of it.*

5

Roseanne listened to the engine outside. A large vehicle, truck or SUV, turned off the road and ground across the hard ruts in the dirt yard. She pulled her knees into her chest and pressed herself into the corner. The walls bit at her spine; the chill of the linoleum floor ran through her. She had gone outside for a while last night, had a couple of beers, made sure Dwayne and Lionel saw her. A robot, going through the motions, couples dancing under the cottonwoods, moonlight flitting in the branches and the hard beats of music pounding in her ears, but in her mind she was still at Ned's house, watching the front door, knowing something was wrong, feeling the wrongness even before Lionel and Dwayne had come running out. After a while she had slipped through the party back into the house and found the corner in the bedroom.

She had spent the rest of the night there,

listening to footsteps coming and going, the slurred, laughing voices, the gagging and retching in the bathroom, her thoughts on Ned. The ambulance might have gotten to the house in time. He could be alive. God, let it be. The shivering was like death coming over her. Her tee shirt was smashed against her chest with perspiration. She had wanted to cry. She should cry for Ned, but she had no energy for it, as if the thought of his death had sucked the life out of her. The window across the room glowed red with the dawn when she finally heard the sounds of the party winding down, cars and pickups pulling out of the yard. The sun was blasting the window now, and she could hear Berta snoring on the bed.

The engine outside switched off. A door slammed, footsteps scuffed the dirt and pounded up the steps. The loud knocking on the front door sent tremors through the floor. Roseanne managed to get to her feet. Her legs felt wobbly, and she had to steady herself against the wall a moment before she stumbled to the window. A white SUV was parked a few feet from the house. The knocking came again.

She leaned over the bed and shook Berta's shoulder. "The fed's here," she said. And now she would know the truth. The fed would tell her if Ned was alive.

"What?" Berta shook away, pulled a gray blanket over her shoulders and flopped to the other side of the bed.

"Berta, wake up," Roseanne said. "The fed's here about last night."

The woman sprang upward. She turned to Roseanne. "Answer the door," she said. "Let him in, but don't say anything 'til I get there. Where's Mervin?"

Roseanne said she didn't know.

"Who else is in the house?"

Roseanne shrugged. It could be anyone, she was thinking. Dwayne and Lionel could have crashed in one of the bedrooms. There could be people sleeping all over the place, wherever they had fallen down.

The knocking sounded again, hard and rapid with impatience.

Roseanne made her way around the bed and down the hallway. Combing her fingers through her hair, wiping at her eyes. Across the living room, past Mervin sprawled on the sofa, his face crunched into a pillow, a guttural noise spitting from his mouth. The knock, knock, knock came again.

She floated toward the sound, managed to grip the knob and pulled the door open. She knew who the man was before he held up the wallet with the badge and said that he was Special Agent Ted Gianelli. He had big hands and thick fingers. She had seen him driving by on the rez once and someone — Ned, she remembered — had said, "There goes the local FBI. Don't get in his way."

She was in his way now, because it was obvious he intended to come inside. "I'd like to talk to you and whoever else is in the house," he said. She hung on to the door. He could push past her, if he wanted. He looked too big for the stoop — boots planted near the sides, shoulders squared, a cowboy hat tipped back. He blocked the sun.

Roseanne moved backward, holding on to the door as he walked past, afraid she might crumble to the floor. She knew the truth now. Something in the fed's manner — serious, official, and worn-looking, as if he carried a heavy burden.

"Looks like you had quite a party last night," he said, tossing a glance backward.

Roseanne looked past him. Beer bottles and disposable cups littered the yard; a beer keg lay on its side. Little trails of smoke rose out of the smoldering campfires. Tracks and ruts crisscrossed the dirt.

"What's your name?" he said.

"Roseanne Birdwoman." Her voice sounded unfamiliar, as if a stranger had spoken her name.

"Who's that?" Gianelli nodded toward Mervin who had propped himself up a little and was staring past half-closed eyelids.

"Mervin Oldman," Roseanne said.

"Time to wake up, Mervin." The fed walked over and held the wallet about a foot from Mervin's face. "I have some questions about last night. Anybody else here?" he said, turning back to Roseanne.

"I'm here," Berta called. She was still halfway down the hall. She had stuffed herself into a white tee shirt and blue jeans that looked too small. There was a roll of fat above the top of her jeans. She padded into the living room in bare feet. "Berta Oldman."

"This your place?"

Berta shrugged. "Sometimes."

Roseanne watched the white man's face. It was hard to make him understand. Probably the house belonged to Mervin now, but she wasn't sure. It had been his father's, but his father was dead. And Mervin had a couple of brothers who lived in Colorado, so maybe it belonged to them, too. But Mervin was here most of the time, and Berta was here to look after Mervin. And Roseanne had found herself coming here more and more often after Ned had gone to

58

Jackson Hole. All those days and weeks waiting for him to call and ask her to come. And the call never coming. Berta was the only one she could talk to.

"Get anybody else out here," Gianelli said.

Berta shifted around and went back down the hall. Roseanne could see her leaning past the doors to another bedroom and the bathroom. She padded back. "Just us," she said.

The fed retraced her steps down the hall, looking past the doorways. Then he walked back. "You know Ned Windsong?" he said, glancing from Berta to Roseanne and finally Mervin, who had set both feet on the linoleum and was wide-eyed, a pink blanket thrown over his shoulders like a cape.

"Yeah, we know Ned," Mervin said. "He okay?"

"He was shot to death last night."

Roseanne felt as if she were spinning about, doing the grass dance at a powwow, her feet lightly tapping the floor, barely connecting. She realized it was the room that had started spinning. She threw herself toward a wood chair and dropped onto the hard surface.

"You all right?" The fed took a step toward her, one arm extended, ready to hold her up.

She gripped the sides of the chair. "Why didn't they save him?" Oh, God. She should have called 911 right away. Jumped out of the pickup and dialed the number. So what if Dwayne and Lionel had tried to stop her? If they had killed her? What did it matter?

"He was dead when the ambulance arrived," Gianelli said. "Did you call 911?"

Roseanne shook her head. He could see through her, she thought. See that she should have called. She sank back against the chair. The room had gone blurry at the edges; Berta, behind the sofa, and Mervin, standing up, clutching the blanket around his naked shoulders.

"Somebody made the call from this house." Gianelli turned toward the sofa. "Who was it?"

"Could be anyone," Berta said. "Fifty, sixty people around here last night."

"Where's the phone?"

Berta nodded toward the kitchen.

"Somebody went to the kitchen and used the phone," Gianelli went on. "Anybody go into the kitchen?"

"Lots of 'em," Berta said. "Looking for beer or something to eat."

"How long were you here?"

"I been staying here."

"What about you?" He nodded at Mervin.

60

"Same."

"So you were both here last night. You must have seen someone use the phone."

Berta shook her head. "There was a party going on. People coming and going. You think we're some kind of policemen? We don't watch everybody."

"What about you?"

Roseanne forced herself to look up into the man's white face. He had black hair streaked with gray, and she wondered if he had kids. There was a kindness that protruded through the tough exterior.

"Roseanne come with the others after the party got going," Mervin said. "Around eight o'clock, I'd say."

Gianelli turned back and waited. A second passed before Mervin said that he noticed the time because he was wondering when they were going to show up.

"They?"

"Ned. Dwayne Hawk. Lionel Looking-glass. Some girls. Party never gets going 'til they get here."

"You're saying Ned was here at eight o'clock last night?"

"Ned never come." Mervin shook his head. "Dwayne and Lionel and Roseanne come about then. Ain't that right, Roseanne?" he said, a pleading tone in his voice.

61

Roseanne saw the look that Berta threw along the sofa. Don't say anything, Berta had told her. You don't have to say anything.

The fed turned to her. "Ned was supposed to be with you?"

Roseanne shook her head. "I haven't seen him for a while." Two weeks ago — another lifetime, another world — she was thinking. She saw herself standing on the stoop, rapping at the door. She had heard that Ned was back from Jackson Hole. It was all over the moccasin telegraph, how he moved back into his grandfather's house. She had waited two or three days, sure that he would call, before she had gone to his house.

"Ned never showed up," Mervin said. "That's all I know."

"What about you?" Roseanne watched the fed's boots moving in her direction. "Ned a friend of yours?"

"He was friends with lots of people." Berta's voice came from behind the sofa.

"How good a friend?"

The tears started then. She dipped her face into both hands, feeling the warm moisture seep between her fingers. She could sense the room freezing into place. From far away came the sounds of breathing. She saw herself back on the stoop outside Ned's house. She had knocked two or three times before the door opened and he stood in front of her. He looked thin and tired. She was struck by the worry lines that creased his forehead. She hadn't remembered them. "Hi," she said, and her voice had sounded weak and scared. She had pushed on. "I just wanted to see how you're doing."

He had walked outside and sat down on the top step. He was still handsome, the curve of his cheekbones and the black eyes set back under the hood of his brow, strands of black hair brushing the top of his ears. She had sat down beside him, conscious of the warmth of his body close to hers, the slender, graceful curve of his fingers. "I was gonna call you," he said. "Soon's I got things straightened out."

She had asked him what things, and he had shrugged and told her that he had pledged the Sun Dance. It was late, he knew. The other dancers had been preparing for most of the year, but Donald Little Robe had agreed to be his spiritual grandfather and help him get ready. "Everything's gonna be fine," he said. "I'm gonna get the strength I need."

"I thought you didn't call because it was over with us," she had said.

"Things got complicated." He turned

toward her then, and she had seen the look in his eyes — a plea of some kind, for forgiveness or understanding. It had confused her. She could almost see herself blushing. She would forgive him anything. Surely he knew that.

"I'm just gonna get through the Sun Dance," he said. "Start a new life. Everything'll be okay."

What things? she had wanted to say. But the look in his eyes had stopped her. She had gotten to her feet, made her way back to her car and driven out of the yard, knowing it was over, everything crashing down around her.

The boots came closer, and she could feel the white man leaning toward her.

"Your friend was murdered," he said. "If you know anything about it, you had better tell me. You could be charged with withholding information in an investigation, maybe even assisting in a homicide."

"I loved Ned," she said, lifting her face and looking past the fed at Berta.

"I made the call," Berta said.

Gianelli glanced around, then looked back at Roseanne. "Tell me the rest of it."

She swallowed hard. Her throat had turned to sandpaper. "I didn't know we were gonna pick him up," she said. Then she told him how Dwayne and Lionel had stopped at Ned's house, how they were inside only a few minutes before they came running out and said that Ned had been shot. Maybe the white girl, too. She had tried to call 911, but Dwayne had stopped her. She told Berta about it when she got to the party.

"What about the white girl," Roseanne said. "Is she dead, too?"

Gianelli shook his head and said that the white girl was in the hospital. She had been assaulted, but she would be okay. "She saw the assailants, two Indian men," he said.

Roseanne doubled over against the sharp pain that plunged like a knife into the middle of her. A new image now, burning itself into the back of her eyelids. Dwayne and Lionel, insisting they had to stop by Ned's place and pick him up. Going into the house and running out. Shouting that Ned was shot! And now this white man with his facts: shot by two Indians. She tried to fit the pieces together in her mind. Dwayne and Lionel could have gone to the house earlier and killed Ned. They could have taken her to the house later so that she could swear they had found him already dead. If the fed suspected them, she was their witness. But the pieces didn't fit; nothing made sense. If they'd had anything to do with Ned's death, they wouldn't have gone back to the house. They had told her to keep her mouth shut. They would kill her if they knew what she had told the fed.

"What is it?" Gianelli said.

From outside came the explosion of a motor gearing down, the sound of tires digging into the earth. Roseanne got to her feet. The fed was already at the front door, and when he threw it open, she saw the white truck jump the borrow ditch and careen onto the road, dust balls rolling behind. She could make out the shapes of the familiar heads in the front seat.

"I swear to you," Berta was saying, "I didn't know they was coming around here."

"Hawk and Lookingglass?" Gianelli said.

It was Mervin who said, "Looks like their truck, all right."

6

Vicky Holden had just sat down at her desk and turned on the computer when she heard the front door open and shut. The brick bungalow on a side street in Lander, with the plaque on the door that said Holden and Lone Eagle, Attorneys-at-Law, was quiet this morning, the faint sounds of wind tapping the windows. Sunshine glowed in the beveled glass doors that separated her private office from the reception room. Usually, Annie Bosey, the secretary, opened the office, started a pot of coffee in the alcove that served as a miniature kitchen, and was tapping on the computer keys when Vicky arrived. But Annie hadn't been at her desk this morning.

Now Vicky saw the dark figure of Annie dart past the corner of the beveled-glass doors. There was a thudding noise — a stack of books dropped onto a hard surface — followed by drawers squealing open. The phone rang. Annie's voice, sharp and impatient. Vicky waited until the red light disappeared on her own phone, then went into the reception room. Annie was at the computer, her index finger stabbing the keyboard.

"Everything okay?" Vicky said.

"Why is this thing so slow." Annie kept her eyes on the blank screen.

Vicky walked over and perched on the edge of the desk. She could still picture Annie Bosey the day she had come through the front door. "I hear you need a secretary," she had said, "and I'm a good one." It was a one-woman law firm then, specializing in DUIs, adoptions, wills, and criminal cases. "Bottom line," Annie had pushed on, "I got two kids and a lousy husband that I just kicked out. I need a job and I'll work my butt off." Vicky had hired her on the spot.

She had insisted on taking Annie along when she and Adam Lone Eagle formed the firm dedicated to natural resources law on Indian reservations and moved into a fancy office on the second floor of a glass-and-brick building on Main Street. Then the bungalow had become available again, and she had moved the firm again. With Adam spending most of the time working for the Crow tribe in Montana, the bungalow was just the right size for her and Annie and Roger Hurst, the associate lawyer that she and Adam had hired.

"What's going on?" Vicky said.

"New client." Annie nodded toward the phone, her eyes on the screen. "Wants to talk to you right away. Says it's an emergency. Donna Bearing had to cancel her appointment this morning." She looked up. Her eyes were puffy and red. "So I told the guy you'd see him."

"I meant, what's going on with you?"

Annie sat back and clasped her hands in her lap. The screen had come alive, icons popping on the purplish background. "Robin's back," she said. "Out on parole. He was waiting for me when I got home from work yesterday. Said we had to talk."

Vicky glanced away for a moment. She had seen herself in Annie that day five years ago. On her own after she had divorced Ben Holden, two kids to support. She had left her kids, Susan and Lucas — so small then, little brown faces forever etched in her mind — with her parents and fled to Denver to go to school so that she could take care of them. Waitressing tables, sending home most of what she earned, pushing through college, then law school, seeing her kids for a day or two, a stolen week now and then.

And now Annie's ex-husband was back, just like Ben Holden had tried to come back.

"Let me guess," she said. "He still loves you. Wants another chance. Everything will be great."

Annie put a fist against her mouth and stifled a sob. "Trouble is, I'd like to believe him. He's the kids' dad."

"What about Roger?" Vicky said, tipping her head in the direction of the front bedroom that served as his office. Whatever was between the Arapaho secretary and the white lawyer, they had been discreet, and Vicky was grateful for that. The ups and downs of her own relationship with Adam had roiled the office enough.

"He doesn't know." Annie shivered and pulled her shoulders forward. "He had to stop by the county court to file some documents this morning. I've got to pull myself together before he comes in."

"You don't have to make any decisions right away," Vicky said. She had never met Robin Bosey, but she could picture him: tall, handsome, charming and drunk, shouting, fists flailing. The image always blended with the image of Ben Holden. "Just because he wants to come back," she said, "doesn't mean you have to take him back."

70

"I feel so guilty," Annie said.

She got to her feet and set a hand on Annie's shoulder. "Don't forget what it was like before," she said. "Don't let anyone tell you that things will be different." She waited a moment before she said, "You're okay now. You're safe. Your kids are safe. Anytime you want to talk . . ."

Annie nodded. She swiped the back of her hand across her eyes and scooted her chair closer to the desk. "Mr. Morrison'll be here any minute."

Vicky went back into her own office and sat down at her desk. She planned to spend most of the morning revising the logging contract between the Arapaho and Shoshone tribes and the Martinson Corporation, and the black text filled her computer screen. She had just started working when the phone buzzed. She picked it up and told Annie to show in the new client. Then she exited the contract.

Larry Morrison stood six foot three and looked to be in his mid-forties — close to her own age, with a wide, pink face and curly gray hair that made him look like an overgrown, mischievous boy. He advanced on her desk and extended his hand. A diamond set in a wide gold band glimmered on his finger. Vicky stood up and shook

71

hands. Her hand felt thin and fragile in his grip.

"How can I help you?" She motioned him to the side chair and waited until he had sat down before she resumed her own seat.

"I'm here about my girl," he said. "Looks like she might've gone and gotten herself mixed up in a mess, and I want her protected." He turned his attention for a moment to creasing the pressed seams of his khaki slacks between his thumbs and index fingers. "You know who I am?"

Vicky studied the man a moment: the dark eyes set far apart, the fine nose that was like a woman's. Something familiar about him. A celebrity of some kind, perhaps. An actor or entertainer. "I'm sorry," she said. "You'll have to tell me."

"You ever heard of the Glory and Success Ministries? Reverend Morrison, founder and pastor. We reach twenty million souls every week from the palace cathedral in Tulsa with the good news that the wealth of the earth belongs to the poorest of the poor. All you gotta do is trust in the Lord and work hard, put your shoulder to the plow like the Bible says, and allow the wealth to come your way. It would appear you haven't tuned in to the Glory and Success Sunday services." He waved a hand between them.

72

"Neither here nor there. What I want is a top-notch local lawyer to look after my little girl's interests. I'd stay right here myself and make sure nothing happens to her if I didn't have the work of the Lord to do. But I believe the Lord puts helpers in our path, and it's our job to recognize them. From what I hear around town, anybody need a lawyer who knows the ins and outs of the reservation would be a fool not to hire you."

"Who is the girl?" Vicky said.

"My only kid, Marcy." Morrison widened his eyes and stared at a point beyond her shoulder a moment. "Got in the middle of a nasty situation last night. Indian boyfriend she took up with got shot on the rez. Marcy seen it happen. Couple other Indians had it in for the guy. Knocked her around a bit, but she's okay. In shock, what you might expect. Hospital's gonna release her today."

"What do you expect from me?" Vicky said.

Morrison leaned forward and fixed her with a look that, she guessed, he used on the television cameras. "You kidding me? White girl on an Indian reservation in the middle of a murder? She's gonna need legal protection, make sure none of them hotshot Indian policemen get the idea she had anything to do with it."

Vicky lifted one hand. "The FBI will be in charge of the investigation."

"FBI. Police." Morrison shrugged. "All the same. Trust me, I know what I'm talking about. I wasn't always walking around in fancy duds," he said. "Before the Lord called me to his saving prosperity, I was a police officer for a few years down in Oklahoma. I know how things work. There's an outsider on the premises, little girl too pretty for her own good, and some hotshot investigator gets the idea she had a part in her boyfriend getting shot. Easy to pin the homicide on her. Case closed."

"Better start at the beginning," Vicky said. Last night's murder was probably on the moccasin telegraph, and Annie usually had the news by morning. But if Annie had heard anything, she had been too distracted by her own problems to mention it. "Who was murdered? Where did it happen? Where was your daughter?"

"Who was murdered? Some Indian, name of Ned Windsong. They was staying at his house in a place called Arapahoe." He lifted the diamond-ring hand again. "Not that I approve of such goings-on, as a minister of the Holy Gospel, but human flesh is weak, and sometimes we gotta make allowances. They was gonna get married. Had a place all picked out on the rez for the ceremony, even though I said to Marcy, 'Honey, you got the whole palace cathedral, if you want it. I'll throw you the gosh-darnedest shindig the television congregation ever seen. Show 'em what the prosperity of the Lord can do.' But she told me her fiancé didn't like showy stuff. They were gonna get married by the Wind River." He rolled his shoulders as if he were working out a kink in his neck. "Neither here nor there," he said. "Poor guy's dead."

"What happened at the house?"

"Like I said, two guys come in, knocked her outta the way and shot the boyfriend."

"What about the weapon?"

"Used a gun, of course."

"I mean, was any weapon found at the house?"

"Nah. Nah." Morrison gave his head a quick shake. "Most likely took it with 'em."

Vicky waited a moment before she said, "What kind of evidence would implicate your daughter?"

"Evidence!" He spit out the word. "That's the point. There's no evidence. All that leaves is a lot of conjecture and theories running around in the investigator's head. Sooner or later, he's gonna come up with the idea that Marcy could've planned the whole thing and arranged for them Indians to come to the house to kill her fiancé. Like I said, he'll start leaning on her, pushing her to incriminate herself. A girl like Marcy! I always protected her, ever since her mother took off."

He glanced sideways, as if he were looking for a different road to go down. Then he drew in a long breath that expanded the chest of his blue shirt, reconciled to the fact he had already started down one road and might as well continue. "Not that I'm laying any blame on my ex-wife for what she did. We was poor as church mice back then. I was starting my ministry on one side of the carport, and the truck was parked on the other. Never had more than fifteen people come by on Sunday mornings, but they give what they could. Dropped quarters and dimes on the collection plate. And you know what? They took the message to heart and began to see their lives change for the better. Pretty soon we was out of the carport and meeting in a parking lot, and the congregation just got bigger and bigger. I told 'em we're gonna be meeting in the biggest, most beautiful cathedral in the whole world, and they believed. Only Janet, my wife, she quit believing. And one day she up and left. I never seen her since. Never heard of a woman of the Lord that could leave her kid, did you?" He hurried on. "I forgive her seven times seventy, like the Bible says. The Lord sent me LuAnn, my wife for eight years now, and she and I did our best by Marcy. I want you to see that her rights get protected in this. I don't want her implicated in a murder she didn't have anything to do with. You gonna help us out?"

Vicky sat back. She had handled cases like this in the past, before the firm had hired Roger Hurst to handle what Adam called "the little cases" so that she and Adam could concentrate on protecting the rights of Indian tribes to the oil, gas, water, timber, and minerals on Indian lands, the important cases. She could hear Adam's voice in her head: Let Roger handle it. But this was the reason she had gone to law school in the first place — out of some naïve belief, she supposed now, that she could protect the rights of innocent people, make certain the force of the justice system didn't sweep away somebody who happened to be in the wrong place at the wrong time. She had wanted to help her people on the Wind River Reservation. But here was a white man asking her to help a white girl on the reservation.

"Where can I find Marcy?" Vicky said, getting to her feet.

Morrison stood up and held out both arms, as if he could embrace her across the desk. "FBI agent wants her hanging around for a while," he said, dropping his arms to his sides. "She can identify the killers. I'm gonna move her into the mission for a few days. You know the priest, Father O'Malley? You think she'll be safe there?"

"I know Father O'Malley," she said. Of course John O'Malley would be in the midst of this. He always knew what was going on with her people, usually before she did. They had worked on dozens of cases together, the white priest and the Arapaho lawyer. "He'll do everything he can to keep your daughter safe," she said. "But you should understand she's in a dangerous situation until her fiancé's killers are arrested. She is under no obligation to stay here. She could return home with you."

"No. No." Morrison lifted one hand. "Better Marcy stays out of the media glare. Soon's she IDs their photos, those two jokers are gonna be behind bars. I just want you to make sure nobody puts her there with 'em."

7

"My heart is falling down to the ground." Donald Little Robe's voice was raspy with sorrow. He was in his eighties, a wiry, work-hardened frame folded into the corner of the sofa. He had white hair caught in braids that flowed down the front of his red shirt and a face crosshatched with wrinkles. Blue shadows circled his narrow, black eyes. "Ned was a good boy," he said. "He was walking straight."

"I know you'll miss him." Father John sat on the edge of a chair across from the old man. The July sun poured past the white curtains, splashing the linoleum floor and shining on the surface of the lamp table. He had driven to Ethete this morning — the clarinet glissando of *Salome* blaring from the CD player beside him — to see the old man who had been preparing Ned for the Sun Dance, knowing that in the hour and a half in which he had managed to catch a little sleep, shower, and down a couple cups of coffee, Donald Little Robe would have heard the news on the moccasin telegraph.

"First time he came to see me," Donald said, the black eyes blurred in memory, "I listened with one ear. I knew the boy since he was small as a grasshopper. Seen him go straight and seen him go crooked, so I waited to see how he was going now. I didn't say anything. Next day he came back. Sat right there where you're sitting." He tipped his head forward. "Said he wanted to start over, leave the past behind. I didn't say anything, and he went away. Third day, he was back. Said it was his last chance. He was falling down crying, asking for help. He wanted to go into the Sun Dance. I spoke to him then, 'cause I knew he was in earnest. I said, 'My boy, the other dancers have been preparing for most the year. You have little more than a month. It will take all your time. You must work hard. You'll have to learn the prayers and rituals and understand what they mean to our people. You have to dance for three days. No food. Nothing to drink. You have to get your body and spirit ready.' 'I'm ready to leave the trouble behind, Grandfather,' he said. So I started teaching him three weeks ago. Now he's dead."

The old man blinked in rapid succession, as if he wanted to refocus. "Looks like the trouble came and found him. Couple Indians shot him, I heard." He leaned forward, stiff-backed, the gray head tilted to the side, and for an instant Father John saw the image of the white truck careening across the mission grounds, out over the baseball diamond, the rock with the message flying out the window. "Boy like Ned had a lot to give the people," Donald said. "What do them killers have? Nothing but destruction."

"Did Ned say what the trouble was?"

The old man dropped his eyes to the gnarled hands clasped in his lap. After a moment, he lifted his chin and fixed Father John with the steady look that reminded him of the look an elderly Jesuit professor used to shoot straight into the core of him. "Folks talk to you in the confessional," he said. "They're looking for forgiveness. It's between you and the sinner and God, ain't that right?" His smile pulled at one corner of his mouth. "Trouble is, the authorities could walk away from this," he said. "Push it off, like it's not important. Indians killing Indians. Don't let 'em do that, Father."

They both knew the rules, Father John was thinking. Donald would never repeat anything Ned had told him in confidence.

But there were other ways. "Is there anything you can tell me that might help to find Ned's killers?"

The old man took a moment, staring into space. His eyes were rheumy, the whites flecked with red dots. "Heard some Indians might've been getting into trouble," he said finally. "Maybe Ned was part of it, maybe not. It was about the time he went up to Jackson Hole."

"What kind of trouble?"

"Kind that gets young men sent off to prison, ruins a lot of lives. Breaking into houses and stealing stuff."

Father John sat back. He set his elbows on the armrests, blew into one fist and tried to search his memory for any accounts of burglaries. An article or two in the *Gazette* about break-ins in homes outside Lander, but that was several months back. About the time Ned left for Jackson Hole, just as Donald said. Both times Ned had stopped by the mission after he got back, Father John had sensed something gnawing at him. He should have confronted him, but he had decided to wait, thinking Ned would talk to him when he was ready. He'd been wrong.

Father John told the old man how sorry he was, then got to his feet. "The FBI agent will be around to talk to you," he said, wanting to prepare him.

"Nothing else I can tell him." Donald scooted himself forward, boots planted on the floor, and Father John set a hand on his shoulder and told him not to get up. The bones beneath the rough fabric of his shirt felt sharp and fragile at the same time. "You gonna do the funeral?"

Father John nodded. Ella had asked him to see that the boy was buried in the Arapaho Way. Not longer than three days after his death — that was long enough for his soul to walk the earth before he went to the ancestors. "Ella would like you to handle the Arapaho ritual," he said, repeating Ella's request, the image of the woman bent in grief floating around him like the memory of a sad melody.

Donald nodded. He blotted the moisture beneath his eyes with the back of one hand.

Father John left the old man leaning sideways in the sofa, eyelids drooping until his eyes had turned into black slits. He plucked his cowboy hat off the chair where he had tossed it, let himself out, and crossed the dirt yard to the Toyota pickup. The sun was hot on his shoulders and the bare strip of skin on the back of his neck. The wind ruffled his shirt, and the hot, dry smell of dust filled his nostrils.

He backed across the yard, then shifted into forward and bumped out onto Ethete Road. The music of *Salome* burst out of the CD player on the seat beside him the instant he pressed the on button.

Gianelli's white SUV was nosed against the steps in front of the administration building when Father John pulled around Circle Drive. He could see the agent peering out the window of his office. He parked next to the SUV and grabbed the CD player. Walks-On, the golden retriever he'd found in the ditch that first summer he'd been at St. Francis, came bounding across the grounds toward him on his three legs, all that the car that had hit him had left him with. What had always amazed Father John was how Walks-On accepted what he had, as if it were enough. He patted the dog's head a couple of times, then took the steps two at a time. He had left a message on the agent's phone this morning after the two visitors in the white truck had tore around the baseball diamond and tossed out the rock with the message.

"Helped myself." Gianelli waved a coffee mug as Father John came through the door. The coffee smelled fresh and strong, Bishop Harry Coughlin's trademark. The muffled voice of the old man speaking on the phone came from the office in the rear. "Your new assistant said to make myself at home."

Father John set the CD player on the desk, filled a mug for himself, then walked over and sat down in the worn chair that bore the imprint of his body. He guessed that Bishop Harry was the new assistant, although nothing was official. Just as nothing was official about his own position. He was still at St. Francis Mission, and that was what mattered.

Gianelli had already settled in one of the side chairs. "You read the message?" he said, nodding at the rock and the small white sheet of paper in the plastic bag at the corner of the desk. He had added the bag.

"Did you recognize either man?"

Father John shook his head.

"What kind of vehicle?"

Father John told him they drove a white Ford truck with damage on the left side that looked as if the driver had run into something solid.

"You think this is about Ned Windsong's murder?"

"What else?" Father John pressed the button on the CD player and *Salome* swelled in the air. Something calming about opera, he thought, even the tragic dramas. With the first notes, he could feel himself begin to relax.

"Nobody captures the character of Salome with more lyricism and expression than Karita Matilla," Gianelli said, waving his mug like a baton in the rhythm of "Ich will nicht bleiben." Father John smiled at the thought of a former linebacker and a Jesuit priest listening to opera. It was a toss-up who loved opera more, or knew more about it. He had to admit that Ted Gianelli had an encyclopedic knowledge of opera trivia.

"Never know what you pastors have going on," Gianelli said, pulling himself away from the opera and zeroing in on Father John. "Anybody who might be carrying a grudge?"

Father John shrugged. Parishioners sat in his office almost every day, pouring out their fears and problems, the broken relationships, the shattered hopes. He had counseled people that sometimes they had to let things go, let people go. There were women who had divorced abusive, drunken husbands. There had been times when the husbands had blamed him.

"This was about Ned," he said.

"You know his fiancée witnessed the killing," Gianelli said. "She's got a lawyer.

Vicky's representing her."

Father John took a drink of coffee and considered this. "Why would she need a lawyer?"

"Not unusual," Gianelli said. "Smart thing to do, looking at it from her point of view. Right now, everything's on the table. No-body's been cleared. The Wind River Police spent most the night bagging evidence. We'll have the forensics report on fingerprints, boot prints, types of blood." He rolled his shoulders and took a sip from the mug. "We'll know if two men were actually in the house. What I don't know is why a couple of Indians went to a lot of trouble to leave you a message. What is it they don't want you talking about?"

Father John clasped his hands around his mug. "I figure they knew that Ned came to the mission a couple of times after he got back from Jackson Hole."

"So what do they think Ned told you?"

Father John shook his head. He could feel the regret stabbing at him like a dull knife. "I had the sense that he wanted to talk, but he didn't tell me anything."

"Nothing?"

"He said he planned to dance at the Sun Dance, that he was changing his life."

"That's something."

Father John stared at the man across from him — the thick head of black hair streaked with silver, the sunburned cheeks and forehead, the dark eyes staring out of a band of light skin left by sunglasses, the thick, linebacker's shoulders inside the white shirt. Gianelli was right. Ned had wanted him to know that, whatever he may have done before, he intended to change his life.

Bishop Harry's voice floated toward him as Father John walked down the corridor. The sepia-toned photographs of past Jesuits at St. Francis Mission — the serious eyes behind wire-framed glasses — followed him. He gave a little rap on the door jamb, stepped into Bishop Harry's office and dropped onto a metal folding chair. The old man had arrived a month ago. Retired after thirty years at a mission in Patna, India, two heart attacks and two bypass surgeries. Looking for a place to recuperate, except the man wasn't the recuperating type. He intended to earn his keep, he said. He would take his turn saying Mass, and he could answer the phone and run the computer as well as any pink-faced priest fresh out of the seminary, and he knew a few more things, too.

The bishop sat huddled over the desk with

the phone pressed against his ear. He gave Father John a lifted eyebrow and nodded at something the caller had said. "Two months before the expected birth? Never too early to prepare for your child's Baptism. We'll expect you at the class Thursday, seven thirty p.m."

Father John had to smile. The Right Reverend Harry Coughlin, used to overseeing the spiritual well-being of thousands of Catholics in Patna, India, registering an expectant mother for a baptism class.

"Yes, yes," the bishop said. "Don't worry. There's no charge for the classes."

Finally the call ended. The bishop hung up and swiveled toward Father John. He squinted in the sunshine that burned through the window. "I heard about the poor young man who was shot last night," he said, tilting his head toward the phone. "Half a dozen calls. Folks upset, wanting to talk to the pastor. I told them they'd have to settle for the bishop. You had a late night. Pretty tough, huh?"

Father John nodded. "I guess I expected it might get easier," he said.

"You would be the first priest who ever had that happen." Bishop Harry shook his head. "Did you know the man?"

"Since he was about twelve," Father John

said. "Played for the Eagles a couple of seasons. Came by the mission from time to time, wanting to talk." He let the memory gather in his mind. Ned Windsong, a teenager, all skinny legs and arms and brown, pimply face, saying he had dropped out of high school. Sitting on the stoop, scuffed boots planted on the step below, knees jutting toward his chin. He hadn't wanted to come inside, he said, and Father John had sat down beside him.

"Why did you want to do that?" Father John had asked.

"What was it gonna get me?" The wind had been blowing that day, and he had turned sideways to catch what the boy was saying.

"What do you like to do?" he had asked.

The boy had leaned against the metal railing. "What do you mean?"

"You were a good outfielder. Had a strong arm. Seemed like you enjoyed playing ball. Anything else you enjoy?"

"Maybe." Ned had shrugged. "I like building things. I'm good with my hands. What's that got to do with high school?"

"You get a diploma, it will be easier to find a job where you can get some training. Learn to be a carpenter or electrician or plumber."

"Yeah, right." Ned had jumped to his feet. "Like anybody's gonna hire an Indian."

Father John had stood up beside him. "They're going to hire somebody good at what he does, Ned."

The kid had shrugged and gone down the steps, hands jammed into the pockets of his blue jeans. He was shaking his head as he got into a dark pickup with rust streaks across the side. "See you around, Father," he had called, slamming the door.

Ned didn't return to the mission, and three or four times, Father John had gone to Ella Windsong's house to see how he was doing. He hadn't been home, but his aunt had assured him Ned was doing just fine. Sooner or later he would find himself, she had said.

Then, last year, Ned had shown up. A young man, with knotted muscles in his arms and a confident look about him. He was an electrician, he said. Got his GED and graduated from a trade school in Casper. Working as an apprentice for the Silver Electrical Company in Lander. Might even get married one of these days.

"Any time you'd like to help coach the Eagles," Father John had told him, "come on out."

He had smiled at that, and a faraway look

had passed across his eyes.

Father John realized the bishop had asked a question, something about the possibility that Ned had gotten himself into trouble. "Little Robe, his spiritual grandfather, thinks so," Father John said. "God knows there's all kinds of trouble on the rez. Alcohol. Drugs." He paused. "Last time I saw him, he didn't appear to be using, and he hadn't been drinking." He felt a surge of gratitude for the way the bishop had nodded and looked away, not pressing the point. They both knew Father John was an expert on alcohol. He could smell whiskey on someone walking down the street toward him. He hurried on: "He was preparing for the Sun Dance. He wanted the strength to live a new life."

"That would suggest he intended to leave something behind," the bishop said. "Perhaps someone did not agree with his plan."

"He wanted to talk the last couple of times I saw him," Father John said. "Maybe, if I had encouraged him . . ."

"Listen, my boy," the bishop leaned forward. "All the talking in the world wouldn't have kept him alive, if somebody intended to kill him. You mustn't blame yourself."

Father John waited a moment before he got to his feet. He gave the bishop a nod of acknowledgment and headed back down the corridor. It was good to have an older man around, he was thinking, an experienced pastor. No telling how many hard and unbearably sad things Bishop Harry had dealt with in India, how many senseless deaths. How many had he blamed himself for? Believed that if only he had done something else, said something, the world would have been different?

He turned into his own office, dropped into his chair, and snapped on the lamp. A circle of light flared over the stacks of papers. The bishop seemed strong and resilient, unbent. Lord, let me learn to be like that, he prayed.

8

Engines geared down outside, tires crunched the gravel. Past the corner of the window, Father John saw a caravan of vehicles coming around Circle Drive, a blue SUV leading a silver Hummer, a red pickup in the rear. He stacked the papers he had been going through into a pile and headed for the corridor. He had reached the stoop as the three vehicles lined up side by side at the foot of the steps. A large man with a head of curly gray hair sprang out of the SUV with the agility of an acrobat. "You Father O'Malley?" he called, waving a bear-like paw.

Marcy Morrison lifted herself out of the pickup as a heavyset man with strips of brown hair combed over a balding pate got out of the Hummer next to her. "Hi, Father," the girl said, giving a little wave. The bruise on her cheek had turned dark purple. Her eyes were lost in circles of blackness.

Father John went down the steps and shook hands with the gray-haired man. Probably still in his forties, maybe a year or two younger than he was, Father John thought, with a pinkish complexion and a smooth shave. The man's palm was smooth; his fingernails glistened with clear polish.

"Reverend Larry Morrison," he said. "I'm entrusting my little girl to this here" — he threw a glance around the mission grounds, his gaze lingering for a moment on the white stuccoed church, the blue and red stained-glass windows shining in the sun — "Catholic mission," he said. "I take it you're the pastor." He looked over at the man leaning against the front of the Hummer. "My assistant, Reverend Angelo Crispie," he said. Father John stepped over and shook the other man's hand.

"I reckon you already know my daughter." Morrison reached around and pulled the girl to his side, keeping a thick sunburned arm draped over her shoulders.

"How are you, Marcy?" Father John said.

"How am I supposed to be?" The breeze caught a snatch of her blonde hair and blew it across her face. She pushed the hair back. She looked like a little girl with thin arms dangling from the sleeves of a white tee shirt and thin legs beneath the cutoff blue jeans.

She wore sandals, and the dust curled over her toes. She barely reached her father's shoulders.

"Ned's still dead," she said. "Nothing's gonna change that."

"FBI agent's making things difficult," Morrison said. "I want to take Marcy home with me . . ."

The girl cut in: "I'm not going back to Oklahoma, Daddy." She ducked out from under the large arm and looked up at her father. "We've been over that. It's not happening."

"You'd be safe there," he said.

She shrugged. "Yeah, whatever. Soon's they arrest those guys, I'll be safe in Jackson Hole. I just want to get back to my own life. I mean, I want things to go on like they were. Well, not exactly like they were, 'cause Ned's gone and all that, and we're never gonna be getting married like we planned." She swung toward Father John. "You get it, don't you, Father?"

Father John hesitated. There was a look of desperation in the girl's eyes, but something trivial about it, like the look in the eyes of students at the Jesuit prep school where he had taught American history, begging to be excused from yesterday's class because they hadn't heard the alarm. He had marked it

96

off to the self-absorption that came with immaturity. But Marcy Morrison was no longer a teenager.

"I'm sure you want Ned's killers found," he said.

A startled look came over the girl. She flinched backward. "Well, naturally. I loved Ned." She glanced up at her father. "We were gonna make a real family together. I mean, a really good family with everybody looking out for one another."

Larry Morrison drew in a long breath that expanded his chest. He cleared his throat and stared down at the girl. "No sense in going off to places the good Father here has no interest in." He turned his attention back to Father John. "I want assurances that my daughter will be safe here."

"You know our so-called family was a big fake," Marcy said.

"Marcy, please," her father said, and the Reverend Crispie lifted himself off the front of the Hummer and moved in closer, like a bodyguard, Father John thought, on full alert.

"Everything was a lie," the girl said, a controlled hysteria coming into her voice. "All that smiling and waving for the TV cameras, all that bullshit about how the family that stays together prospers together, only our family wasn't exactly together, right? Not after Mom took off. I never blamed her, 'cause all I wanted to do was get the hell out myself." She seemed to settle back inside herself. "Well, maybe I blamed her for not taking me with her. She should've done that."

"When all this is over, I want you to go back into therapy," Morrison said. A distant note had come into his voice, as if he were counseling a parishioner.

"Therapy!" The girl spit out the word. "You never could face it, could you? You're the one needs therapy. Living a lie for a long time. That's gotta take it out of you. My therapist told me that. She said I needed to distant myself from toxic relationships with my family. So I did, and I was gonna start over, get me a new family." She started moving backward, holding out both hands. "Oh, my God. Now I get it," she said. "You sent those Indians to kill Ned. You didn't want me to have another family. You didn't want me to have a new chance. You'd do anything to stop me."

"That's ridiculous, Marcy," Morrison said. "I want whatever makes you happy. I told you we could have your wedding in the palace cathedral . . ."

"Where you could show the gazillion

dupes — oh, excuse me, followers in the Lord of prosperity — what a happy family we are, and so progressive! I mean, the reverend's daughter marrying an Indian. Wow, that would have brought in a whole bunch more money."

Morrison stared at the girl a long moment, not saying anything. Then he turned to Father John. "My apologies, Father, for this little scene."

"Little scene! Little scene!" Marcy shouted. "My whole life is falling apart, and you call it a little scene! Nothing ever mattered to you, did it? You drove my mother crazy. She had to get away to save herself. Well, you know what I think? I think she did save herself. I think she's real happy somewhere. Tahiti, maybe. Yeah, I think of her in Tahiti, getting it on with some gorgeous guy with brown skin . . ."

"Stop it, Marcy." Morrison held the girl in his gaze for a couple of seconds. Drawing in another long breath, he looked at Father John. "I'm afraid this was a very bad idea. The best thing will be to take her back to the hospital for further evaluation. It's obvious this unfortunate incident has affected her balance."

"Oh no you don't," Marcy said. "You're not locking me up again in any crazy ward."

She leaned toward him. "You don't have the right. I'm not your little girl anymore. Oh, Marcy's rebelling again, causing trouble? Lock her up! I'm twenty-three years old. You'd need a court order, and you're not going to get it."

Father John put up one hand. "Hold on," he said, glancing between the girl and her father. He was aware of the hulking shape of the bodyguard shifting from one foot to the other, watching the girl. Father John kept his gaze on Marcy. "It's quiet here. It's a good place to take a little time away from everything. I expect Gianelli will have the men in custody in a day or so, and you can go back to Jackson Hole."

"You don't understand . . ." Morrison began.

"He understands a helluva lot more than you ever did," Marcy said. "Just go, okay? Go back to Oklahoma and all the love pouring out of those TV cameras. I shouldn't have brought you into this. It's none of your business, really. I can handle this myself. I'm good at handling things all by myself. I learned early."

"I can't leave without the assurance that she'll be safe," Morrison said, as if the girl weren't standing next to him. Then he shrugged, as if absolving himself from whatever stood between him and his daughter. "I've hired a lawyer to see to her rights."

"I don't need a lawyer," Marcy said. "You can unhire her."

"Trust me in this."

"Right. Just like in all the rest of it."

"As I said, what I'm concerned about at the moment," he went on, locking eyes with Father John, "is her safety."

"Marcy can stay in the guesthouse." Father John hooked a thumb in the direction of the alley that ran between the administration building and the church. At the end of the alley was the little guesthouse where all kinds of people had stayed — people in hiding, people looking for themselves, people needing time away. "We'll keep it quiet that Marcy's here," he said. The tough part, he was thinking. If the truth got to the moccasin telegraph, Dwayne and Lionel would hear about it. But if the girl stayed in the guesthouse and walked the grounds when no one was around, it could work. He hurried on. "Gianelli will have the men in custody soon," he said. He hoped he was right.

"I don't call that assurances," Morrison said, and the bodyguard gave a little laugh.

"There are no guarantees," Father John said. He turned to the girl. "You're a witness in a murder case. It's up to you whether you feel secure staying here. If not, I'm sure Gianelli would find a safe house for you."

"He offered." Marcy gave a quick, dismissive shrug. "Policemen at the door, just like at the hospital. Wouldn't that be lovely? Like those Indians wouldn't hear about a policeman hanging around a house? No thanks. I'll take my chances here."

"Reverend Crispie will be close by," Morrison said.

"What? Are you crazy? I don't want that goon anywhere near me," Marcy said. Out of the corner of his eye, Father John saw the Reverend Angelo Crispie square his shoulders and lower his head so that his chin set on his chest, staring at the girl out of slitted eyes. "Get him out of here," Marcy said.

Morrison took his time removing a small folder from his shirt pocket and selecting a business card. He handed it to Father John. "In case of any trouble, call me at this number. My associate will be on the next plane to Wyoming."

Marcy clasped her head in both hands and started walking around in a circle. "I don't fricking believe what I'm hearing. You playing the role of the all-caring dad. A little late, isn't it?"

Father John slipped the card it into his own shirt pocket. He hoped there wouldn't be any reason to summon the man next to the Hummer. "I'll show you the guesthouse," he said to Marcy.

"Good idea. Why don't you do that." Marcy slid behind her father, walked back to the pickup and got inside. The engine growled into life. She backed up and rolled down the window. "See you on TV, Daddy," she called.

Morrison kept his back to the pickup, his gaze on some point past Father John. There was something firm and resolute in his stare, his eyes as opaque as dark marble. "My daughter is very troubled," he said, his voice low. "I'm sure you're used to counseling people, but you can see she needs professional help. It would be for the best to leave her alone. No sense in her stirring up past issues. Don't you agree?"

Father John glanced between the two men, the father and the bodyguard. He wondered who they wanted to protect, the girl or themselves. "Thanks for coming by," he said.

He left them standing in front of the SUV and the Hummer and headed down the alley, in and out of the shadows that ran down the sides of the buildings, the breeze stirring in the cottonwoods and the pickup's engine purring behind him. The guesthouse was a small white bungalow nestled in the trees. He unlocked the door, then went over and took the bag that the girl was struggling to lift out of the bed of the pickup. "The TV works," he said, ushering her into the small living room with a kitchen in the corner. He immediately regretted the words. Probably the last thing she wanted to be reminded about was that her father was on TV. He set her bag down and nodded toward the refrigerator. "The refrigerator's stocked," he said. He had asked Elena to bring over some bread, milk, lunchmeat, and fruit. "You're welcome to join us for meals at the residence, or you can take your meals here. There's a nice walk along the river." He moved toward the door and pointed in the direction of the Little Wind River that wound around the southern boundary of the mission.

The girl had flopped down on the sofa and crossed her legs. She swung one sandaled foot in his direction. "This is gonna be just fine," she said, a calm, control in her voice. For an instant, he had the sense that he was talking to someone he had never met before, a total stranger. The girl who had shouted at her father and gripped her head

— that girl was gone.

"I want to ask you something," she said.

Father John was about to step out onto the stoop. He turned back. "What's that?"

"You said you knew Ned."

He nodded. Not very well, he was thinking. He hadn't known Ned Windsong well at all.

"What about his girlfriend? You know her?"

"I thought you were his fiancée."

"I mean before. The girl that hung around him before he came to Jackson Hole."

"What about her?"

"So, you know her."

Father John shook his head. "I never met her."

She shrugged. "I was just wondering how she's taking it. No way Ned's ever going back to her now."

"Is that what he wanted?"

"What?" The girl flinched backward. "Of course not. We was gonna get married."

9

A half mile down the road, Vicky spotted the cars and pickups jammed into the yard, the people milling about, dust lifting in the air. Everything just as she expected. A death on the reservation brought out all the relatives and friends. There would be gallons of fresh coffee, and kitchen counters groaning under casseroles, plates of fry bread, and cake. She had visited the houses of death since she was a little kid, staying close to her parents, wanting to run off and play with the other kids. She slowed for the turnoff into the yard, aware of the tension in her muscles. Beneath the camaraderie, the earnest, heartfelt wishes was always the horrible reality.

She parked behind a red truck and threaded among the people moving back and forth like tumbleweeds. Most of the faces were familiar. A few had been clients. Adoptions. Wills. DUIs. Minor assaults. The cases blurred together. Past the screen door, she saw the shadowy figures in the living room. The smell of fresh coffee wafted toward her as she rapped on the side of the door.

"Hey, Vicky." Marie Adams, about her own age, with a large bust, rolls of fat around her middle and short, black hair, pushed open the door. A picture flashed in Vicky's mind: three little girls, she and Marie and her sister, Ella, at the mission school, tearing about the grounds at recess, giggling in class. She and Ella were in the same class. Marie was a year older, which placed her in command, like a colonel over the troops. The day after Marie graduated from high school, she had joined the army. Twenty years later, she was back in the area living on a ranch, a retired sergeant with a white husband who, Vicky had heard, was also an ex-sergeant.

"How's Ella?" Vicky said, stepping into the living room. The sofa and chairs were occupied by elders and grandmothers, balancing disposable cups and paper plates half filled with food on their laps. Little groups of people huddled together. A short, gray-haired woman holding a coffeepot moved about, refilling the cups thrust in her direction. A low buzz of conversation, like the noise of a beehive, filled the room.

Marie was shaking her head. "She's in shock. Ned meant the world to her. Me, too, for that matter. He was all we had left of our brother. Jerry and I came over last night, soon's we heard. She's in the kitchen. She'll want to see you."

Marie spun around and cut a path through the crowd. Vicky started to follow when she felt someone tug at her arm. She turned sideways toward a young man, still a teenager with thin shoulders and an anxious look about him. "You remember me? Mervin Oldman?" he said.

"Sure," she said. She knew the Oldman family. Berta Oldman would be his aunt. She couldn't remember the last time she had seen Mervin. He had probably been a kid, a brown face in a sea of brown faces at a powwow.

"Ned was a good guy," he said. He had black hair slicked back and shiny, and enormous hands that flared from thin wrists. "You gonna help find the guys that did it?"

"The fed will do that," Vicky said.

"They shouldn't get away with it."

"Who do you think killed him?"

He shrugged. "I don't want to say. I mean, they could be dangerous. They think I'm going around saying they killed Ned, they could come after me."

"Have you talked to Agent Gianelli?"

The young man went quiet. He glanced around the room, as if to make sure no one was close. Then he leaned in and said, "He come to the house this morning. Asked a lot of questions. Roseanne said we gotta watch our backs." He threw another glance about.

"Who's Roseanne?"

"Roseanne Birdwoman. Used to be Ned's girlfriend, 'til he got mixed up with that white girl in Jackson Hole and she followed him here. Broke Roseanne up real bad. I seen her a couple times with . . ."

"With the guys that might have killed Ned?"

Mervin gave a halfhearted attempt at a shrug. "Ned wouldn't've liked it. He didn't hang around with them guys after he got back. They come to the house last night with Roseanne. We was having a party. Bunch of people was there. No harm done."

"Who are you talking about?"

"You gonna help get 'em get arrested?"

"I'll do my best."

He was so close now that Vicky could smell the coffee and tobacco on his breath. "Dwayne Hawk. Lionel Lookingglass.

They're not from around here. You know 'em?"

Vicky tried to put faces with the names, but the faces were blanks. "What're they into — drugs?"

Mervin kept shaking his head, as if once he had started, he couldn't stop. "I don't do drugs," he said. "I don't hang with druggies."

"I'm not accusing you. Why didn't Ned like them?"

"I never asked." His head was still shaking. A piece of black hair dropped over his forehead. "Ned was straight with me, give me good advice. Told me to stay in school, so I did. Graduated two months ago. I've been looking for a job. Ned was gonna get me lined up to be an apprentice. You know, so I could learn to be an electrician like him."

Vicky had to look away from the earnest young face. She remembered reading somewhere that when one person dies, the whole world changes. "Is Roseanne here?" she said.

Mervin stepped sideways and surveyed the house. "I guess she hasn't shown up yet. She spent the night at the house. Berta ran her home this morning." He looked back at Vicky. "Like I say, she was pretty torn up over Ned breaking up with her. Now that he's dead . . ." He began shaking his head again. "I don't know how she's gonna take it."

At the periphery of her vision, Vicky could see Marie waiting in the doorway to the kitchen, leaning against the jamb, as if the jamb were necessary to hold her upright.

She set a hand on the young man's arm. "Tell Roseanne to call me," she said. It was possible the girl might know something that could lead to Ned's killers, and it was also possible that she was too scared to tell Gianelli. At the edge of her thoughts, hovering like a shadow, was the image of a white girl caught up in a murder on the reservation.

She tried for an encouraging smile and left Mervin Oldman standing in the middle of the living room, the enormous hands dangling at his sides, and headed for the kitchen. Marie pushed herself off the doorjamb, and Vicky followed her past the dishes and plates of food that covered the countertops to the table in the far corner. The window framed a view of the Wind River range, brown, rolling humps lifting into an azure sky. White cotton clouds floated past. Ella sat at the table with two other women, all backlit by the sunlight framed in the window.

Marie pulled out a chair across from her sister, and Vicky sat down. Immediately, Ella laid both arms on the table and stretched out her hands. Vicky set her own hands on top of them. The woman's hands felt chilled and lifeless. She was aware of Marie sliding a cup of coffee onto the table.

"Appreciate your coming." Ella looked past Vicky, across the kitchen. "I feel like I'm floating on everybody's strength, 'cause I don't have none of my own." She took a moment and studied Vicky's hands before she nodded at the women on either side of her, "You know Linda Rigs and Patsy Yellowman?"

Vicky gave a nod and smile to each woman. Black hair, both of them. One tied in braids that rode down the front of a red blouse, the other curling over the shoulders of a white tee shirt. Cousins or second cousins to Ella and Marie. It was hard to keep the relatives in an Arapaho family straight.

"Where's Ned's fiancée?" Ella said. "Seems like she oughtta be here. Maybe she doesn't know this is our custom. Everybody that loves Ned is gonna come by, say how sorry they are, say how much they're gonna miss him."

"She'll be released from the hospital

today," Vicky said. Then she told her that Marcy would probably remain in the area, since she's a witness. She hurried on: "I'm sure she'll do everything she can to help Agent Gianelli find Ned's killers."

Ella pulled her hands free, questions popping in her eyes. She glanced at the women beside her, and Vicky saw the look of encouragement they gave her. Then she squared herself at the table and said, "I been thinking, maybe she had something to do with it. Maybe that's why the fed don't want her getting away."

Vicky sat back and took a sip of coffee. This was what Larry Morrison feared. Sooner or later, someone would start to wonder if the white girl had anything to do with the murder of an Arapaho man. She told Ella that the girl's father had hired her to look after his daughter's interests.

"Interests?" Ella said. "Like getting away with murder?"

"What makes you think Marcy's involved?" The other women were nodding. Obviously they had been discussing the possibility. They had all agreed.

Ella let her gaze drift sideways over the edge of the table. "I never liked her. First time I seen her, I got a bad feeling. She showed up here like she owned the place, said she was gonna marry Ned. She wanted to know where he was. I didn't tell her. I figured if Ned wanted her to know, he'd tell her. Few days later I stopped at Ned's with some extra groceries, the kind of cereal he always liked and a bag of apples. She was there. I don't mind saying, it sure surprised me when this blonde girl with green eyes opened the door. Okay, I said to myself. Ned was getting ready to tell me in his own time. She took the groceries. Even offered to give me some money, but I said, no, no, they're for Ned. She said he'd come by and see me."

"And did he?" Vicky said.

"Yeah." Ella nodded and went back to following the edge of the table, pulling the memories together, Vicky thought, imagining Ned. "He didn't say anything about her. Finally I asked him, 'So, you gonna get married?' He didn't say yes or no. All he said was he was real busy preparing for the Sun Dance." She let out a little sob at this piece of memory and set the palm of her hand against her mouth. "He wanted to take part in the Sun Dance for a long time, but he didn't feel worthy."

"He told you that? He didn't feel worthy?"

Ella nodded. "I told him that was silly. He was as worthy as anybody. But he said no.

114

Not yet. When he got back from Jackson Hole, he said he wanted to try to become worthy. That was all he wanted to do. He was making changes in his life, he said."

Vicky took another sip of coffee and waited. After a moment, Ella went on, "There were things Ned never wanted me to know. That's the truth. I don't like to think about it." She let out a little sob. "Things he might've done he wasn't proud of. But he was trying to do better. That was Ned, always trying to do right, even if he was doing wrong. When he started preparing for the Sun Dance, that was his way of taking a stand. From then on, he was just gonna do right. The Sun Dance was gonna give him the courage."

"Wouldn't Marcy have been part of the changes?" Vicky said. "Why do you think she would want Ned killed?"

Ella shifted forward and gripped the edge of the table, as if the table might prevent her from floating away. "I been turning everything over in my mind, trying to make sense out of it. Maybe she didn't like Indian ways. Maybe she didn't like living on the rez."

"But she was living with him," Vicky said. "She was looking forward to a wedding down by the river."

Ella stared straight ahead, as if she hadn't heard.

"What about Dwayne Hawk and Lionel Lookingglass?" Vicky went on. "Did Ned have anything to do with them?"

Ella gave a quick shake of her head, like a reflex. "Far as I know, he never wanted those Indians around. Jerry hired them on the ranch last summer. Said they were more trouble than they were worth. Drinking, fighting. Beat up another ranch hand. They weren't like Ned. Never see them two pledging the Sun Dance." She shook her head again, slowly this time. "Ned was an electrician. Had a good job in Lander. Worked in some fancy houses. One time he drove me by a house up in the mountains outside town. Put in a chandelier as big as this table. Then went to Jackson Hole and got a better job in Jackson." She rapped her knuckles on the tabletop. "There wasn't any way he was friends with losers like Hawk and Lookingglass."

10

There was a familiarity about St. Francis Mission, the cottonwood branches arched above the narrow road, the glimpse of buildings past the tree trunks, the white steeple against the blue sky. Vicky guided the Jeep around Circle Drive toward the administration building, feeling as if she were coming home. It had been several weeks since she had been here. She parked next to the old red pickup, hurried up the concrete steps, and let herself in the wooden doors that groaned on the hinges.

"I understand my client is your guest," she said, leaning into the front office. John O'Malley was at his desk, bent over a fan of papers. He jerked his head up, and the familiar smile creased his face. His eyes came alive. She could have closed her own eyes and seen everything about him — the reddish hair fading a little, the smudges of gray at his temples, the sculpture of his features, the squareness of his chin.

"Vicky!" He got to his feet. "How are you? Have a seat. How about some coffee?" All of it spilling out as he cut a diagonal path across the office to the coffeepot on the metal table behind the door. The smell of recently brewed coffee permeated the air.

"No, thanks." She moved into the office, catching him with a cup in one hand, a half-full carafe of coffee in the other. "I'm here to see Marcy Morrison. You've probably heard that I'm representing her interests."

"I've heard." John O'Malley set the carafe and cup down and faced her. It struck her that his eyes were the color of blue wildflowers. "She's staying in the guesthouse."

"What do you know about her?"

He shook his head. "Not much. She came here two weeks ago looking for Ned."

That was strange, Vicky thought, and she could see in John O'Malley's eyes that he had formed the same conclusion. She stepped back and dropped onto a hardwood chair. "She didn't know where her fiancé was?"

Father John sat across from her. "She said she didn't have directions to the house where he was staying. No one would help her, including Ella."

Vicky let it pass. Some things didn't make

118

sense, looking from the outside. People moved through the days working things out the best they could. "Anything else about her?" she said.

"I suspect she's still in shock," Father John said. "Her father brought her here a couple hours ago. She seemed angry with him. Maybe she was just expressing her anger over Ned's murder, and her father happened to be a handy target."

"Maybe she resents the fact that he's not staying to look out for her himself," Vicky said. "She's a witness to a murder, and Gianelli probably hasn't ruled her out as a suspect. He wants her to view some photos on the chance she can identify the men she claims burst into the house and killed Ned," she said, standing up. "I'd better go meet my client. I know my way to the guesthouse." She put up one hand, but John O'Malley was already on his feet. She was aware of his footsteps behind her in the corridor. His hand shot around and pulled open the front door.

She gave him a wave and hurried down the steps. In a couple of minutes, she parked in front of the guesthouse sheltered in the shade of the cottonwoods. There were times in the past when she had fled to the guesthouse, the sounds of the mission floating through the walls — people coming and going, calling to one another, vehicles crunching the gravel, and the wind whistling in the trees. It was a place of refuge. A white face peered past the edge of the front window, then disappeared.

Vicky knocked at the door. Inside, a phone rang twice. Then she heard the girl's voice, muffled and tentative, like the voice of a frightened child, saying, "Okay." After a moment, the door opened. The girl stood perfectly still, blonde hair hanging about a small, pretty face with wide green eyes circled in black and a purplish bruise running across her cheek. She wore a tee shirt that showed her pink midriff, and faded cutoff jeans. She blinked into the sunshine. "You're my lawyer?" she said.

"Vicky Holden." Vicky held out her hand. The girl hesitated a moment before she slid a small hand across Vicky's palm.

"Nice to meet you," the girl said, stepping back into the small room. Thick shadows lay over the sofa and side chair, and the air was filled with the smell of soap. "Father John called and said you were on the way."

Vicky followed her inside and shut the door. "We need to talk," she said, ushering the girl over to the worn, comfortable chair in the corner, an impulsive gesture, she re-

120

alized, like a flashback to the times she had spent curled up in the chair as a fugitive in the guesthouse.

The girl sank into the cushions and pulled her feet up beneath her. She crossed her arms and hugged herself. "Is it okay if we don't talk about it?" she said. "It's too terrible."

Vicky perched on the sofa a few feet away. "I understand," she said. "But if I'm going to help you . . ."

"What do I need a lawyer for? I didn't do anything."

"You're a witness," Vicky said. "Until the investigation is closed, everyone's a suspect."

The girl unfolded her hands and spread her fingers. "They put that stuff on my hands. Daddy said they were looking for gunshot residue. They're not going to find any residue. I didn't shoot anybody." Her face folded into tears. "I wish I'd had a gun," she said, fingertips mopping at the moisture on her cheeks. "I would've shot those bastards before they killed Ned."

"Your father has hired me to protect your interests," Vicky said.

"Don't bring my father into this!" The girl spit out the words. "Daddy's only concerned about himself and his precious ministry, and all those millions of people that think he's God strutting around the stage with his fancy ruffled shirt and big diamond ring. What he's concerned about is keeping any scandal out of the newspapers. You know: TV Evangelical's Daughter Mixed Up in Murder." She shifted into a cross-legged position. Bony knees pressed against the armrests. "Oh, did he forget to mention that part?"

Vicky took a moment. An image had moved at the edge of her mind from five or six years ago. Her own daughter, Susan, nineteen years old and on drugs, anger running through her at the lost years when Vicky was in Denver. But Susan was twenty-five now, clean and happy, working in LA, almost mended.

It could be the same for Marcy Morrison, she was thinking. The broken places could begin to mend.

She said, "Your father doesn't want any harm to come to you."

"He's got you convinced at least." Marcy blew out a stream of air. "Let's make a deal," she said. "We don't talk about Daddy."

"And you'll tell me what happened last night?" Vicky waited. A blank look had come into the girl's face. "I need to hear from you exactly what took place."

"Agent Gianelli already asked me," she said, a sulky frown creasing her forehead.

"All the more reason for you to tell me."

Marcy stretched out her neck and rolled her head around. Finally, she said, "I heard 'em driving up, so I went to look out the window 'cause Ned hadn't said anybody was coming over. They busted through the door. They were inside before I knew what was happening. Two Indians, shouting, 'Ned! Where are you, you bastard!' Stuff like that. They had a gun. I was scared to death they were gonna shoot us. Ned was in the bedroom, and I tried to keep 'em from going in there. That's when they hauled off and let me have it, slammed me up against the wall. Next thing I knew, I was on the floor. They started pulling open the drawers, tossing things around, like they were crazy. I heard Ned shouting, 'Get out!' There was a loud gunshot. He quit shouting, and they ran past me out the door."

"Did they both have a gun?"

Marcy shook her head. "Just the big guy with a ponytail. The other guy's the one that hit me."

"What did you do?"

"I crawled into the bedroom. Ned was on the bed." She lifted her hands to her face and sobbed quietly, the thin shoulders shaking, as if she were waking from a nightmare, Vicky thought. She fought the impulse to go to her and cradle her in her arms, the way she had cradled Susan and Lucas when they had awakened screaming from the childhood demons that had invaded their dreams.

"Make it go away," the girl said, slurring the words. "Make it so it didn't happen. Ned was all I had. He was everything."

"I know this is hard," Vicky said.

"Do you? Do you really think you know what I've been through?" Marcy threw her head back against the chair. "Nobody cares what happened to me. I got hit hard," she said, brushing a hand over the red bruise. "Maybe they kicked me or something. My ribs are sore. I feel terrible."

Vicky took a moment, watching the girl shifting about, squeezing her hands together. She wondered if Marcy was on drugs. "Did they give you something at the hospital?" she said. "For the pain?"

"They gave me some pills." Marcy nodded toward the bedroom at the back of the house.

"Any other drugs?" Vicky said.

"You accusing me of something?"

"I'm your lawyer, Marcy. I need to know

124

anything that could possibly implicate you in Ned's murder."

"What?" The girl's legs sprang forward, and she jumped to her feet. "You think it was about drugs? You think Ned was dealing drugs?"

"I'm only asking what Gianelli's going to ask."

"He already asked me." Marcy stood over her, hands hooked on her waist, and Vicky understood. This was the reason Larry Morrison had shown up at her office this morning wanting to hire a lawyer to look after his daughter's interests. He had suspected that somehow drugs could be involved.

"I told him what I'm telling you," the girl said. "Ned didn't have anything to do with drugs. He was going into the Sun Dance. You can't be on drugs when you do that."

"What about you?"

The girl sat back down. She leaned forward and clasped her hands around her knees. "I got clean after I got away," she said, not taking her eyes from Vicky's. "Soon's I escaped Oklahoma, I didn't need drugs anymore. Then I met Ned in Jackson. You don't need drugs when everything's perfect."

"Tell me about you and Ned," Vicky said. "How did you meet?"

Marcy was looking at something inside her head now. The faint trace of a smile came into her face. "I got a condo in town. The manager sent him to install new smoke detectors. I gave him a cup of coffee, and we talked while he worked. I never met anybody like him. You believe in love at first sight?"

Vicky smiled. "When I was your age," she said.

"Well, that's the way it was. He felt the same way. I went out and bought a big crystal chandelier for the dining room so he'd have to come back. I had to buy a couple more fixtures before he finally asked if I wanted to see a movie or something, 'cause he was shy, you know. Him being Arapaho, and me white, that made him shy. But I could tell he felt the same way. That's how it was with us. We could read each other's minds. We didn't even have to talk, 'cause I knew what he was thinking. Same for Ned. We both knew we would get married. Like we'd been waiting for each other all our lives." She blinked at the tears that started bubbling again.

"I understand he came back to the rez a couple of weeks ago. Father John said you stopped by the mission looking for him. Didn't he tell you where he was staying?"

"Why's everybody making a big deal of it? So I didn't write down the directions." The girl's voice was rising into hysteria. She pulled her hands into her lap. They were shaking. "He was waiting for me. He came and found me at the motel where I was staying and took me home with him. He loved me."

"There's something else Gianelli will want to know," Vicky said. She waited until the girl looked at her. She could see the effort the girl was making to concentrate. "Why didn't you call the police?"

"You think I didn't want to?" The hands flew out; the white face contorted in anger. "Is that what everybody here thinks? That I didn't want to get help?" She stopped and stared straight ahead a moment. "I don't remember. I don't remember anything. Maybe I did call 911, I don't know. Next thing I knew, boots were stomping around me, people were shouting. They put me on a stretcher and took me to the hospital."

"It makes sense," Vicky said. The girl had probably been unconscious. But a good prosecuting attorney . . . She shut down the thought. "Nobody's going to make a big deal out of it." She let the words hang between them a moment. She would make sure nobody made a big deal out of it, she thought, watching the girl settle back into herself, her chest rising and falling at a steadier rate. "Agent Gianelli would like you to look at photos," she said. "I'll take you to his office." When the girl didn't respond, she pushed on. "You want the men who killed Ned arrested, don't you? It's for your own safety, Marcy. You could be in danger."

Marcy waited before getting to her feet, as if she didn't trust her legs to hold her up. "What the hell," she said. Then she scooped a small bag off the chest under the window and started for the door.

11

The local FBI office sprawled across the top floor of a flat-faced brick building on Lander's Main Street. Vicky found a parking place a half block away and guided Marcy Morrison past the novelty stores, boutiques, and coffee shops, aware of the images of a black-haired woman and a small, light-skinned girl flashing in the plate-glass windows. It was mid-afternoon, the sky a burned-out blue and the day's heat rolling off the sidewalk. There was a lazy summer feeling to the traffic that flowed past — tourists on the way into the Wind River range to fish and hike and camp. People in shorts, tee shirts, and sandals, cameras bumping on their chests, strolled along the sidewalks. Flowers overflowed the planters at the curb, and the smell of geraniums drifted in the air.

She opened the framed glass door and ushered Marcy into the shadows of a small entry and up the narrow staircase. The girl climbed slowly, pulling herself along the railing. Vicky wanted to assure her, tell her everything would be all right, a comforting thought that may or may not be true. She didn't say anything. At the top of the steps, she leaned in close to the intercom next to the pebbled-glass door. "Vicky Holden with Marcy Morrison," she said. The girl slouched against the wall across the corridor. She still had on the white tee shirt and cutoff blue jeans.

The door opened, and Ted Gianelli, black hair silvery under the fluorescent ceiling light, waved them inside. Vicky waited as the girl rowed herself over, swinging her shoulders as if she were paddling a kayak in the Wind River. Gianelli turned and led the way down a corridor of shelves piled with books and cartons into the office itself. "Have a seat, ladies," he said, motioning to a pair of side chairs. He walked around and sat down behind a desk, the surface lost under stacks of folders and papers.

"I'm representing Marcy," Vicky said.

"So Mr. Morrison has notified me." Gianelli clasped his hands on a stack of papers, rolling his shoulders, making himself comfortable. His face was immobile. He could be Indian, Vicky thought, taking in

130

every detail — the clothes they wore, the expressions on their faces — giving nothing back. She had known the local agent for more than six years now, sitting across from him, bantering over the guilt or innocence, the evidence or lack thereof, of dozens of clients. She knew the way his mind worked, the logic with which he marshaled evidence and drew conclusions, a lot like John O'Malley. The two men had more in common than opera.

"Is my client a suspect?" she said.

"What?" Marcy turned sideways, and Vicky could feel the anger shooting from her eyes. "You're supposed to be on my side."

"The investigation is ongoing," Gianelli said. "Nobody's been cleared yet."

Vicky reached over and set a hand on the girl's arm. The muscles felt tight, capable of propelling the small body out of the chair. Keeping her eyes on the agent, she said, "Let's get something clear. My client had nothing to do with Ned Windsong's death. She saw the men who killed him, and she's willing to cooperate to see that they are prosecuted."

Gianelli nodded. He opened a folder, pulled out a stack of photos and handed them across the desk. "Recognize anyone?"

he said to Marcy.

Vicky took the photos and held them out, but the girl kept her fingers laced together, her eyes on the floor. "I don't want to look at those guys again," she said.

"It will only take a moment." Vicky held the photos in front of the girl.

"We want to pick them up before they can get too far away," Gianelli said.

The girl's head snapped back. "You think they left?"

"It's possible."

Marcy took hold of the photos then and stared at the image of a man with long, black hair and a pockmarked face. "I never seen this one." She tossed the photo onto the desk and looked at the next photo and the one after that. All with black hair and dark skin and dark, wary eyes. Vicky wondered if they looked the same to a white girl.

Marcy held up the next photo. "He's the one that hit me," she said. She handed the photo to Vicky and studied another. "He's the guy with the gun." Vicky passed both photos to Gianelli.

"Dwayne Hawk and Lionel Lookingglass," he said, laying the photos side by side as if he were dealing two poker cards. "Do you know them?"

"Why would I know them?" A whine came into Marcy's voice.

"Seen them before?"

"Look, Ted," Vicky said, "she's ID'd . . ."

"I think so," Marcy said.

The office went quiet. Vicky was aware of the traffic sounds floating up from the street below. She glanced at the girl clasping and unclasping her hands, the blonde hair draped like a veil along the side of her face.

"Tell me about them," Gianelli said.

"They came to see Ned last week."

"Why didn't you say so earlier?"

"I didn't remember." The whine came into her voice again. Vicky turned toward her, and she said, "I didn't, Vicky, honest. You gotta believe me. I didn't recognize them until just now when I saw the photos."

"Okay, okay." Vicky patted the girl's arm. She looked at Gianelli. "My client has been through a horrific experience," she said, starting to get up. "I suggest we continue this interview at a later time."

"No!" Vicky felt the girl take hold of her arm, the thin fingers digging into her flesh. "They're the Indians that killed Ned. I want them punished. I want them in prison forever."

Vicky settled back in her chair. "Okay," she said.

133

"What happened when they came to Ned's place?" Gianelli said, a patient note sounding in his voice, as if he had just kicked over a rock and spotted something new and interesting to probe.

"They hung around, that's all."

"Hung around?" Gianelli said, still probing.

"They never came inside. I didn't see them up close 'til . . ." Marcy let her voice trail off, then she went on, and Vicky could sense the effort she was making. "I heard them arguing outdoors," she said. "After they left, I asked Ned who they were, and he told me not to worry, it didn't have anything to do with me. Just something between him and some guys on the rez."

"Any other time that you saw them?" Gianelli said. He had pulled a notepad out from under some papers and was jotting something down.

"Three, four times," Marcy said.

Gianelli let the pen drop on top of the pad. "You've been on the reservation for two weeks, isn't that what you said? You're telling me you saw them three or four times in the last two weeks?"

Marcy shook her head. "I never said that. Only the one time last week. The other times were in Jackson."

"Let me get this straight," Gianelli said. "You saw Hawk and Lookingglass in the Jackson Hole area?"

"And that girl."

Vicky shifted sideways. "We have to talk before you say anything else," she said.

"No," Marcy said. "I want to tell what I saw. Roseanne Birdwoman was with them in Jackson, and she came to the house with them that one time." She leaned forward and grabbed on to the edge of the desk. "You should arrest her, too. Maybe she was waiting for them outside when they killed Ned. She could've been in the truck."

"Did you see the truck they were driving?"

"White Ford. I looked out the window when I heard 'em drive up the night they killed Ned. I remember shouting, 'Ned, those freaky guys are here again.' Then they burst through the door."

"Let's get back to Jackson Hole," Gianelli said. "Where did you see them?"

"At my condo in town. They stayed outside and talked real loud. I was watching out the window. They were real mad about something. They took some cartons out of Ned's van."

"What are we talking about?" Gianelli said. "Drugs?"

Vicky was on her feet. "Okay, this interview is over," she said. "My client has positively identified Dwayne Hawk and Lionel Lookingglass as the men who came to Ned's house last night, assaulted her, and shot Ned. There's nothing else she has to say."

"This goes to motivation, Vicky," Gianelli said, standing up. "Why did they contact Ned Windsong? What were they involved with?"

"You'll have to ask them." Vicky leaned over and tapped the girl's shoulder. "Let's go," she said.

It was a moment before the girl started to unfold herself from the chair. Vicky placed an arm around her shoulders and led her across the office, back down the corridor, and out the door. She could hear her heart pounding in her ears as they retraced their steps down to the sidewalk.

There was no one in the office. The surface of Annie's desk was cleared, the chair pushed in, the computer turned off. Annie and Roger had both left early. "This will take a few minutes," Vicky said, ushering the girl into her private office.

Marcy dropped into a side chair. "You're mad at me," she said, and for a moment, Vicky thought she might burst into tears.

"I'm not mad at you, but if I'm going to represent you, you'll have to trust me," Vicky said, walking around the desk to her own chair. "Tell me everything you know about Dwayne Hawk and Lionel Looking-glass and Roseanne Birdwoman. There can't be any secrets between us, because if there are, I can't help you."

"I don't understand," the girl said. "I was telling the truth."

"Okay, okay." Vicky waved a hand between them. "You didn't mention them to me."

"I already told you. I didn't think about them until I saw the photos. Then I knew who they were, and I remembered that Roseanne was with them. Ned said she wouldn't leave him alone, like she was obsessed with him. He couldn't get away from her. He had to go to Jackson Hole to get away. No way was he ever going back to her . . ."

"He had a relationship with her?"

"It was over." Marcy scoffed, as if she were clearing her throat. "He met me, and he never wanted to see her again. She just wouldn't get the message."

"What was inside Ned's van?"

"What?" The girl blinked as if she were trying to shift her thoughts away from Roseanne Birdwoman.

"Drugs? Is that what this is all about? Ned was killed over drugs?"

"No! I told you, he didn't do drugs."

"Listen, Marcy," Vicky said, leaning forward. "If Ned was involved in drugs, if he had possession, if was dealing and you knew about it and helped him in any way, you could be charged as an accomplice. You could be in serious trouble."

Such a blank look came on the girl's face that Vicky wanted to shout at her. God, no wonder Larry Morrison had hired a lawyer. The man knew his daughter.

"It wasn't drugs," Marcy said, the little girl voice again. "I think they might've been, you know . . ."

"I'm not clairvoyant," Vicky said.

"Stealing stuff. Breaking into houses. But Ned wasn't doing that anymore. I told you, he was gonna dance in the Sun Dance."

Vicky sat back and studied the girl on the other side of the desk. A white girl with a televangelist father who had said, "Send me your bill. I don't care what it is. Just take care of my little girl." A white girl with a condo in Jackson and a pickup and no doubt an annual allowance that was more than Vicky had seen in the first twenty-five years of her life. And she had no inkling that if Ned was involved in a burglary ring, she could also be implicated. She wondered how long it would take before Gianelli had Hawk and Lookingglass in custody. A day or two. The minute they told him what was going on, he would want to talk to Marcy Morrison again.

"Did Ned tell you what he had been doing?"

Marcy was shaking her head. "I figured it out. He never wanted me to know, 'cause he didn't want me to get into trouble." She started panting, as if she were having trouble getting her breath.

Vicky stood up. "Are you all right?"

"He's dead now," she said. "Doesn't anybody get it? Ned is gone forever, and what am I gonna do?"

"Maybe you should go home." Vicky sat back down. "Stay with your father for a while."

The girl's lips began moving silently. The blue vein pulsed in her forehead. Then she started speaking, enunciating carefully, letting each word hang in the air before she uttered the next one: "I will never go back there."

"Then think about going back to Jackson Hole," Vicky said. "You've identified the two men. There's no reason you can't go home."

"They killed him," she said. "I'm not leav-

ing here 'til they're arrested. All of them.
That girl, too."

12

Roseanne darted past the automatic glass doors and across the Walmart entrance, the day's heat trapped with the rows of metal carts. "Have a nice evening." The greeter, the old man with the sunken chest, waved a bony hand in her direction. She kept going. Out the glass door that swung toward her, across the sidewalk and down the rows of parked vehicles to the far lot where employees parked. The sun was dropping behind the mountains, and red, orange, and magenta shot across the pale gray sky. At some point, she realized, she had stopped thinking and become a robot. Going through the motions — bending, gripping, smiling. All of it a blur — the shelves and the fluorescent lights that glowed through the flat white panels overhead.

She stayed close to the parked vehicles, sunlight sparkling in the bumpers and dancing on the hoods. Swinging her backpack around, she pulled out her keys, robot eyes straight ahead, feet moving toward the blue sedan. The hot asphalt burned through her sneakers. A dry breeze snatched up pieces of trash and tossed them in the air. She inched sideways between the sedan and a pickup, letting the backpack drag over the asphalt, and jammed the key into the lock.

He grabbed her from behind, an arm like an iron bar pressing against her neck, a fist dug into her stomach. "Shut up," he said. Dwayne's voice in her ear, the sour breath flowing across her cheek. Then she was spinning about like a puppet and jammed against the door, her vertebrae pressed into the window frame. The scream erupted in her throat, but he had placed a hand over her mouth and dug his fingers into her cheeks.

"You gonna scream?" He leaned over her. The black eyes were wide with the joke of it. "You think them fat white tourists are gonna come running and save you from a big, bad Indian?"

She tried to push down the terror rising inside her. No one could see them. They were at the far end of the parking lot scrunched down between her car and a pickup. She could scream her lungs out, but in the heat and wind, with the traffic grinding along Federal Boulevard and vehicles belching in the lot, no one would hear.

"You snitch on us?" he said, and she felt the pressure of his hand giving way.

"No," she managed.

"Come on, Roseanne. Word's out the fed's looking for me and Lionel. How did he freaking hear about us? I told you to keep your mouth shut."

She could feel herself slipping downward, her legs folding beneath her. "I don't know," she said. Her mouth had gone dry, her tongue was a piece of sandpaper grating her teeth. She could picture herself in the front room at Berta's, spilling out her guts when all she had to do was keep quiet. Except that Berta had blurted out the truth.

"The fed already knew," she managed. She could hear the hollowness in the lie, and she pushed on. "All I told him was that you and Lionel found Ned's body. I told him that Ned was already dead when we got to the house. It'll help you. Don't you see?"

He made a grunting noise under his breath and looked away, and for the first time, Roseanne glimpsed the fear running through his eyes. "How did the fed know we went to the house? Nobody could've told him but you."

"Somebody must've seen us," she said.

He stared at her for a long moment, but she could see that he was beginning to accept the possibility. "What if the fed thinks we killed Ned and went back to the house afterward? He'll pin it on us. Lionel and me will rot in prison."

"There's no reason for him to think that." She was shivering, arms shaking. There was reason. She could feel the truth of it. Something between them and Ned. He had warned her to stay away from them. Oh God. Why didn't she listen? All she had been thinking about was getting back at him, doing what he had told her not to do.

"What else did you open your mouth about?" he said.

"I told you all of it."

"What else, Roseanne?" The tips of his fingers plunged into her shoulders like darts.

"I told him you came running out of the house like you'd seen a ghost."

"What about the business?"

Roseanne stared at the brown face a few inches from her own, the missing curve of his left ear, the narrow, black eyes as opaque as stones, the purple lips and the pores cratered in the hooked nose. "What are you talking about?" she said.

"The way Lionel and me got it figured"

144

— the fingers loosened; he took a half step back — "you snitched to the fed about the business, so he figures we had reason to take out Ned. Some business problem, like maybe he was cheating on us. Is that a fact? Was he cheating on us?"

"You're crazy," she said. The dark eyes pulled into slits, and she put up one hand. "I didn't mean that. I don't know anything about any business. I haven't seen Ned since he got back from Jackson Hole." Except for that one time, she was thinking, but no one else had been there. "He broke up with me. He was with the white girl. Maybe she said something to the fed." God, she was going to cry. She could feel the moisture gathering behind her eyeballs.

"The white bitch that was in the house." He seemed to consider this. "Where is she?"

She was aware that he had let go, and she had to grab on to the door handle to keep from crumbling onto the pavement. "The fed might have her in hiding," she said. " 'Cause she saw Ned's killer."

"Yeah? Well, she didn't see me or Lionel." His muscles seemed to relax; he ran the palm of his hand over his forehead, pushing the sweat into the edges of his black hair. "She keeps her mouth shut about the business, we'll be okay. Unless . . ." He straightened up and looked past her across the roof of the sedan. "Who else would he have shot off his mouth to?"

"I told you, I didn't see him."

"That priest at the mission? Talked to him, didn't he? Used to go over there, hang around, confess his sins, whatever." He shrugged. "He knows what'll happen if he says anything to the fed."

Roseanne could feel her breath stopped in her throat.

"You hear where the white girl is, you call my cell." He dropped the slit-eyes to her and smiled out of the corner of his mouth. She had called him yesterday. Going crazy, locked up in the house that reeked with whiskey, Aunt Martha on a tear, ordering her about — clean the kitchen, take out the trash, wash the freaking clothes. The house, the job six hours a day, and the image never leaving her mind of Ned and the beautiful white girl he wanted more than her. "Anything going on tonight, Dwayne?" she had said when he answered. "I need to get outta here."

"You hear me?" he said.

She nodded.

"The fed comes around again, you stick to your story. About how we was shocked at finding Ned." He swung around and started

146

for the back of the pickup, then glanced around. "No hard feelings," he said.

Roseanne stayed against the door, watching the white truck damaged on the left side back up and jerk forward. It shot past the rear of her car. She listened to the engine roaring across the asphalt until the sound blended into the low hum of traffic out on Federal.

She drove across Riverton, south on Highway 789, right onto the reservation, all of her senses on alert, as if a thousand needles had pricked her skin, replaying in her mind everything Ned had said that last time. Maybe he had told her about the business, and she hadn't realized what he was talking about. She pushed away the idea. He would never have told her anything that would cause her trouble. She felt a brief tingle of something she remembered as happiness: maybe Ned had still loved her after all.

She kept coming back to this: If Dwayne found out that she had seen Ned even once, he would think she was lying about the business. He would find her again — anyone could find her. The same hours at Walmart, the stupid, reeking house. She had to find someplace else to stay. Talk the supervisor into giving her another shift. Everything had to be different.

She took another right and fishtailed onto a dirt road. The plains floated outside the windows, rising and falling with their own rhythm. The miles clicked on the odometer. She tapped the brake pedal, swung into a dirt yard, and stopped at the corner of the gray house. She jumped out of the car, slamming the door behind her, and raced up the wooden steps. The door was unlocked, as usual. She pushed it open and went inside. Aunt Martha was sprawled on the sofa, staring at the flashing images on the TV. Cartons crusted with days-old takeout lay scattered over the coffee table and linoleum floor, and odors of burned coffee, mustard, and old hamburger mingled with the smells of whiskey.

"About time you got home." Aunt Martha lifted one eye in her direction. She wore a baby blue robe, and her breasts hung over the tie that had worked its way up from her waist. Her gray hair was matted, sweat-pressed to her head. "Some guy was here to see you."

"Some guy?" Roseanne stopped next to the sofa and looked down at the woman who had gone back to staring at the TV. A rerun of *Beevis and Butt-Head* jumping around. "Who was it?"

"When did I get to be your secretary, Miss High and Mighty?" The pink spot wiggled at the top of the old woman's scalp. Roseanne felt disconnected, floating in space. How had she come to be living in a gray house with an old woman she called Auntie, when Martha wasn't her auntie at all. She was no relation, except she had married Roseanne's uncle, and somehow, after accidents and diabetes and alcoholism had run their course, they were all the family left on the rez. The survivors.

"I need to know who it was." Roseanne felt her muscles stiffen.

"Dwayne somebody." Martha fumbled for the remote in a stack of cartons and turned up the volume. Cartoon voices rose over the laughter and tinny music.

"You told him where I was!" Roseanne screamed at the woman. It took all of her strength not to pick up an empty whiskey bottle and hurl it at the woman's head.

Aunt Martha turned sideways and stared up at her, daring her, Roseanne thought. Begging her, even. Make it easy for her, put her out of her misery. "Some big secret, you working at Walmart?"

Roseanne spun around and hurried down the hall. She went into Aunt Martha's bedroom and shut the door. The room smelled of the old woman, the unwashed hair and dirty nails, the dry, flaking skin, the whiskey odors rising off the tangle of blankets on the bed. She pulled open the top drawer in the dresser and rummaged through scraps of underwear, nothing more than rags. Then the second drawer, a jumble of tee shirts and shorts, a wadded up black skirt. Inside the bottom drawer were the same kind of torn and soiled shirts and slacks. Her fingers ran over the surface of a box in the corner, and she yanked it past the clothes and flipped back the lid. An assortment of necklaces and bracelets, chains broken, glass stones missing. She closed the lid, put the box back, and kicked the drawer shut. God, it was pathetic the sum of the old woman's possessions.

She bent forward, resting her forehead on the edge of the dresser. She had wanted so much more. How they had talked, she and Ned, about the ranch he would buy: their own house, fine horses in the corral, a small herd of cattle, bales of hay in the pasture. He was saving most of his salary, he had told her, and she was saving, too, a little bit out of each paycheck after she had bought food and given money to Aunt Martha. "We'll get it," Ned had said. "Trust me, Roseanne. Someday, we're gonna have our own place." They had hiked up in Sinks Canyon and were sitting on rocks, boots propped against the rocks down slope, listening to the sounds of the Popo Agie rushing by below. She pressed her eyes shut. She could see them now up on the mountain. Wearing blue jeans torn at the knees, Ned in his red plaid shirt, she in a pink tee shirt. Last summer, another lifetime. "It won't be long now." She could almost hear his voice.

She pushed herself off the dresser, flung open the closet door, and started slamming the hangers aside, kicking at the mismatched shoes and boots strewn over the floor. Then she lifted herself on her tiptoes and rummaged through the piles of faded blankets and towels until her fingers hit a hard surface. This was it — she knew by the weight as she pulled the cigar box off the top shelf, the sound of metal knocking inside. She sank to the floor, lifted the lid, and took out the black M1911 Colt .45 automatic pistol that her uncle had brought home from Vietnam. She jammed the gun inside the waistband of her blue jeans and picked up the loaded magazine.

"What the hell are you doing?" Aunt Martha swayed in the doorway, blinking down at her. "Get out of my closet!"

Roseanne pushed the cigar box into the debris of shoes and got to her feet. "None of your business," she said, pushing past the old woman, the magazine tight in her grip. She ran back down the hall, grabbed her backpack off the floor where she had dropped it, and flung herself past the door out onto the stoop. In a moment, she was backing across the yard. Then she put the gear into forward and drove out onto the road, the image of Aunt Martha in the side-view mirror, gray hair straggling over her shoulders, leaning out the front door.

13

Vicky read through the corrected pages of the logging contract with Martinson Corporation of Dover, Delaware, as if the largest logging and timber company in the West were actually run from Delaware. A soft nighttime quiet had settled over the bungalow, broken by the intermittent sound of a dog barking outside, a car crawling down the street. Evening was a good time to work, after Roger and Annie had left and the phones had stopped ringing. She told herself it had nothing to do with the empty apartment, now that Adam wasn't around, or that he hadn't called in a week. She was used to being alone. *Hi sei ci nihi,* the grandmothers called her. Woman Alone.

She forced her thoughts back to the contract. Similar to the previous contracts, except for the section titled "Revenues." The Wind River tribes would collect a higher percentage of revenues, a change that the company lawyers had hardly blinked at, as if they had been expecting it for years. Well, it had taken years — she could hear Adam's voice in her head — before Indian people had their own lawyers to look out for their interests. She hit another key and sent the document to Annie's computer. Tomorrow Annie would clean up the spacings and titles, check the spelling, and print out two copies. One for the Joint Business Council of the Arapaho and Shoshone tribes and one for the law firm in the modern brick building on Main Street that, not long ago, had been the offices of Holden and Lone Eagle.

Then she hit another key and typed in a search for burglaries, Lander, Wyoming. Lines of black type filled the screen, most about burglaries in Cheyenne or Sheridan or Cody. A few with Lander in bold type. She clicked on the first site: a rash of burglaries in Lander in the 1930s, executed by an outlaw gang that broke into houses, stole everything they could carry off, and vanished into the Wyoming wilderness. White men, she guessed, by the tone of barely suppressed admiration for the gang's audacity and success.

She moved to the next site, a small article about burglaries in the spring of 1955.

Police had been called to the break-ins at two houses in the western part of town. There was a follow-up article under the headline "Arapahos Guilty." She skimmed down the text: three Arapaho men in their twenties charged, convicted and sent to prison. Witnesses swore they had seen them loitering in the neighborhood of recent house burglaries, and one witness placed them near the late-night burglary of a shoe repair shop.

She wondered what kind of shiny lawyer straight out of law school had been appointed to represent the three Arapahos. She knew by the tone of the article that they had been convicted before they had ever stepped inside the courtroom. Guilty of being Indians.

She scrolled through other sites looking for recent break-ins, an uneasy feeling starting to nag at her. Marcy had seen Dwayne and Lionel taking cartons out of Ned's van, but what did that mean? It was possible she was mistaken. Maybe she imagined what was going on, made up a story to explain what she hadn't understood.

Vicky scrolled to the next page and looked down the list of sites as irrelevant as the others. The problem was, Marcy had told Gianelli about the cartons, and now they would take on a life of their own, become their own reality.

She stopped on the bold black words: "Break-ins, Lander." A brief article from the Lander newspaper:

Three vacation homes in the mountains were burglarized last week, according to the Fremont County sheriff's office. No one was in the homes at the time of the break-ins. Security systems had been disabled, which allowed the burglars to break through doors, enter the homes, and leave without being detected. Out-of-state owners are still being contacted, and inventories of stolen items are not available. "These types of break-ins usually result in the theft of electronics and jewelry, anything that can be quickly sold," the sheriff's spokesman said. He urged residents in mountain areas to be good neighbors and notify the sheriff's office of any suspicious behavior or suspicious vehicles.

Vicky scrolled back to the top and studied the date: March 16. Ned Windsong was still in the area.

She typed in another search looking for burglaries in Jackson Hole, and this time, every site on the first page looked relevant.

She clicked on the first site. An article from the *Jackson Hole Daily* filled the screen:

A rash of home burglaries have plagued our community in the last month, according to a police spokesperson. The burglars overrode the security systems. "We didn't hear about the break-ins until the owners went to the houses and found household items missing," the spokesperson said. "We believe a sophisticated burglary ring has moved into the area. The burglars look for unoccupied homes likely to have high-priced items that can be fenced easily."

Vicky read through the next site, a blog by one of the homeowners.

Imagine walking into your house and realizing something's missing, like the flat-screen TV that used to be on the living room wall, and the telescope in front of the big dining room windows, and the other TVs and DVD players and radios. I immediately ran into the bedroom and guess what? Cameras were gone. About broke my husband's heart to lose his favorite Canon. But the worst was my jewelry dresser. They took the whole fricking dresser, costume jewelry along with the good stuff. I'm trying to maintain my Zen mind-set. They are only material things. I trust the burglars must need those things, and they have gone to the right people. The insurance agent was here today. All is well.

There were six other sites. All follow-up newspaper articles, urging the police to capture the outsiders that had set the town on edge, urging people to lock their doors and report any unusual behavior.

Vicky closed the last site and stared at the screen that went from black to swirling blues, reds, and yellows. The burglaries had taken place while Ned Windsong was in Jackson Hole, just as the burglaries in Lander occurred while he was here. Circumstantial evidence, to be sure, like the testimony of witnesses in the 1950s who happened to spot three Arapahos at the time of the break-ins, but strong enough, coupled with Marcy's story, to tie Ned to a burglary ring with Dwayne Hawk, Lionel Lookingglass, and a girl named Roseanne. Gianelli would have pulled the information on the burglaries by now. He would make the connections, draw the conclusions, and start wondering whether Marcy might have also been involved. It was only a matter of time before he would want to interview her again.

Roseanne leaned against the door and knocked again. She had been knocking for five minutes, she was sure. She glanced around. The only vehicle parked in front of Berta's house was her own. Darkness was pressing down, filtering through the cotton-woods. She could make out the remnants of last night's party, the beer cans scattered about, the little clumps of trash, the gray ashes of campfires. The backpack felt heavy and awkward over her shoulder. She went back to knocking. "Be here, Berta," she said, under her breath.

"Roseanne?"

She swung around. Mervin was standing at the corner of the house, all arms and legs and skinny neck popping past the collar of his white shirt.

"Thought I heard somebody knockin'," he said. "I been in the barn feeding the horses. Berta's not here."

"Can I come in?" Roseanne said.

Mervin stomped across the hard-packed dirt and jumped onto the stoop. She had to squeeze herself against the wood railing while he shoved a key in the lock and pushed open the door. "Berta says we gotta keep things locked up 'til Dwayne and Lionel get arrested. You never know about them two. They could come around, start trouble." He stepped inside, expecting her to follow, she knew. He turned on a table lamp, and she watched the way the circle of light burst across the sofa and coffee table, pushing the shadows back into the edges of the living room.

"I'm gonna stay here awhile," she said, dropping the backpack on the sofa.

The boy shrugged. "Okay by me. You want some stew or something?"

Roseanne sank onto the sofa. "Do you think Dwayne and Lionel killed Ned?" she said.

"What?" The question seemed to take him by surprise. He pulled over a wood chair and straddled it backward, wrapping skinny arms across the top. "What do I know?" he said.

"You know what they were doing, don't you?" Mervin stayed quiet, biting at his lower lip. Light flickered in his dark eyes. "The business," she prodded. "Come on, Mervin. Berta thinks you were in on it, too. She told you to stay away from Dwayne and Lionel."

"I wasn't ever involved," he said, glancing into the corner of the room. "They give me a chance to come in." He shrugged. "Ned got wind and went ballistic. Said I'd end up in jail, be a nobody all my life. What did he know? It was my chance to get some good money."

"Doing what? Selling drugs?"

"Drugs didn't have nothing to do with it." He took a long moment, then went on. "Stealing stuff, that's all. Fancy TVs, cameras, jewelry, that kind of stuff."

Roseanne tilted her head against the back of the chair. Oh, man, she should have seen it coming. That day last summer — that hot, stuffy August day when she had stripped down to her underwear and thrown a bucket of water over her head out in back of Ned's house, and he had come out and found her and laughed so hard, he'd sat down on the ground — that was the day Dwayne and Lionel had roared up in front. She had thrown on her tee shirt and shorts and followed Ned through the house out to the front stoop. "Get inside and shut the door," he'd called, like she had done something that really got to him, and he'd deal with her later. She had backed into the house and shut the door. But she had peered past the edge of the window and watched him open his van with Silver Electrical Company lettered in black on the side. Dwayne and Lionel had pounced on the cartons, dragging them out of the van, but real careful, as if whatever was inside could break.

"Where'd they steal the stuff?" she said.

Mervin gave a quick shrug. "I don't know where they got it, and I don't know what they did with it. All I know is Dwayne said, 'You want in on a deal? You do what I say.' Ned come roaring over here, said he'd break my legs if I got into anything with them two."

Roseanne looked away. Ned's voice had started playing like a recording in her head. "I'm gonna change my life. Start over. Cut it off with Dwayne and Lionel. Stay away from them, Roseanne. I'm warning you. They're no good."

"I'm gonna go into the Sun Dance next year, in memory of Ned," Mervin said.

"You do that." Roseanne pushed herself off the sofa, went into the kitchen and opened the refrigerator. Then she leaned against the edge of the door, trying to focus on the cartons and containers, wondering which one contained stew left over from last night's party. There was a hollow place in her stomach; she couldn't remember the last time she had eaten.

"Almost forgot . . ." Mervin was standing in the doorway. "Vicky Holden said you

162

should call her. She's the white girl's lawyer."

"Why would I do that?"

"She wants to find Ned's killers."

And get her involved, Roseanne was thinking. Blame her somehow. She shooed him away. He shrugged and disappeared into the living room. The front door slammed shut, sending a small tremor through the linoleum floor. Papers rattled on the bulletin board clipped to the side of a cabinet.

She wondered how long Ned had been in the stealing business with Dwayne and Lionel before he decided to get out. Long enough, she thought, to get enough money put away to buy a little ranch. She leaned into the refrigerator, letting the cool air wash over her. She had convinced Dwayne once that she knew nothing about the business. But he'd go over and over it; he'd tell Lionel. "Bullshit!" Lionel would shout. They would convince themselves that she could tie them to Ned, provide the motive for his murder. They would come after her again. And even if the fed picked them up first, Gianelli would learn about the business soon enough. He would assume she was an accomplice, all those months living with Ned, and he would come after her.

She had to get out of here. She slammed

the refrigerator door, went into the living room, and grabbed her backpack. She had put the Colt and the magazine in the outside pocket. She could feel the gun's hard edges. Then she let herself out and ran to the car. In a moment she was speeding across the reservation through the darkness.

14

Roseanne stared at the yellow cones of headlights floating ahead, barely aware of the sides of the road, the drop-offs into the borrow ditches. The sound of the engine filled up the silence. A pickup had passed ten minutes ago, but there was no other traffic. Like driving off the edge of the world, she thought. Her mind was spinning. How had she gotten caught up in this? If Dwayne and Lionel had killed Ned over some stupid argument about stolen stuff, then they would kill her if they thought she could connect them to Ned.

"I didn't know!" The sound of her own voice slammed into her. She hunched forward and tightened her grip on the steering wheel. Her fingertips cut into her palms. Out of the corner of her eye, she could see the dark outline of the backpack riding on the passenger seat. The Colt was in the pocket. God! She hardly knew anything about guns. Ned had wanted her to go target shooting, and Aunt Martha told her to take the Colt. "No damn good to me." Roseanne could still hear the slurred voice. "Tommy give it to me before he died. Told me to shoot any burglars that broke in." The old woman had thrown her head back and let out a howl of laughter. "I hid the damn thing 'cause I was afraid I'd shoot Tommy."

They had gone out to the Red Desert, a place of red, sheer-faced cliffs that lifted out of the brown earth, the sky as blue and clear as water. It was mid-April, the air crisp and the sun just beginning to warm. There were antelope, coyotes, wild horses, and even wolves in the Red Desert. They had shot at piles of rocks stacked on a boulder. She could feel Ned's arms around her, his warm breath on her neck, his hand steadying hers. "That's it," he said. "Lift the gun higher. Brace with your other hand. You got the rocks in sight? Okay, pull the trigger."

The rocks had splinted into a thousand pieces, hanging in the air a moment, then dropping to the ground. They had shot a dozen rounds. Ned had an old pistol, the only thing he had of his dad's, he said. Helluva thing to leave your kid.

Afterward they had spread a plastic tarp in the shade of a red cliff, eaten sandwiches and sipped on the cold Cokes. "Why are we doing this?" she had asked.

"What'd'ya mean?" He had a way of teasing her, drawing her out until she answered her own question.

"We're gonna have a ranch," she had said.

She could see him nodding and smiling, as clearly as if he were in the headlights ahead. "We're gonna have the best spread in these parts," he said. "We're gonna raise white-faced Herefords and Appaloosas. Acres of hay."

She had started laughing, she remembered. Laughing so hard she had doubled up and lay on the tarp, trying to get her breath. Laughing with the joy of it, as if the dream were real. Then she had sat back up. The pain in his eyes was like a fire bolt that burned through her.

"You don't believe me," he said.

"No, Ned." She had scooted over to him, put her arms around his neck, tried to bend him to her, wanting to kiss away the pain. "I believe you. I do. It will be wonderful. I just don't know how it's possible."

She remembered the tiniest flicker of doubt in his eyes, but he had smiled. They had made love in the shade, then driven back to the rez. A few days later he told her he was moving to Jackson Hole.

The house was up ahead somewhere, she thought, forcing herself back into the present. She scanned the dark plains rolling outside like a black sea. Set back from the road was the tiniest glow of lights. She slowed down and stared past the headlights, pulling herself so far forward that the steering wheel dug into her chest. She passed the turnoff and had to back up. Then she was jolting across the dirt. Two pickups were parked ahead, the bumpers gleaming in her headlights.

She stopped alongside the pickups, grabbed the backpack, and ran for the little house, stumbling in the dim light that glowed in the front windows. Before she could knock, the door flung back. A square-shaped woman stood in the opening, backlit by an overhead fixture inside, gray hair springing about her head. Roseanne felt her heart skip. She had come to the wrong house.

"Come in," the woman said, and at the sound of her voice, Roseanne recognized Marie, Ella's sister. The woman moved sideways, ushering her inside, and Roseanne caught her heel on the edge of the step as she pitched herself forward. Ella sat on the sofa against the far wall.

Roseanne walked over and dropped down

next to her. "I should've come sooner," she said.

"You're here now." Roseanne felt the woman's hand, warm and moist, close over her own. She had dark, wide-set eyes and a round, kind face. "You loved him, too," she said.

"I don't have anywhere else to go," Roseanne said. The sound of her own voice surprised her. The words had tumbled out on their own. How could she explain? She could never tell Ella that Ned had been involved in a burglary ring.

Puzzlement flickered in Ella's eyes. "You'll stay here," she said.

"You'll be safe here." It was a man's voice, and Roseanne glanced around. Jerry Adams, big shoulders and puffed-out chest and shaved head, stood in the doorway to the kitchen. He took his time moving past the chair where his wife had sat down and perched on the edge of a round ottoman.

"Thing is, Ella, moccasin telegraph is saying Roseanne here was with Dwayne and Lionel when they found Ned's body," he said. "Course that was a setup. They'd already shot him. They pretended to find him so Roseanne could say that's what happened. They could get real mean with her, make sure she tells a good story for them."

"He never liked 'em," Ella said. "Why do you think he moved to Jackson Hole? He needed to get away from guys like that, make a fresh start with new friends." She glanced at Roseanne, then went back to patting her hand. "Not you, honey. You were what kept him going."

She looked back at Adams. "Why do you suppose he was living over at Dad's house after he got back? He didn't want anybody knowing where he was. Didn't want Dwayne and Lionel coming around again, stirring up a lot of trouble. Ned was smart. He was saving up to buy a ranch . . ." She dipped her head and gave way to the tears a moment. Then she wiped at her cheeks. "He didn't have nothing to do with Dwayne and Lionel. You ask me, there's a whole lot the fed don't know."

Adams was shaking his head. "They had a beef, Ella. There's nobody else with any reason to kill Ned."

"What about the white girl," Ella said. The words hung in the silence.

"We've been over that, Sis," Marie said. Her fist thumped the armrest. "There was no gun in the house, no residue on her hands. The hospital checked her out. She was bruised, beaten up. She tried to help Ned, and the killers pushed her around."

170

Roseanne shifted toward Ella. "You think she had something to do with it?"

"Look." Adams leaned forward and punched a fist in the air, as if he were knocking on a door. "Nobody's ruled out at this point. That's how the fed's gonna get to Dwayne and Lionel, by ruling out everybody else. Sure, he's gonna look at the white girl — what's her name? Mary?"

"Marcy," his wife said.

"Yeah, Marcy. I heard her old man's that big televangelist, Larry Morrison, rakes in the dough from true believers. You ask me, the girl's a rich, spoiled brat, took up with an Indian to rile her old man. Now she's a witness to murder. Gianelli's gonna get to the bottom of it and find out what their beef was with Ned, soon's he finds them."

"I wish I could be sure," Ella said.

"Listen to me." Adams stretched out his hand and took hold of Ella's arm. "He's the FBI. What else you think is gonna happen?"

Ella dropped her face into her hands. Her shoulders were shaking. After a moment, she started to her feet, and Roseanne took her elbow, rising with her. "It's been a long day," Ella said. "Sometimes I think I been dreaming, and I'm gonna wake up. Ned's gonna come in the front door, plop down at the kitchen table, and I'm gonna pour him some coffee and give him fresh fry bread with gooseberry gravy, and he's gonna say to me, 'Auntie Ella, you're the best cook on the whole rez.' " She was crying so hard that the words sounded muffled and water-logged.

"Then I get a flash," she went on, "like I'm back in my normal life, only it's not normal anymore. There's a big hole in the middle. Everything's going on around me, people in and out, the food laid out on the counter, everybody saying they're sorry, and I'm just stuck in this hole."

Marie was at her sister's side. "Come on, sweetheart," she said. "I'll take you to the bedroom. You need to get some sleep. I'm gonna give you one of my sleeping pills." She started leading Ella along the sofa, past an armchair. "It's gonna help you," she said, her voice fading in the hallway.

Roseanne took hold of her backpack and started to get up. She could feel the energy draining out of her arms and legs, the fatigue settling like a rock inside her. She would crash wherever there was an extra bed.

"Hold on a minute." Adams put up a beefy hand, and Roseanne dropped back onto the sofa. "How'd you figure it out?" he said.

Roseanne didn't say anything. She threw a glance down the hallway. Ella and Marie had disappeared.

"Ella doesn't know what Ned was up to," the man went on. "I seen the way you was trying to keep it from her. How did you find out? Who told you?"

Roseanne clasped her arms around the backpack and drew herself in close. "How do you know what Ned was doing?" she managed.

"He talked to me," Adams said. "I'm his uncle. He knew I'd help him, give him good advice. He said he wanted out of the burglary ring. He had enough money saved up for his ranch. That's all he wanted, but Dwayne and Lionel weren't gonna let him out. They needed him to disable the security systems. Those dumb shits weren't gonna figure it out, even though he showed them how to do it. They'd probably electrocute themselves."

"You think they killed him because he wanted out?"

"The fed'll figure it out, sooner or later."

"Ella will have to know." Roseanne closed her eyes, remembering how she had felt when Mervin told her, as if he had driven a fist into her stomach.

"We'll worry about that later," Adams

173

said. "You haven't said how you found out? The telegraph? People talking about it? How many people know?"

"Nobody knows," Roseanne said. She was thinking of Mervin, just a kid. He didn't need to be dragged in by the fed and asked a lot of questions. Ned had kept him out of it. "I put it together," she said. "I remembered some things."

"Oh, yeah," Adams said. "Like what?"

"Nothing important. Boxes that Ned stored in an old barn out on North Fork Road. We went there once." She could feel herself in the passenger seat of the van, the dusty road unrolling ahead. Ned had made a couple of turns, then they were jolting down a rutted track, equipment banging in the back, an old barn rising out of the plains ahead.

"Ned made me stay in the van," she said, "but soon as he opened the doors, I saw the boxes. Dwayne and Lionel showed up and they loaded boxes into their truck and drove off. I didn't know what was in the boxes, but I figured it wasn't drugs. Ned wouldn't have anything to do with drugs. Ned told me it was just some stuff he'd been storing for them. But I've been putting things together, and I figure the stuff was stolen. That's how he was getting money for our ranch."

"Old barn, you say? Who else knows about it?"

Roseanne shrugged against the backpack. "How would I know."

"The fed might wanna hear about the barn."

"I'm not talking to him," Roseanne said. "He'll think I was part of it. I don't wanna go to jail."

Adams didn't say anything, and Roseanne stood up.

"Dwayne and Lionel came after you, right?" Adams said, getting to his feet in front of her. "That the reason you don't have anyplace else to go? You're hiding from them?"

Roseanne nodded. "Dwayne was waiting for me after work. He warned me to keep my mouth shut."

"I'll bet he did. Didn't say what hole they've crawled into on the rez, did he?"

"Why would he tell me?" Roseanne slipped past him and started down the hallway toward the bedroom at the far end. She knew where Dwayne and Lionel were hiding, she realized. God, she had known all along. Adams's voice followed her: "Nobody's gonna be at peace around here 'til those bastards get caught."

15

Fewer than two dozen parishioners occupied the pews this morning, wrinkled, brown faces turned up to the altar, missals and rosary beads gripped in knobby, swollen hands. They sat in the same place every morning, as if the places had been assigned. Mary Hunting, second pew on the left, James White Eagle, last pew on the right, Jonathan HisManyHorses, middle pew behind Josephine Yellowbear. Father John knew them all — the regulars who came to daily Mass, steering old pickups and Chevy sedans around Circle Drive, stopping outside the church.

"Let us pray for the soul of Ned Windsong," he said. The heads dipped in front of him. Everyone was thinking about Ned, he knew. Another one of the younger generation gone. All that might have been, the good Ned might have done, the children and grandchildren he might have had — all gone.

He said the first prayers of the Mass slowly, waiting for the gravelly voices to catch up. Then he lifted the paten, a pottery plate a young woman had made for him when he first came to St. Francis. Her name was Jo Eastman, he remembered; she had died in an accident a few months later. *This is my body.* Then he lifted the chalice. *This is my blood. Shed for you for the forgiveness of sins.*

Amen. The word rippled softly around the pews, and Father John felt the familiar sense of peace come over him. This was the heart of the Mass, the heart of his own priesthood. Without this — the faith in the Real Presence, that Jesus was among them — nothing made sense. This was the reason he had become a priest. *Walk with me. Walk with my people.* Sometimes he wondered if he had actually heard the words when he was struggling with the notion that had come out of nowhere, like a bolt from heaven, that he should become a priest, or whether he had only dreamed them.

He stepped into the aisle and distributed the consecrated pieces of bread to the elders and grandmothers moving toward him in a solemn line. The morning sun glowed in the stained-glass windows, and thin columns of sunshine lay over the pews. The church was suffused in quiet broken only by the shush of footsteps on the carpet, the sounds of people settling back into the pews, heads bent in prayer. This was his favorite time of the day, when, for a moment, everything seemed whole somehow.

When the Mass was finished, he walked down the aisle and waited at the door, shaking hands with the old people who filed past. "Who would've wanted to kill that boy?" Mary Hunting asked, holding on to his hand. He was surprised at the strength in her fingers. "Nobody deserves to die like a dog."

"Don't worry." Jonathan HisManyHorses had come up behind and leaned around the old woman. "What gets sent into the world always comes back. Them men that killed Ned are gonna pay a heavy price."

Father John gave a little nod of what he hoped looked like affirmation. It was a comforting thought; it might be true. But there were killers who walked around free, never brought to justice. He pushed the thought away. He could see Ned Windsong bounding across the grounds, arm raised: *Hey, Father. How's it going?* He didn't want to think of his homicide left unsolved, a box of evidence in the back of a warehouse.

He waited until the last pickup had disappeared down the tunnel of cottonwoods toward Seventeen-Mile Road. Then he headed back inside, checked the pews for any items left behind, and hung his vestments in the sacristy closet. Five minutes later he walked across the field of wild grasses moving in the sunshine and let himself into the residence. Walks-On was at the door, wagging his tail, hopping about. "Later," Father John said, patting the dog's head. "We'll play Frisbee later."

The dog trailed him down the hall to the kitchen where Elena was scooping oatmeal into a bowl and helped himself to a cup of coffee. Walks-On curled up at his feet when he sat down at the round table. "Bishop Harry already eaten?" He could hear the man moving about upstairs. They took turns saying daily Mass, but even on the days when it was Father John's turn, Harry was up early, a thousand plans running through the old man's head.

"Good thing somebody around here eats." Elena set the bowl of oatmeal on the table. She had already sprinkled on brown sugar and some raisins. He reached for the carton of milk and poured it around the edges.

"You know how I eat everything you put

in front of me," he said. "I'm a grateful man."

"When you're around, you eat," she said. "The bishop could eat you under the table. That man likes food." For a moment, he wondered if she appreciated the bishop's appetite or was going to complain about the extra work. She had looked after the priests at St. Francis Mission for longer than anyone could remember. Part Arapaho and part Cheyenne, sharp-featured and round-faced at the same time, probably in her mid-seventies, but that was a subject Father John never brought up. He couldn't imagine the place without her.

Elena plopped down on the chair across from him, and tucked a piece of gray hair into place. "That girl staying in the guest-house never touched a bite of dinner I brought her last evening. Left the plate on the stoop, never even brought it inside." She lifted a hand before he could say anything. "I knocked on the door, told her I brought dinner, and she calls out, 'Just leave it.' Like I'm the maid. What's she think this is? Some fancy hotel?"

Father John took a sip of coffee and tried not to smile at the idea of Elena as the maid. "I guess she didn't know she was speaking to the boss," he said. Then he saw the frozen look on her face, the worry in her eyes. "Look, Elena." He set the mug down. "The girl's still in shock. She probably wasn't hungry."

"She needs to keep up her strength." Elena raised her eyes over his head. "Could be more coming at her."

"What do you mean?"

"She was the only one in the house, besides Ned," she said, bringing her eyes back to his. "Maybe she had something to do with it."

Father John took a bite of oatmeal, then another bite. He hoped that wasn't true. The girl loved Ned. They were going to be married. And yet there was something about her that was not quite whole, as if an invisible fracture ran through her. "She seems very sad," he said. "It doesn't mean she had anything to do with Ned's murder."

"He had a real nice girlfriend," Elena said. "Roseanne Birdwoman. Why'd he ever get mixed up with that white girl?"

Father John laughed. "You expect me to explain that?"

She swooped a hand along the table and got to her feet. "Everybody's wondering the same thing," she said.

"When they figure it out, let me know." He finished the oatmeal and drained the coffee, watching Elena move about the kitchen, wiping the counters, his thoughts on the gossip weighing down the moccasin telegraph, the urge to blame the white girl, the outsider. He felt a stab of pity for the girl. She would be convicted before Gianelli had the killers in custody.

He thanked Elena for another gourmet breakfast and retraced his steps down the hall, Walks-On clipping behind. Outside he threw the Frisbee a half-dozen times, squinting in the sun as the dog ran through the grass, pivoted on his single hind leg, leaping in the air, and trotted back with the red Frisbee clenched in his jaws, a triumphant look on his face. Across the grounds, at the far side of the administration building, Bishop Harry was swinging his fishing rod, casting into Circle Drive.

"Gotta go to work," Father John told the dog. Still he gave the Frisbee another toss before he started across the grounds. The morning sun burned through the back of his shirt and pricked his neck. Walks-On trotted ahead, tossing and catching the Frisbee himself.

"Morning," Bishop Harry called, waving the fishing rod like a flag. Father John laughed at the sight of the man in the middle of the plains, a long walk from the river, in a fisherman's vest with bulging pockets and brown waders, too large for his skinny legs, pulled up to his hips.

"Caught anything?" Father John called back.

"Not yet." The old man reeled in the line and started over. "I have high hopes," he said. "How's our guest doing?"

Father John walked over. "Elena says she's not eating."

The bishop nodded. "I remember a girl who came to the mission in Patna. Pretty little thing, big brown eyes. Scared-looking most the time, expecting her father to find her. She'd been sold in marriage, you see, and she'd run away."

"What happened to her?"

"The father came with a whole phalanx of police. Dragged her away." He gazed out over the grounds. "I had an old Flintlock somebody had left at the mission. Probably hadn't been fired in fifty years. Type of weapon people carried when they rode out in the howdahs on top of elephants. Used to shoot lions that tried to scale the elephants. It was of no use against armed policemen. I couldn't protect her. I try not to imagine what happened to her."

Father John took a moment before he said, "I'm not sure we can protect Marcy if the killers find out she's here."

"The police are on her side," the bishop said.

Father John gave the bishop a little wave and bounded up the steps to the administration building. The phone was ringing inside. He pushed through the heavy door, cut a diagonal path across the corridor into his office. He leaned across the desk and picked up the receiver. "Father O'Malley," he said.

There was no response. He could hear the faint sounds of breathing. "How can I help you?" he said.

"You don't know me." It was a woman's voice, tentative and trembling. "I'm calling about Ned."

He waited for her to go on, but the line went quiet again. "Is this Roseanne?" It was a guess, but he heard the truth of it in the gasp that came down the line.

"How do you know?" she said.

"I know you and Ned were once . . ." He hesitated. Ned Windsong had planned to marry Marcy Morrison. "Together," he said.

"I need to talk to you."

"I'll be here," he said.

"No." She seemed to go away, and Father John wondered if she had pressed a button that ended the call. Then she said, "The Sun Dance grounds in Ethete. Can you come there now?"

He told her he was on the way.

Father John drove west on Seventeen-Mile Road, the sun bursting through the rear window, the wind crashing through the open windows. "Salome, komm trink Wein mit mir" blared from the CD next to him. He had left Bishop Harry plodding down the corridor to the back office in his waders, the fishing rod upright in one hand like a spear. "You go along," the old man had said when he told him there was an emergency call. "I'm reporting for duty."

He tapped on the brake pedal, turned onto Yellow Calf Road and drove toward Ethete. The old pickup lumbered up a rise, coughing and sputtering. The Sun Dance grounds lay below, surrounded by golden plains that melted into the blue distances. "Go to the Sun Dance, if you want to know the Arapahos," Father Peter had told him that first summer at St. Francis. The old pastor had taken pity on him and given him a job when no one else wanted him. "Nobody knows how old the ceremony is," Father Peter said, "but the people say it has always been part of them. Arapahos come from all over and camp in tipis. It's like all the people coming home."

Father John had driven out to the Sun Dance grounds alone that first summer. He remembered feeling like a grad student again, off to do field research. At the crest of the hill, he had pulled off and gotten out. He felt as if he had stepped into the past. Spread across the grounds below were hundreds of white tipis, like a village in the Old Time. Sounds of children playing and dogs barking flowed up from the camp. A baby was crying. He could imagine warriors preparing for the hunt, women tanning buffalo hides, grinding wild vegetables into the meat and drying it for winter. A whole people going about their lives, unaware of the storm about to break across the plains and change everything. He remembered getting back into the pickup and driving down into the village, feeling humbled before all that was lost.

He turned into the grounds, stopped on the flat expanse of wild grass and got out. The sun burned down, unforgiving. He walked away from the pickup. Then he saw her, a slight figure with black hair blowing back in the wind, dressed in jeans and a dark tee shirt and white sneakers that flashed in the sunshine. She kept her hands in her jeans pockets. Surprise crossed her face as she came closer. "You the priest?"

186

she said.

"Father John," he said, aware of her eyes taking him in, the blue jeans and plaid shirt, the scuffed boots and cowboy hat. "And you're Roseanne."

She nodded. "I hope it's okay, meeting out here. I didn't know where else to go. I don't want anybody seeing me." She glanced over her shoulder, a hunted look about her. "It's always quiet here. Sacred grounds, you know. We come here for the Sun Dance. Otherwise, nobody's here."

"What are you afraid of?" he said.

"Can we walk?" she said, swinging about and starting off. He fell in beside her. "I guess I was hoping the ancestors might help me. Ned was going to dance this year, you know. He said the spirits would give him courage, the Creator would take pity on him. That's where the Sun Dance Lodge will be placed. The Rabbit Lodge will be right behind it. It'll be taken down as soon as the Sun Dance Lodge goes up." She gave a little wave. "The Rabbit Men have already completed their vows to dance the Sun Dance, and they help the Four Old Men run the dance." She stopped and turned toward him, a searching look in her expression. "Do you understand?"

"The Four Old Men are the ceremonial

elders. They preserve the traditions."

Roseanne nodded and started off again. "The ceremonial people pray for three days in the Rabbit Lodge before the Sun Dance starts. They pray for the Creator's blessings. On the fourth day, the center pole that the dancers dance around is brought to the grounds. It's a special time," she said. "Traffic is stopped on the roads outside the grounds, and everything becomes very quiet. It's like the whole world goes silent. The dogs don't bark and children stop crying; it's amazing. I remember how much I loved watching the men bring in the center pole. Then volunteers start to erect the Sun Dance Lodge. Over here," she said, picking up her stride and waving him on. "Have you ever seen that?"

He told her that he had come to the Sun Dance every year since he had been on the rez.

"Pretty impressive, wouldn't you agree?" she said. "Funny, how I remember all of it. I can almost see it taking place. The volunteers bringing in lodge poles and laying them out in a circle, and people tying pieces of cloth onto the poles. Prayer flags, symbols of our own prayers. Then volunteers set up the center pole and build the lodge around it. They set up other poles and pile up cottonwood branches between them for the walls, and then they lay the poles with the prayer flags across the top and push them up to the center pole. The prayer flags dangle over the lodge."

She turned and started toward the opposite corner of the grounds, wandering through her memories, he thought. "The White Bulls always camped over there." She waved toward a sweep of wild grasses. "The Yellowmans were next to them, then the Water family and behind them, the White Horse camp. Every family has a place, like in the Old Time. We were here." She stopped and stared at the vacant patch of land. "The Birdwoman family. Grandmother and Grandfather ran our camp. My aunt Martha was the camp cook — every camp had a cook that either volunteered or got drafted. She used to be real pretty, I remember, flipping pancakes on the little portable stove, brewing coffee on the campfire. You could smell coffee everywhere."

"What are you afraid of, Roseanne?" Father John asked again.

The girl took in a gulp of air. She looked as if she might burst into tears, nostrils flaring, eyes narrowing. She turned to the side and pressed her fingers against her eyes. "I'm afraid of losing all this," she said, lifting a hand toward the grounds. "I can't stop thinking about Ned. How he should be one of the dancers. He should dance every morning to the rising sun, pray all day in the lodge. Not eat anything. Not drink anything. Make a sacrifice for the people. It's all gone for him." She dropped her face into both hands and sobbed, her thin shoulders shaking.

He found a handkerchief in the back pocket of his blue jeans, handed it to her, and gave her a moment. "Are you afraid someone will try to kill you?" he said, taking a stab at it.

She crunched the handkerchief and ran it over her cheeks. Finally she looked up at him, and he saw that he had hit on the truth. The girl was not only mourning Ned Windsong, she was mourning her own life. "I know Ned trusted you," she began, the words ragged and halting. "Did he go to see you after he got back?"

The sense of regret washed over him again. There were sins of commission and sins of omission, he was thinking. He said, "I had the sense he might have been in some kind of trouble. I'm sorry." He took a moment. "I didn't find out what it was."

"I just found out." The girl was searching his face, he thought, for anything he hadn't told her. "He got mixed up in a burglary ring. First in Lander, then in Jackson Hole. I know Ned," she said. "I know him better than anybody, better than that white girl he got involved with. He didn't want to do that kind of thing. It wasn't like him."

"He did it anyway," Father John said. This was what had been weighing on the young man, what had brought him to the mission. A need to confess, be absolved, go forward? But he hadn't said anything about confession. What, then? The desire to talk about what was going on? Ned knew what he would have advised him: get out, make restitution in any way he could, do the right thing.

"It was his chance," Roseanne said. "His only chance to get enough money for the ranch he wanted. All his life, he wanted his own ranch. We were gonna live there." She was choking up again, swiping at her eyes with the balled-up handkerchief. "Soon's he got enough saved up, he would've gotten out."

"That's why he was killed?"

"Lionel Lookingglass and Dwayne Hawk," she said. "They wouldn't let him out. They were afraid he'd snitch to the fed, but Ned would never have done that."

"Anyone else involved?" Something wasn't

right, Father John was thinking. Ned and two other Arapahos — how did they plan the burglaries? Fence the stolen goods? Keep the whole operation quiet on the rez?

"Lionel and Dwayne, that's all I know. I think they were running it. I think Ned must have been working for them. That's why they killed him."

Father John watched the girl a moment, the quick, nervous movement of her hands, the way her eyes shifted between the road and the place where the Birdwoman family had camped and Aunt Martha, who used to be pretty, had been the cook, as if what was coming down the road might erase the memory. "They're afraid you'll talk to the fed?" The white girl was in danger for the same reason, he was thinking. Not only was she a witness, she could provide the motive.

"They're convinced I knew all about the burglary ring," Roseanne was saying, "but, I swear, Ned never told me anything. Dwayne warned me to keep my mouth shut." She looked hard at him. "They think Ned talked to you. They could come after you, too."

"Is there someplace you can go until they're in custody?" Father John said.

She gave a bark of laughter. "Like the fed's gonna find 'em? They know the rez inside and out. They'll move from house to house, and nobody's gonna turn 'em in."

"They killed an Arapaho."

"That's why nobody's gonna call the fed, 'cause they don't wanna be the next one to get shot."

"What about you?" he said. "Any relatives they wouldn't know about?" She was shaking her head, and he pushed on. "In Casper or Cheyenne?"

"Aunt Martha and me," she said. "All that's left of the Birdwoman family, except for some cousins in Denver. We hardly ever see them." She looked away. "Now Ned's gone. I don't have anybody."

He wanted to tell her she could stay at the mission, but Marcy Morrison was at the guesthouse. "How can I reach you?" he said. He was thinking of the parishioners, the brown faces in the pews this morning, the grandmothers and the elders. Someone would take in a girl with nowhere to go.

A light flickered in the girl's eyes, as if she had guessed his thoughts. She recited her cell number, and he took out the pad and pencil that he carried in his shirt pocket and wrote it down.

16

The sun was like a blowtorch when Father John drove into the mission. On Seventeen-Mile Road, the pickup rattling, *Salome* blaring, Ned Windsong had consumed his thoughts. How did Ned get involved in a burglary ring? Who brought him in? Why? The need always came first, the fertile ground. Ned had wanted his own ranch. Then came the reality. On an electrician's wages, it would mean years of saving, scrimping, dreaming. Then the opportunity had presented itself, and he had made a choice. He had chosen the ranch.

Father John pulled in close to the administration building and turned off the ignition. "Und wars die Hälfte meines Königreichs" rose into the wind a moment before he turned off the CD. He raced up the concrete steps, a question still pulling him: Who had brought the opportunity? Two men he tried to avoid and didn't like?

He had yanked open the door when the Jeep came out of the alley, past the corner, and pulled to a stop. Vicky jumped out. The wind whipped at her skirt, and she held her hair back with one hand. "Where's Marcy?" she said, hurrying up the steps.

"I don't know," Father John said. The girl's pickup had been parked at the guesthouse this morning. He hadn't checked on her, but Elena had taken over a bowl of oatmeal and a plate of toast. At least Marcy had opened the door — half-asleep, Elena said — and taken the food. "Bishop Harry might know," he said.

"Your assistant is a bishop?" A flash of mirth replaced the worry in her eyes.

"Harry Coughlin," Father John said. "Retired bishop, spent the last three decades in India. He's supposed to be recovering from a heart attack." He shrugged. "He likes to help out."

Vicky brushed past the door he was still holding open, and he could see that the worry had implanted itself again. "Marcy shouldn't have left," she said over her shoulder. Father John followed her into the corridor, and she turned to face him. "She's scared, John. She's like a little girl. She doesn't realize the danger she's in. Now she's gone off somewhere . . ." She lifted

195

both hands, as if nothing made sense.

"Ah, John, you've returned." Bishop Harry's voice came down the corridor. The fluorescent light glinted in the old man's glasses, and the soft soles of his shoes made a squishing noise on the old wood floor. "I'm afraid your guest has flown the coop," he said.

Vicky let out a gasp. "Flown the coop? Her things are still there. You don't think . . ." She broke off, and Father John could sense the apprehension in the stiff way she turned toward him.

"Bishop Harry, meet Vicky Holden," he said. "Marcy Morrison's attorney."

"Always good to have an attorney close by." The bishop extended a thin, vein-riddled hand, which Vicky took for a brief moment.

"Did she say anything to you?"

"Oh, yes." The bishop nodded. "Stood right in the doorway." He tilted his head in the direction of Father John's office. "Demanded to know where you were, John. I explained you were out. She didn't like that very much. Naturally I offered my assistance, and she asked me to convey the message that she had to get out of here."

"Did she get a call?" Father John said.

Bishop Harry shook his head. Calls to the

mission came through the office. Still, she could have gotten a call on her cell.

"I spoke to Gianelli this morning," Vicky said. "Every cop and deputy in Fremont County is looking for Hawk and Looking-glass. They've burrowed in somewhere. It could take days to find them. I should have insisted that Gianelli arrange for a guard." A hint of reproach had come into her tone, and Father John knew that she reproached herself. "Her father could have hired a guard. Marcy's like a child, and she needs protection."

"May I interject?" Bishop Harry leaned forward, and Father John realized the old man had stepped back and had been watching him and Vicky. "The girl strikes me as quite headstrong. I believe she will do as she pleases. She said she was going stir-crazy — those were her words — locked up in a chicken coop." He shook his head, and specks of light danced in his glasses. "I had the distinct impression that had you been in, John, she would have made the same announcement. Nothing you could have done would have stopped her, aside from physical restraint, and I assume we are not in the business of physically restraining our guests."

"Did she say where she was going?" Vicky

asked. She would go after the girl, Father John was thinking, if she had any idea of where to go.

"I'm afraid I did not have the presence of mind to inquire," the bishop said. "May I add that I doubt she would have told me."

"Anybody could spot her red pickup," Vicky said, resignation seeping into her tone. "Hawk and Lookingglass could hear about it."

"I'm afraid I must leave you to sort it out." The bishop wheeled about and started back down the corridor.

"Do you have a minute?" Father John said, indicating his office. Vicky moved ahead of him. "Coffee?" he said. The coffeepot on the metal table behind the door was empty. It would take five minutes to brew another pot, but she shook her head. He tried not to smile. Somehow he had known she would refuse. He walked over and half-sat on the edge of the desk. "It's possible that Ned was part of a burglary ring, along with Hawk and Lookingglass," he said. "Others could be involved."

Vicky was quiet, not moving from the center of the faded rug, her black bag dangling from her shoulder. "How did you hear this?"

"Someone told me," he said.

She locked eyes with him for a moment before she said, "You think my client was involved?" She hurried on. "She's not involved, John. She didn't have anything to do with whatever Ned might have been up to."

"I hope you're right," he said.

Vicky drew in a long breath that flared her nostrils. "You don't like her, do you?"

"I don't know her," Father John said. He was wondering if she could read his thoughts, the way he sometimes read hers. Something about the girl was off key, not quite right. He looked away, but he could feel Vicky's eyes on him.

"You do think she was involved in Ned's homicide?" she said. "Even though there is no evidence. She loved Ned Windsong. She was going to marry him. You're the last one I ever thought would fall into this trap."

"What are you talking about?"

Vicky started moving about, carving out a little circle on the rug. "Blame the outsider. An Arapaho man is shot to death, the white girl is in the house, so she must have something to do with it. The outsider, the other, must be guilty." She swung around and faced him. "It's easy to turn against outsiders. They never really belong, you know."

"That may be." He felt as if she had hurled a dart into his chest. "It has nothing to do with my misgivings about Marcy Morrison."

"You admit that you don't like her."

"What difference would it make?"

"Gianelli will pick up on it. He'll wonder why the pastor doesn't trust the white girl. He'll want to interview her again, probe into her life, instead of arresting the killers and letting Marcy Morrison go back to Jackson Hole and forget about this nightmare." Vicky made another circle around the rug, slower this time, as if some of the anger had begun to dissipate. "You don't understand her," she said, stopping in front of him. "She's absurdly naïve. Her mother left when she was six. Something stops when that happens, some emotional development. A part of her is still six years old, wanting her mother and trying to understand why her life has changed."

"Vicky," Father John said, reaching for her, then pulling his hand back. "She is not your daughter."

She stared at him a long moment, then looked away. "You think I'm too involved," she said.

"What do you think?"

"I want to help her. I don't want her

charged as an accomplice to a murder she couldn't have committed."

He could hear the thrum of an engine on Circle Drive, the sounds of scattering gravel. He pushed to his feet and went over to the window. The red pickup slowed past the administration building, the girl hunched over the wheel, blonde hair folded around her shoulders. The pickup disappeared into the alley.

Father John turned back to Vicky. The way she was looking at him made him feel as if he had failed her somehow. "Your client is back," he said. Vicky swung around, hurried into the corridor, and slammed the door. Little tremors ran through the old floorboards.

Father John sat down at his desk. He could hear the bishop's footsteps approaching. The old man stopped in the doorway a moment, then walked into the office and settled into a side chair. "Couldn't help but overhear," he said.

Father John waited for the rest of it: the innuendos and accusations that surfaced from time to time, like little campfires never completely put out. The pastor and the lawyer — such good friends. What else was between them? Even the old man had heard the rumors.

"She seems like a very nice lady," the bishop said.

"She's a good lawyer," Father John said. "She cares about her . . . clients." He had started to say "people," but Marcy Morrison was not Arapaho.

The bishop remained quiet, like a confessor waiting for the penitent to continue.

"It's not what you think," Father John said, and the bishop nodded.

"I make no judgments about the lives of others," he said. "When I was sent to India, I was young, wet behind the ears, and lonely as hell, stuck out in Jharkhand for five long years. Not many of my own kind around. There was a young woman, red-haired, beautiful, working in a dispensary. She was a nun. Went out with a cart every day, collected sick children, brought them to the mission. We often worked together, and I must admit, I thought about leaving. The priesthood, you understand. I had dreams that she and I could do the same work, but we would be together. I came to love her."

"Why didn't you leave?" Father John said.

"The same reason I became a priest in the first place. It was my journey." He set both hands on the armrests and lifted himself to his feet. "In time I was transferred to Patna. I heard she was transferred to the

Philippines. I daresay our lives went on as they were meant to do." He started for the door, then turned back. "I tell you this so you'll know you are not the first priest to find yourself attracted to a worthy woman."

Then he was gone, the soft noise of his footsteps in the corridor, the muffled sounds of a chair scraping the floor in the back office. Father John set his elbows on the desk and dropped his face into his hands. He could still see her — that first time she had come to his office. Black shoulder-length hair and large black eyes, and not beautiful exactly, but something about her — intelligence, intensity, and compassion shining through. *So you're the new pastor I've heard so much about.* He had felt his heart stop.

He supposed he had decided even then that he could love her from a distance.

17

Vicky started the Jeep and left the gear in park. Sunlight splayed the administration building. Behind the windows on the right, John O'Malley had probably gone back to his desk. She felt a sharp pang of guilt over what she had said. After all, there were times when she felt like the outsider, and he was the insider. He cared about the people as much as she did. They had always been on the same team, and that was what had stung her, she knew. She had expected him to see Marcy Morrison as she did: a young woman caught up in something dreadful, with consequences that were more serious than she realized. But something about Marcy Morrison bothered him. She had sensed that and lashed out. She slammed a fist against the edge of the steering wheel. She wanted John O'Malley to be with her, on her team.

And yet he wasn't the only one with

misgivings. What was it Ella had said? *Maybe she had something to do with it?* Other people on the rez probably thought the same thing. She closed her eyes against the sharp fact that what she had said in the office was often true: sooner or later, outsiders were turned upon. She had never meant to say it to John O'Malley.

She backed into Circle Drive, then shifted into forward and drove to the guesthouse. She stopped next to the pickup. It was quiet except for the sound of the wind swooshing through the wild grass and moving in the cottonwood branches. She was about to knock on the door when it opened a few inches and Marcy peered around the edge. "I didn't know you were coming," she said.

"We need to talk." Vicky waited, and when the girl didn't move, Vicky placed her hand on the door and pushed it open. Shadows swallowed the living room — tee shirts, jeans, towels tossed over the sofa and chair, bottles of fingernail polish and lotions crammed on the little table. "We can talk outside, if you prefer," she said.

Marcy started forward, and Vicky stepped sideways, making room for the girl on the stoop. Marcy pulled the door shut and folded onto the top step. She leaned forward, hugging her bare knees. A silver watch with tiny diamonds that Vicky hadn't noticed her wearing before looked like a bracelet on her thin arm. She wore her cutoff jeans, ragged at the edges, and a white tee shirt that outlined the knobs of her spine. She was barefoot, her feet turned inward, pigeon-toed. Bright red polish shone on her toenails. "Why are you here?" she said. "The SOBs that killed Ned got arrested and want to drag me into it?"

Vicky sat down beside her. The question came like a bolt of lightning. "Why would you think that?" she said.

The girl shifted toward her. Her eyes were dull, encased in black bruises. "Isn't that what everybody's saying? Everybody hates me here. They want me sent to prison for something I never did."

"That's not true." But there was truth in it, Vicky knew. "In any case, I intend to see that doesn't happen." She took a second before she went on. "I want you to think hard. When Hawk and Lookingglass burst into the house, what exactly did they say?"

"Roseanne Birdwoman was probably waiting outside. Don't forget her."

"Were they looking for stolen items?"

"What? I don't know?"

"The house was ransacked, Marcy. They were looking for something."

Marcy dipped her head into her knees. "I don't know anything about this," she said out of the side of her mouth, her voice slurred.

"You never saw any of the stolen items? You don't know what they were or where Ned might have kept them? Except for that one time in Jackson where Hawk and Lookingglass took cartons out of Ned's truck. Is that right?" Vicky held her breath. The less the girl knew, the harder it would be for Gianelli to tie her to the burglary ring or, for that matter, to Ned's murder.

"All I know is what he told me," Marcy said.

"He told you?" Oh God. This wasn't good.

"Told me he had some stuff he was gonna unload. Never said where he got it. I put it together." Her head sprang back and she stared straight ahead. "I'm not stupid. I mean, when he gave me this watch, I said, 'Wow! Where the hell did you get this?' All he said was, 'Never mind.' I didn't need to know."

Vicky reached over and lifted the girl's arm. The watch was beautiful. She had no idea of what it must be worth — more than she could imagine spending on a piece of jewelry. Stolen from a home outside Lander or from one of the vacation homes in Jackson Hole. She had a sinking feeling, as if she were bobbing about on the hard concrete stoop. Marcy Morrison had accepted a piece of jewelry from Ned that even she admitted she wondered how he could afford. Gianelli could make the case — it would be easy — that she had accepted goods knowing they must have been stolen, which would make her an accomplice.

"It's the only thing he ever gave me," Marcy said. "Course when we got married, he was gonna give me a gold ring. He said he had it ready."

Vicky sank against the black metal railing. "Did he ever actually tell you he had stolen the jewelry?"

The girl turned sideways. Her eyes had become green saucers. "I told you, I didn't have nothing to do with it." She ran a finger over the face of the watch. "You think 'cause I've got this watch, the fed'll think I was involved?" For the first time, a note of fear sounded in her voice.

"If he asks whether Ned gave you anything, whatever you do, don't lie," Vicky said, trying for a calm, reassuring voice that would mask her own nervousness. "And don't volunteer any information." She was thinking that Marcy Morrison was capable of saying anything off the top of her head, even with Vicky sitting beside her. "Do you understand?"

The girl looked as if she was about to burst into tears — small face scrunched, pink lips pulled in. "I'm in trouble, aren't I?" she managed. "Soon's those guys get arrested, they're gonna lie. They're gonna say things about me. It'll be my word against theirs. What am I gonna do?"

"Nothing. You let me worry about it." Vicky got to her feet and went down the steps. She looked back at the girl still huddled over herself. "Don't go anywhere," she said. "Someone could recognize your pickup and follow you to the mission. Hawk and Lookingglass could hear where you're staying." The girl flinched backward, as if she had been hit. "I'm not trying to frighten you," Vicky said. "Just stay close by until they are in custody." She glanced around at the grounds — so peaceful and quiet. It was hard to imagine any danger here. "I'm sure your father would hire a guard —"

"No bodyguard!" The girl jumped to her feet. Her legs were shaking; goose pimples were popping on her pink skin. "You don't know my father. He wants to watch me all the time. He'd never take the guard away. I can't have any guard!"

"Okay." Vicky put up her hand. "Call me

if you need anything. And . . ." she hesitated. "Father John's good to talk to, if you want somebody to talk to."

She left the girl standing on the stoop as she drove back down the alley. She wasn't sure why she had mentioned Father John, except that — in the smallest moments — she had glimpsed something in Marcy Morrison that John O'Malley must have seen, something broken and patched back together in rough, uneven pieces.

"Larry Morrison called," Annie said as Vicky let herself into her office. "I said you'd get back to him."

Vicky stood at the desk a moment, reading over the message sheet that Annie had handed her. Then she said, "How are things with you and Robin?"

"Everything's going to be fine." Annie tossed her head back, and Vicky watched her trying for a confident stare.

"The court issued a restraining order this morning," Roger said, emerging from the hallway. He walked over and set a hand on Annie's shoulder. "Robin comes anywhere near her, all Annie has to do is call 911. And I have no intention of leaving her side."

Vicky let out a long sigh. He had no idea, she was thinking, no experience with the determination of men like Robin or Ben Holden. Annie had the experience; she knew Robin would never give up, that he would stalk her, stay on her every move, plead and promise until she weakened and forced herself to believe he had changed. But Annie had deferred her own judgment to the man patting her shoulder.

"Be careful," Vicky heard herself saying. Then she asked Annie to call Larry Morrison and went into her own office. She sat down at her desk and stared at the copies of the timber contracts arranged in a neat stack. She would check them over and have Roger deliver them this afternoon. The phone rang once, and she picked up the receiver. "Mr. Morrison," she said. "I understand you called."

"How's my little girl?" The voice was hurried and gruff.

"I just saw her at the mission," Vicky began.

He interrupted. "Well, how is she?"

"She's scared," Vicky said. "The FBI agent has interviewed her, and she identified the killers' photographs."

"You telling me them bastards aren't in custody yet?"

"Every law enforcement agency in the county is looking for them. They'll be arrested soon."

"Soon! Soon! Soon isn't good enough. My little girl's in danger."

"I suggested that she return to Jackson, but she insists on staying here until they are arrested." She took a second, then went on. "It looks like Ned was part of a burglary ring with them. They probably killed him over some disagreement."

"My little girl know about this?" For the first time, Vicky heard a note of fear sounding in the man's voice.

"I'm afraid she did."

"My God, the fed will pull her right in. I know how these investigations go. Cops, they're all the same. Grasp at anything to solve a case, don't matter if innocent people get trampled. You make sure they don't trample her, understand?" He hurried on without waiting for a response. "I want her to go back to her condo in Jackson today. She has to get away from them killers, and she doesn't need to be under the fed's nose. Tell her to leave."

"I suggest you tell her," Vicky said.

"If I didn't have commitments here with my television show, I'd come up there and take her away myself. I'm counting on you to look after her interests, and I want her in Jackson."

"I'll do my best," Vicky said. She realized she was speaking into a dead phone.

18

The drive to Lander was long and slow, the roads clogged with out-of-state cars and campers, tourists peering into the distances. Father John had passed a couple of vehicles, then settled back, resigned. It wasn't possible to pass them all. "Jochanaan, ich bin verliebt" blared on the CD. He had meant to get away earlier, but it had taken longer than he anticipated to respond to the messages on his desk — arrangements for baptisms, parishioners admitted to the hospital, couples in need of counseling. He had made four phone calls trying to find a safe house for Roseanne Birdwoman before Betty Mock had called from California. She'd heard he was looking for a house — it seemed the moccasin telegraph even reached California — and she volunteered her own. She wouldn't be back on the rez for another month.

He had called Roseanne and told her to

stop at Betty's brother's place for the keys. There was nothing to connect Roseanne to Betty Mock. He reminded the girl not to tell anyone where she would be staying, and she had mumbled a tentative and frightened "okay" that sounded as if it had come from the dangerous depths of her situation.

He followed the traffic through Hudson and on into Lander. The town spread before him, wide streets of bungalows and ever-greens. He made a left off Main Street and pulled onto the concrete apron in front of a boxlike building with Silver Electrical Company splashed in white paint across the plate-glass window.

Inside, a woman with a wide pink part in her gray hair sat behind a counter, studying the pamphlet in front of her. She looked up as he approached. A friendly look of surprise came into her face. "Aren't you the mission priest?" she said.

"Father O'Malley." He clasped his hands on the counter. On the white plaque next to the door behind her was the name Bud Silver. "Is the manager in?"

"You mean the boss." She gave a little laugh. "We call him the boss around here 'cause he manages and owns the whole darn place. Need some electrical work at the mission?"

"Not that I know of," he said. Something always needed attention, he was thinking. Leaking roofs, broken windowpanes, peeling paint, lights that flickered on and off in the corridor outside his office, as if there were ghosts in the place. "I'd like to speak with him, if he's available."

"Hold on." She pushed backward and got to her feet, gripping the edge of the desk, then the back of the chair. She headed to the door, knocked once and let herself in. A couple of seconds later, a short, dark-haired man, with the build of a bull, came out, the woman smiling behind him.

"Bud Silver," he said, extending a thick hand with an antelope head silver ring on one finger. "How can I be of help to the clergy?"

"I'd like to talk to you about Ned Windsong," Father John said, shaking the man's hand.

"Should've figured." Silver nodded Father John around the counter and into his office. He shut the door and gestured to the folding chair that stood at an angle to the desk. Papers spilled across the surface. Some kind of spreadsheet took up the computer screen. The window behind the desk framed the backyard view of a yellow two-story house. "FBI agent said he was gonna stop by this

216

afternoon," he said, taking the swivel chair. "I thought you was him. You conducting your own investigation?"

"Not exactly," Father John said. "I've known Ned since he was a kid. Used to play on the Eagles."

"Good little outfit you got there," Silver said. "Beat the socks off my kid's team a few years back."

"Ned was preparing to dance in the Sun Dance," Father John went on. "His Sun Dance grandfather . . ." The man's eyebrows shot up, and Father John said, "The elder who was teaching him the prayers and rituals asked me to see what I could find out about why he was killed."

Silver nodded. "He was a darn good electrician's apprentice."

"How long was he here?"

"Five months, one week, six days. Hired him right out of that training program in Casper. His uncle, Jerry Adams, gave me a call, wanted to know if I had a place for a new apprentice. Now mind you" — he leaned sideways over the armrest and lowered his voice, as if there were someone else in the office — "I don't cotton to hiring Indians. Not that I'm prejudiced, you understand."

Father John nodded. The prejudice was

leaking out of the man.

"But they can be trouble. Take off for ceremonies and what have you. Grandmother gets sick, they can't come to work. But times are changing, and I'm trying to change with the times. Look at the individual, I tell myself. Everybody don't come outta the same mold. Besides, Adams was vouching for him. And I gotta say, I admired the kid. Got himself enough gumption to go off and learn a trade so he could make a living. Guy had just quit on me, so I put Ned on the crew. Did real good, too. Always wanting to learn more. Wanted to know every last detail about everything. He could make electricity dance any direction he pleased. Wasn't anything he wasn't catching on to. Wire a new house, install security systems. You name it."

"Why did he leave?"

"Now that's the real puzzle. I had some big jobs coming up, and he marched in here one morning and said, 'Bud, you been real good to me, but I gotta move on.' I said, 'What the hell you talking about? You got a steady job here.' All he said was it was personal. Needed to get his life straight, something like that. Said he had connections in Jackson Hole, so he was going up there and work at Sloan's Electric. I gave him a good recommendation."

"Ever see him with anybody?"

"Yeah." Silver's head bobbed up and down. "I betcha I seen him with the two guys I heard killed him. A couple of scary Indians, you ask me. Come around a couple times when Ned was loading his van out back. Got into a shouting match, then they took off. Driving a white truck. I intend to tell the FBI agent."

"Can you identify them?"

"You bet. He shows me pictures I'll pick 'em right out." He leaned over the armrest again. "You ask me, they was the reason he wanted out of here. You know, the personal thing."

Father John didn't say anything. It was possible there wasn't anybody else in the burglary ring — that Hawk and Looking-glass had gotten Ned involved. He had to look away a moment. Silver was bound to find out about the ring. He had trusted Ned. He would probably never trust another Arapaho.

"Thanks for your time," he said, starting to get up.

"There was another guy," Silver said. "Seen him once. Drove a dark pickup, wore a cowboy hat. Pulled in while Ned was loading up. Getting ready to wire a remodel on a big house up in Sinks Canyon."

Father John dropped back onto his seat. "What did he look like?"

"Stayed inside the pickup. Never got a good look at him. Could've been just about anybody."

Father John thanked the man again and left him standing in the middle of the office, saying how he hoped the killers would rot in prison. He retraced his route to the rez; the traffic thinned out a little. Still he had to pass a series of vehicles so as not to miss the Eagles practice. He had a gut feeling that whoever the cowboy hat was, it was another member of the ring, maybe the one with enough power and persuasive gifts to draw Ned Windsong into something he didn't want to be in.

"Take a look at that kid!" Amos Whitebull called as Father John hurried down the sidelines. He was late; practice had started fifteen minutes ago. Amos's son, Randy, played first base, and Amos had been helping coach the team all season. Their record was 7–2 so far, but Saturday they faced the Riverton Rangers, the toughest team in the league.

Amos was grinning and waving toward the pudgy kid winding up for another pitch.

Marcus White Owl. "Our secret weapon," he said. "Batter gets all relaxed, thinking he can't throw hard, but he can throw some serious heat. He may be small but all his strength's in the lower half of his body, and that lets him really fire the ball in. Look at that!"

The kid opened up with a pitch that just missed the outside corner of the plate. The batter swung and missed. He was doing a little circle dance of frustration.

"Choke up and focus on the pitch!" Father John called.

"The Rangers'll have a tough time handling Marcus," Amos said, still grinning. It was contagious, Father John knew, the excitement of a one-pitch hurler who could shut down a youth baseball team.

"I thought we'd focus on scratching out runs however we can," Father John said. He waved the next kid up to bat, David Oldman, short and round-faced, with big black eyes that squinted toward the pitcher's mound as he adjusted the bat. Father John moved in closer. "Get a comfortable grip," he called. "Bend your knees a little, keep your weight back and your eye on the ball."

Marcus delivered another fast ball, but this time, the batter was ready. Father John watched him shift his weight through his hips, the way they had practiced two days ago, transfer the power of his stocky body, and accelerate the bat through the hitting zone. The ball arched out to left field. Another kid ran underneath, glove lifted, and snagged the ball out of the air.

David was close to first base. He stopped mid-stride, turned around and headed toward home, shoulders slumped. "Good hit," Father John called. "Connect like that on Saturday, okay? The Rangers can't field the way we do."

At the edge of his vision, he saw Bishop Harry hurrying down the sidelines. He motioned the next kid up and went to meet the old man. "What is it?" he said, closing the distance between them.

"I believe you might want to talk to your guest," the bishop said. "She came to the office. Highly distraught."

"Where is she now?"

"I saw her walking back toward the guest-house. Her pickup is still there."

Father John thanked the old man and walked over to home plate where Amos was showing the next batter how to bunt the ball by squaring to the pitcher and getting the bat out in front of the plate. "Can you take over?" Father John said.

The man lifted his head without changing

his stance. "No problem," he said.

The bishop was past left field when Father John caught up and took off running for the guesthouse.

19

The door at the guesthouse hung open. Father John leaned inside. "Marcy?" he called. "Where are you?" Silence gripped the house, and the faint, acrid smell of whiskey floated over him. He went down the steps, glancing about the grounds. The pickup was still there, which meant the girl was somewhere. Across the graveled alley was a stand of cottonwoods and brush bisected by a narrow, dirt path that led to the banks of the Little Wind River.

He cut across the alley and started down the path. He had gone a good twenty yards before he spotted the small prints of what could be sandals, worn by someone so lightweight, they barely disturbed the dirt. He started running. "Marcy!" he called.

The path ran straight, then bent into a little curve, and as he came around it, he spotted a flash of white in the trees ahead. The sounds of the river bubbling over rocks interrupted the quiet. He called out again. She stopped and glanced back, then started running. He took a diagonal route through the trees and came out alongside her. "Hold on," he said.

She darted sideways and leaned over, gulping in air and holding on to her side. The blonde hair fell forward. Her face was red, eyes black and swollen. She pulled herself upright, squared her shoulders and backed away. She stared at him, with a fixed, glassy look as if she had never seen him before. He could smell the whiskey. "Where are you running to?"

The girl shifted from one foot to the other. It was warm in the shade of the trees, a hot breeze passing through, yet she looked cold, thin arms hanging at her sides, knobby knees below her shorts and dust piled over her sandals. She started blinking. "Get away! Get away!" she yelled, backing up, throwing out her hands.

"Marcy, it's me, Father John. I'm not going to hurt you. Tell me what's happened."

The glassy look returned to her eyes, and he had the same uneasy feeling that a stranger was staring at him.

"Talk to me, Marcy," he said, moving toward her. She started screaming, tilting back her head and howling. He took hold of her shoulders. "Stop it," he said. "Try to get control of yourself."

She stopped screaming and blinked up at him. He could feel the tremors running through her. "What's going on," he said.

"They're gonna crucify me." Her voice might have been that of a little girl.

"Who? What are you talking about?" He let go of her shoulders and kept his eyes on hers.

She waited a long moment, taking in gulps of air. Finally she said, "They're gonna make me part of a burglary ring, say I knew all about it. The guys that killed Ned are gonna lie and say I was in on it. My father told me how it was when he was a cop. Killers always want to make a trade so things will go easy for them, and they'll trade me. Agent Gianelli will love that, won't he? Daughter of famous evangelist connected to burglary and murder. I can see the newspaper headlines. It'll be all over the internet, TV, everyplace. All because of this!"

She started scratching at her arm, digging her nails into her skin, and he realized she was yanking off a silver watch. She let it dangle, sparkling in the light. "The only thing Ned gave me. 'This is for you,' he said. 'There's lots more, too,' he said. 'I got you a big ring that you're gonna love.' The lawyer says that means I knew all about the burglary ring, and the FBI is gonna charge me."

"Vicky said that?"

"I know what she meant." Marcy swung the watch in a wide circle, turned sideways and flung it into the trees and brush. A small clanking noise sounded, then nothing. She started crying, flinging both arms about, spinning in a little circle. Then she stopped and began pulling at her tee shirt. "Ned give me this shirt, so that makes me guilty? They'll say he stole all my clothes. I gotta throw 'em away." She ripped the tee shirt into a jagged tear up the middle.

"Stop it, Marcy," Father John said again, his voice low, the tone of a counselor. He felt helpless. There were fractures in the girl that he wasn't trained to mend. "I know a good therapist in Riverton," he said. "She can help you through this."

Marcy flinched, as if he had hurled a rock at her. Her eyes had turned darker; he had the sense again that someone else was looking out of them. "No more therapists!" she screamed, wrapping the fronts of the tee shirt around her. "I had enough of therapists at the institution. Oh yeah," she said, doubling over as if she might throw up, "my father put me there. For my own good, he told me, so I wouldn't hurt myself or something stupid like that. I was twelve years old. I got to spend a whole year with a bunch of nuts, talking, talking, talking 'til it made me crazy." She lifted her head and stared off into the trees. "I figured everything out," she said. "I did what they told me. I smiled all the time. I offered to help out with the nut cases. I was the model patient, and the therapists told my father there was no reason he couldn't take me home."

She was smiling now, a broad, friendly, relaxed smile, the kind she had perfected in the institution, Father John thought. "Only problem was he didn't want me back, 'cause he had a new wife — Deborah, or somebody; she didn't last long. Then he met Lu-Ann. But I kept up my act, and I was good. Pretty soon, my father came and got me. 'We have new rules in the house,' he told me on the drive home." She dropped her voice and lowered her chin. " 'Evenings you will spend in your own room and will not emerge to bother us. You will do your homework, and you will practice your violin. No TV, no internet, no cell phone. You will go to school, do as you are told, and stay out of our lives.' "

"I'm sorry," Father John said. He waited a

moment before he went on: "No one is forcing you to see a therapist now."

She tossed her head back and laughed. "The minute my father got the bill, he'd think I was crazy and have me sent to some institution." Turning slowly toward him, she said, "He could do that, you know. He's Larry Morrison, the great savior. He can do whatever he wants."

"Come on," Father John said. "I'll walk you back to the house."

"I hate the house," she said, but she fell in beside him. She was so small, barely reaching his shoulder, like a child plodding along in her flopping sandals, grasping her tee shirt around her. The faint smell of whiskey wafted toward him, and he swallowed back his own thirst. How quickly it came upon him, waylaid him when he was least expecting it. "It's like the institution, all closed in, nobody around."

"You went to town this morning and bought whiskey," he said. "It won't help, Marcy. I know."

"It's better than sitting there, thinking how Ned and I were gonna get married. He really loved me."

"I want you to pour out whatever's left in the bottle."

"What?" she said. "No alcohol allowed in

this fricking place?"

"One of those hard-and-fast rules. We don't have many," he said. They had reached the stoop in front of the house, and he let her go up the steps. "Ned's wake is this evening. I can ask one of the parishioners to pick you up and see that you get safely back without anyone following."

She spun around and locked eyes with him. "Wake?" She gave a little laugh. "That's funny. Like Ned's gonna wake up, only he's dead forever. 'You must learn to face reality,' they told me in the institution. Well, I been facing it and I'm not going to any wake."

"Bishop Harry and Elena will be here. You won't be alone." It was probably just as well that she didn't want to go to the wake. He wasn't sure she was strong enough to see Ned's corpse in the casket. "If you want company, walk over to the residence."

"Sure, I'll do that," she said, the voice of the good little girl promising to do as she's told. He doubted she would go to the residence.

"Don't forget about the whiskey," he said, but she had already gone inside and closed the door. He would ask Elena to check on the bottle when she brought dinner over. If the girl hadn't poured it down the sink, he would have to do so. For his own sake, he was thinking. Dear Lord, for his own sake as much as for the girl's.

"What the hell are you doin'?" The question sounded like buckshot behind her, and Roseanne swung around. Aunt Martha slouched against the doorjamb, eyes red and cheeks flushed.

Roseanne went back to stuffing a pile of tee shirts and jeans into the small suitcase opened on the bed. "What's it look like I'm doing?" she said. She grabbed the pink cosmetic bag off the bedside table and smashed it on top of the clothes. Then she closed the lid and pressed down hard. Her hands were trembling. She was aware of the key in her jeans pocket, biting at her thigh as she thumped on the suitcase. She had picked up the key to Betty Mock's house immediately after Father John had called. Dwayne and Lionel knew she lived with Aunt Martha, but they would never look for her at the other house.

"You running off with some no-good guy?"

"I'm not running off with anybody," Roseanne said. The woman understood nothing; she stumbled around in her own alcoholic haze.

"You still owe me rent. Just 'cause you're

leaving don't mean you get out of it."

"Don't worry," Roseanne said. She put her knee on top of the suitcase and pulled the zipper. She had no idea where she would get the rent. She'd called work this morning and said she wouldn't be in for a few days. "We got us a problem," the supervisor said. "Store's open every day, so we can't have associates not showing up. You don't take your regular shift today, don't bother coming back." Roseanne had started to beg — she wasn't proud of that. "I just need a few days to straighten out some personal problems. Please." The supervisor had hung up. She had held on to the phone a long time, a part of her hoping the supervisor's voice would come back on: *Of course you can take the time. We need you here. You're a good worker.* Finally she jammed the cell into her backpack.

She bumped the suitcase off the bed and picked up the backpack. She could feel the hard outline of the Colt under the canvas fabric. She started for the door, swinging the backpack over one shoulder, pulling the suitcase. Aunt Martha didn't move. There was so much sadness in her eyes that Roseanne had to look away. Aunt Martha had been so pretty once, the prettiest woman Roseanne had ever seen, bustling about the camp stove at the Sun Dance grounds, singing to herself, calling everybody to come eat.

"I'm sorry," Roseanne said. She could feel something inside her melting. "It's about Ned's murder. Dwayne and Lionel think I know something. I don't know anything, but that won't keep them from coming after me. It'll just be for a few days."

"You're scaring me." Aunt Martha's eyes had gone wide. She looked almost sober. "They might come here?"

"Keep the doors locked." Roseanne stuffed herself and the backpack through the small opening that Aunt Martha left in the doorway and pulled the suitcase past. She went down the hall and across the small living room, conscious of Aunt Martha plodding behind her. The sweet, stale odor of alcohol filled her nostrils.

"That's who that guy was?" Aunt Martha said.

Roseanne yanked open the front door and looked back at the woman leaning against the wall, the picture of a black mustang dangling behind her. "What guy?"

"Dwayne or Lionel." Aunt Martha tried for a shrug that sent the picture clattering to the floor.

"Someone was here?" Dwayne had come

back, Roseanne was thinking. "What did he want?"

"I don't know." Aunt Martha stood very still, pressed against the wall. "I seen him parked across the road. Didn't pay no attention at first, but after a while I seen he was still there. Watching the house. Made me mad. I didn't know he was one of the guys that killed Ned. I went out and threw a bottle at him and shouted for him to go away. He drove off."

Roseanne felt as if all of her muscles had gone into spasms. Her hand was numb around the handle of the suitcase. She drove her other hand hard against the canvas backpack to stop it from shaking. "Maybe you'd better come with me," she said.

"With you?" Aunt Martha glanced wild-eyed about the living room, the half-filled whiskey bottles lined up next to the sofa, the cabinet door hanging open in the kitchen and the bottles jammed inside. "I can't leave here." She pushed herself off the wall and stumbled forward. "Where you going, anyway?" she said.

"Nowhere," Roseanne said. She plunged out the door and crossed the dirt yard to her car. "Going no damn place," she said to herself.

20

Roseanne left the car behind the convenience store and walked around to the entrance. She glanced about, taking note of the pickups at the gas pumps, Indians coming and going across the pavement. No sign of Dwayne or Lionel. She hurried inside past the line waiting to pay for gas and another line in front of the food counter waiting for hot dogs or cheese quesadillas. The blue and red plastic tables in the small eating area were all taken. Black heads bobbed about in the food aisles that ran toward the back of the store. She kept her head down as she headed for the aisles, avoiding the other shoppers. "Sorry about Ned," they would say, and in their eyes she would read the truth: Ned had left her for a white girl.

She stashed a carton of eggs, a loaf of bread, a small carton of milk, and two cans of soup in her arms and made her way back to the cash registers. She could hide out for a while with her little stash. Dwayne and Lionel were like the plains themselves, melting into the distances, indistinguishable features of the landscape.

She paid for the items with her head down, not meeting the eyes of the heavyset cashier with the silver watch that cut into the flesh of her arm. Carol Makepeace, the badge on her black tee shirt said. They had gone to Wyoming Indian High together, at least until junior year when Carol had dropped out.

Thick brown hands counted out the change, then stacked the groceries inside a plastic bag. Hugging the bag to her chest, Roseanne darted out the door and around the corner. Down the little dirt path between the side of the store and the bumpers of parked trucks, reeking of gasoline. A strange feeling — definite and distinguishable — came over her. Someone was watching her. She could sense the eyes trained on her like a rifle. She hurried to the car, tossed the bag of groceries into the backseat, and got in behind the wheel. Her hand was shaking as she started the engine. The house that Father John had found was only a mile away, but she would have to take an indirect route. Whoever was watching would be behind her.

The white truck appeared in the rearview mirror as Roseanne drove across the vacant dirt strip behind the store and exited onto the asphalt. Two men in the front seat, shoulders bunched, cowboy hats riding low. Lionel at the wheel, Dwayne in the passenger seat. She pressed down on the accelerator and took a wide turn onto the two-lane highway, the rear end swaying, the tires skipping. She watched the truck bank into the turn and speed up behind her. A left turn now, and she was heading north, golden plains, dried grasses, and little pastel houses blurring past. The car was more flexible than the truck, the carriage narrower. She pulled the wheel right and took a diagonal route across a vacant field onto a two-lane dirt road that ran east, jolting over the hardened ridges of the sun-packed earth. The truck fell behind. She reached the corner and swung left.

She leaned her whole weight on the accelerator, the speedometer needle bumping at eighty-five. A brown cloud of dust rolled behind her. She made another turn and drove between two houses, then spun out onto a side road. Through the cloud of settling dust, she could see the pickup's bumper glinting in the sun. She turned onto a two-track and drove onto the Sun Dance grounds. She had a feeling of being lifted out of herself, transported back to a hot summer, the sun beating down and her throat ragged with dust and thirst. Aunt Martha frying bread at the cook stove, all the relatives milling about. "Here they come," someone called, and everybody ran out to watch the volunteers bringing in the center lodge pole.

She drove across the Sun Dance grounds. No other vehicles were in sight, except for the truck barreling behind. She was in the area where her family had camped. She could almost see the tipis, the cottonwood branches banked around the shade lodge in the center, the flash of Aunt Martha's white apron. She took a sharp left, and the car started rolling back and forth. For a moment, she thought it would turn over. She gripped the steering wheel hard. There was a ditch that ran along the periphery. She used to run through the ditch with the other kids, splash in the thin stream. She remembered the feel of the cool water on her legs. She tapped the brake and stopped. Grabbing the backpack off the front seat, she jumped out and ran for the ditch as hard as she could. Her lungs were like hot stones inside her chest. Then she was slipping, the backpack banging her ribs, her arms flailing toward the sharp, prickly branches that snapped off as she grasped at them. She tumbled forward, rolled down a steep hill and crashed against the rocks and boulders. Stabs of pain went through her. She came to a stop alongside the foot-wide stream of water. Above, she could hear the noise of the truck's engine, Dwayne's voice over the quiet, peaceful sounds of the little stream: "You can't get away, Rosanne! We got you!"

She unzipped the backpack and pulled out the Colt. She jammed the magazine into place. Gripping the gun hard, she scooted below an outcropping of rocks and pressed herself into the irrigation ditch. The smells of moist earth and rotting bark plugged her nostrils. She could feel the faint tremor in the earth as the truck circled above, Dwayne still shouting and thumping the door, as if he were beating a drum. She was a little girl again, in a sleeping bag inside her family's tipi. Aunt Martha snored softly beside her, the drums beat into the night. She had felt safe then. She listened to the truck coming closer. Then the truck turned away, and the noise subsided. They would see her car. They would figure she had run for the ditch.

She struggled to her feet, flung the backpack over her shoulder and, crouching low, started running down the ditch. She had gone a half mile, not stopping, scarcely breathing, when the ditch emptied into a culvert under the road. They were told to stop here, the kids, but they never did. They would plunge into the culvert, drawn forward by the dark, damp mystery. They could hear their voices echoing around the corrugated metal sides.

Roseanne stayed low, almost bent in half as she edged past the rounded opening. Rust hung off the metal, and the smells of roots and rotting branches were so strong that she thought she might throw up. She had to slow down, wading through the black water that pooled around little piles of plastic bottles and cups. Then she was out in the open again, still bent in half but picking up speed. By now they would have guessed where she'd gone. She had a couple of minutes, that was all, before the white pickup came down the road over the culvert. She could almost see Dwayne and Lionel getting out, sliding down into the ditch, running behind her.

She crawled up the bank and swung the backpack over the lip of hard dirt, her fingers stiff around the pistol. Finally she managed to pull herself over the top. She was like a bird, she thought, perched among the willows, watching and listening just like when she was a kid, only then she had imagined herself a cougar or a great brown bear, afraid of nothing. The road was empty. Across the field ahead was a white house surrounded by parked cars and sheds and a silver trailer. She ran all out for the house, then slowed down, crouching low, trying to blend into the field.

She glanced back. A cloud of dust rose at the far end of the road and moved toward the culvert like a rolling brown tumbleweed. She started running again, her eyes straight ahead on the white house, the silver trailer beaming in the sun. She reached the trailer, ducked past the sheds that leaned sideways as if they had been blown by the wind and hurried down the side of the house. The road in front was empty. She crossed to the borrow ditch on the far side and ran south. She had gone a half mile when she spotted the ranch-style house, half brick and half green siding. A truck was parked in front. She stumbled out of the ditch, made her way to the truck, and dropped down in front of the hood. She had a good view of both directions. Her heart pounded against her ribs; her mouth tasted of dust. She braced herself against the hard ground and tried to fight off the sense of unreality that came over her. She set her cheek against the cool, hard metal of the bumper, a real thing.

Out on the road, an engine revved up. She peered around the truck's bumper. A gray-colored sedan sped past, a woman at the wheel, two kids in back. She shifted back and gave herself another moment before hoisting the backpack and heading back to the borrow ditch. Gripping the pistol at her side, she ran as far as she could, then started walking. The pastel village was ahead now. She could see the houses arranged around a grid of streets, a few trees limp in the sun, cars and pickups parked about. "Go to the second street," the man with the key had told her. "Third house from the corner. Pink siding, gray roof. You can't miss it."

Roseanne took the long way through the area, circling the block, checking the house from the front and the rear, before she was satisfied no one was around. She headed down the side of the house to the rear door, fumbled in the backpack for the key and let herself in. The house had a closed-up feeling, the faint trace of cigarette smoke in the stale air. She locked the door behind her and crossed the long, narrow kitchen with empty counters and a dripping faucet into the living room. A sofa, a couple of chairs, and a television on a table beneath the front window. The curtains were drawn, and the dim light gave the room an otherworldly feeling. She went down the hall and checked the bathroom, the two bedrooms, the closets. She was alone.

She dropped the backpack on one of the beds and set the pistol on the lamp table. Then she slumped down onto the linoleum floor, leaned against the side of the mattress and stared at the wall. Sooner or later she would have to get her car on the Sun Dance grounds. But not for a while. They would be watching. Then they would get bored, start thinking she had called the cops, and leave. She would go back as soon as it got dark. Ned's wake was tonight, and she intended to go. For Ned, she thought. The last thing she could do for him.

She reached up, grabbed the pistol, and studied it. She knew so little about guns. The thought of holding a pistol on someone, pulling a trigger seemed like a bad dream, a story that might happen to someone else. The gun was heavy and warm in her hands. She would have to use it. The truth of it struck her like a physical object. Unless she did the very thing that Dwayne and Lionel intended to prevent her from doing: tell the fed where they were hiding.

21

"I saw Ned last night." Ella Windsong balanced the bowl of stew on her lap and glanced at the mourners milling about Great Plains Hall. Father John noticed that she hadn't touched the stew. They had taken two vacant metal chairs in the corner away from the crowd around the food table. Ned's casket was at the far end of the hall. The wake would begin as soon as everyone had eaten.

"You had a dream about Ned?" Father John said.

"He can't find any peace," Ella said. Her black hair was wound tight, close to her head. She had a blanched, sleep-deprived look. "His spirit is wandering around. He needs justice."

Father John set one hand on top of hers. He could feel her pulse pounding beneath the cool skin. "Ned is with God," he said. "He has gone to the ancestors. It's our spirits that are unquiet. We're the ones who want justice."

Off to the side, he saw Marie and Jerry Adams walking over, carrying bowls of stew and mugs of coffee. Jerry hooked the leg of a chair with his boot and dragged it close to Ella. Marie dropped her bulky frame onto the seat while her husband went after another chair. "You eaten anything, honey?" Marie leaned toward her sister. Then she turned to Father John. "She's hardly eaten a bite since Ned's murder," she said as Jerry sat down beside her. "I been telling her, she's gotta eat to keep up her strength."

"I been dreaming about Ned," Ella said.

Marie shifted back toward her sister. "What's he saying?"

"He's gotta have justice." She glanced at Father John. "He wants to go to the ancestors, but he's stuck until they get his killer."

"Killers," Jerry said. He had placed the coffee cup on the floor and was about to take a bite of stew. "You know those two bastards killed him."

"Why?" Ella fixed the man with a hard look. "That's what I don't know. The fed came around asking all kinds of questions about what Ned was doing with those guys. Was they breaking into houses? Stealing stuff? Did they have a disagreement? Was

Ned holding out?"

The questions hung in the air a moment. No one said anything. It was inevitable that Ella would find out about the burglary ring, Father John was thinking, but a part of him had hoped she might be spared.

"What did you say?" Jerry said. He held the half-empty bowl of stew beneath his chin and scooped in another spoonful. The fluorescent light glistened on his bald head.

"Lies," Ella said. "People like to believe lies. I hear the way they stop talking soon's I walk by. Look at them over there." She nodded in the direction of the food table. "Berta and that no-good kid she looks after."

Father John glanced over. Berta Oldman and her nephew, Mervin, were moving along the table, bowls of stew balanced on paper plates piled with slices of bread. The woman looked over, as if she felt someone watching her, then went back to spooning something onto the plate. Behind her in the line, Vicky was nodding to the grandmothers on the other side of the table. He looked for Roseanne, but he couldn't spot her.

"They got a nerve coming here," Ella said. "Berta's the one let Dwayne and Lionel come to the parties out at her place. I bet she's been passing around the rumor Ned was mixed up in some burglary ring, and it's a damn lie."

"What proof does the fed have of any so-called burglary ring?" Jerry said, working on the coffee now, the empty bowl on the floor.

"Nothing," Ella said.

"Look, Ella," Father John said. "Gianelli has to follow every lead." The woman's eyes were black slits of denial.

"Listening to gossip is what he's doing," Ella said "Whole rez is filled with gossip and rumors that don't amount to anything."

"Father here is right," Jerry said. "Fed's going off in a lot of directions, hoping he's gonna stumble on something. There's no proof of any burglary ring. Don't worry about it."

Father John studied the man a moment, wondering if he knew the truth and was trying to protect his wife's sister, or if he was also in denial. He must have heard the rumors. Yet Jerry was right. There wasn't any evidence that Ned had been involved in a burglary ring. Roseanne had her suspicions, but suspicions weren't evidence.

Marie leaned over her sister and patted her hand. "You should try to eat. Here, you want me to help you?" She spooned some stew and lifted it toward Ella who pressed herself against the back of the chair and shook her head. Marie dropped the spoon into the bowl and shot a sideways you-see-how-I'm-trying? glance at her husband.

"It's all that girl's fault," Ella said.

"What girl," Father John said, but he knew who she was talking about even before she said the name: Marcy Morrison. The white girl, the outsider.

"She's the one started the rumors," Ella was saying, "making it look like those guys had reason to kill Ned, so the fed would go chasing around, asking folks a lot of stupid questions. She's the one the fed oughtta be talking to."

"Honey, we've been over this," Marie said. "What'd'ya think? The white girl shot Ned, beat herself up, threw the gun out the window, or something? The cops would've found the gun if it was anywhere around that house. She didn't do it, honey. You gotta accept reality."

Ella stood up so fast that the bowl of soup on her lap spilled across the linoleum floor. Jerry started peddling his chair backward away from the brown puddle of chunks of beef, potatoes, and carrots that crept toward his boots. "You believe the lies!" Ella leaned over her sister. "Ned was your nephew, too, our own brother's son. How can you believe he'd ever hang around with the likes of that trash and break into people's houses?"

Father John got to his feet and placed a hand on the woman's shoulder. "Take it easy," he said. He was aware of the heads craning in their direction, the sudden halt to the drone of voices in the hall. At the far end, two men had begun setting metal chairs into rows. Donald Little Robe and two other elders were standing at a small table near the coffin, preparing for the ceremony. The wake would start soon.

"Maybe I seen the real Ned," Marie was saying. She tilted her head back and looked up at Ella. "He wasn't perfect, like you always made him out to be. The perfect boy, here to take the place of our brother. Our brother's dead, and nobody can take his place. Ned wanted things like everybody else. He wanted a better life. So what if he —"

"Enough, Marie." Jerry jumped up and clamped a hand on his wife's shoulder. Father John could see his fingers digging past the woman's cotton blouse into her flesh. "Leave it alone."

Ella placed her hands over her ears. "I won't listen to any more lies. My own sister!" She turned to Father John. "That white girl come here?"

"No, Ella," he said. "She's not here." The

crowd had begun flowing past, filing into the rows of chairs. The sounds of metal scraping the floor mingled with the hushed tones of conversation. He felt a wave of relief that Marcy Morrison wasn't anywhere around. In a way, it wouldn't have surprised him if she had changed her mind and shown up. He wasn't sure the girl could ever be believed. "The wake's about to start," he said, but Jerry Adams had already taken hold of Ella's arm and was nudging her along the side aisle toward the chairs in front.

"I'm sorry, honey." Marie stumbled after them. "Just forget what I said, okay? You know I loved Ned."

Ella glanced back, ignoring her sister. "You gonna say a prayer, Father?" she said.

"Yes, of course," he said. He and Donald Little Robe had already talked about the wake. He would begin with a prayer, then turn everything over to the elders. Always two sides, he was thinking. The Christian and the Arapaho. There would be both ways of praying this evening but only one Creator, as Donald had reminded him several times.

Father John followed the little group to the front row set aside for relatives and close friends and waited while Marie and Jerry sat down on either side of Ella, Marie patting her sister's back. The coffin was opened, and he could see the familiar face, the broad forehead and black hair slicked back, the squared jaw of Ned Windsong. And yet the young man was not there. In his mind, he saw the gangly-legged kid sprinting for home, head high in victory.

He realized that Ella was sobbing quietly. He waited a moment before he walked to the front of the center aisle. The hush of voices, the noise of shuffling began to subside. "Let us pray," he said, bringing his palms together. "For Ned Windsong, our brother and friend, that his soul may rest in God's everlasting peace and love. Our Father," he began, waiting a beat for the people to join in the familiar prayer, voices hushed and reverent and out of sync, running past one another. When the prayer had ended, he said, "Let us remember Ned the way he was, a man with a good heart and an easy smile, always planning and hoping for the future. Let us remember the good things, and not forget his name or forget to tell his stories, so the memory of his generous spirit will live on with us."

"Amen," came from someone five or six rows deep. Other "amens" rippled through the quiet sound of sobbing. Vicky was sitting near the back, and for the briefest moment, he caught her eye. He glanced over the rows, looking for Roseanne. Then he spotted her, poised near the opened door in the rear, as if she were ready to bolt outside. She looked small, staring straight ahead at the coffin, one fist clenched against her mouth.

He walked to the end of the first row and took the vacant seat next to Marie as Donald Little Robe and the other elders, Timothy Standing Elk and Richard Marks, stood up. *"Jevaneatha nethaunainau,"* Donald said. He used a formal tone, like the elders in the Old Time. *"Jevaneatha Dawathaw henechauc hauane nanadehe vedaw nau ichjeva."*

Father John recognized some of the words. He had heard the prayers so many times, he could make out the meaning: God is with us. God's spirit fills everywhere on earth and above us.

The elder went on, and Father John listened for the familiar words that would anchor the meaning. *Our bodies will die and return into dust. But our souls live forever. Good souls go to God, to our home on high.*

When the prayers had ended, Donald and the others walked over to the coffin. Now would come the painting, Father John knew. Donald dipped his fingers into the can of sacred red paint inside the cloth bundle that Timothy Standing Bear held out. Working slowly and praying in a whisper-voice, he made a red circle on Ned's forehead, two red circles on his cheeks, and a red circle at the base of his neck above the blue shirt he was dressed in. Now the ancestors would recognize Ned and escort him into the spirit world. He glanced over at Ella. She sat very still, eyes fixed on the painted corpse of her nephew, hands open and relaxed in her lap. He had the sense that the ancient Arapaho beliefs had brought her some peace.

Richard Marks stood at the small table, preparing the cedar. After a moment, he walked over to Donald and handed him what looked like a small iron pot. Donald stepped toward the chairs, lifted the pan over head with one hand, and started down the center aisle. In his other hand was an eagle's wing with which he brushed the cedar smoke over the people, making sure the smoke reached everyone and everything. The other two elders walked beside him, all of them praying in Arapaho as the cedar smoke rolled out of the pan, wafting over the brown heads and curling along the rows. Father John blinked back the burning sensation in his eyes. The hall smelled of cedar. Next to him, Marie, Ella, and Jerry sat with their heads back, gazing up at the smoke. He could hear the sounds of their breathing.

When the wake was over, he got to his feet, leaned over Ella and took one of her hands in his own. He told her again how sorry he was.

"Help him get justice," she said, holding on to him for a long moment.

"I'll do what I can," he told her but he was thinking there was little he could do. Not until Gianelli had arrested Dwayne Hawk and Lionel Lookingglass was anyone likely to know what had happened to Ned.

"I'll be staying with Ella," Marie said, as if she wanted to reassure him that Ella would not have to spend the night in the hall alone. Relatives always stayed with the corpse.

Father John glanced toward the rear door. A few people had begun shouldering their way outside. He couldn't see Roseanne. Most of the people were lining up in the center aisle to speak with Ella, express their condolences. He kept a hand on Ella's shoulder a moment, then shook hands with Jerry, who was on his feet, eyeing those straining to get close to the family, as if he wanted to protect them. Father John told Ella good-bye and started for the side door.

Maybe he could catch Roseanne in the parking lot.

22

Groups of mourners straggled out of the hall, looking as if they had wandered into a neighborhood that was once familiar but had changed now that Ned Windsong was no longer there. They stood about, heads bobbing in and out of the circles of yellow light from the overhead lamps. A column of light washed out the front door across the graveled parking lot. Father John spotted the small, dark figure hurrying past the vehicles at the end of the lot.

He took off running, conscious of the scrape of his boots on the gravel. "Roseanne!" he called.

She threw both arms over her head and ducked around a pickup, as if to shield herself from a wall of falling bricks.

"It's Father John," he said, moving in closer. She was pressed against the passenger door, the whites of her eyes enormous in the shadows.

"You scared the hell outta me," she said, dropping her arms and tossing her head about, taking in the knots of people wandering down the row of vehicles. "What do you want?"

"Are you okay?" He kept his voice calm. "You're settled in the house?"

She gave a half shrug. "They came for me today."

"Dwayne and Lionel?"

"They seen me at the convenience store in Ethete. I shouldn't have gone there, but I needed groceries. They must've been driving by. Jesus, why don't the cops pick them up?"

"It's a big reservation," he said. And they are like smoke, he was thinking. Visible for a moment, then gone. "What happened?"

She ran her fingers through her hair, tucking a strand behind her ears. Her silver earrings glinted when she moved her head. "Followed me to the Sun Dance grounds. I ran down the ditch and got away. They think I been talking to the fed and I can connect them to Ned. I only talked to the fed once, and that was because I couldn't get away. I mean, I was at Berta's when he showed up. What was I supposed to do? I'm not a snitch." She lifted her hands and pressed her fingers under her cheekbones. "They won't believe me. They're gonna keep looking 'til they find me. They're gonna kill me."

"What do you know about them?" Father John said. "Where could they be hiding?"

She gave him a wide-flung look, as if she were taking him in with the whole reservation. Then she pulled in her shoulders and pushed past him.

"Wait a minute," he said following her, but she kept going until she reached a blue sedan nearly hidden between two pickups. She lunged for the driver's door, jammed a key into the lock and started to drop behind the steering wheel. He took hold of her arm and turned her toward him.

"You know where they're hiding, don't you?" he said.

"They'll kill me."

"Not if they're in custody."

"Leave me alone." She twisted in his grasp. "I don't know where they are."

"But you have a good idea." She was staring up at him with the same wide eyes, like a wild animal in a trap, scared and innocent and vulnerable. He had been guessing, he realized, reading in between the lines, following his gut instincts, but now he knew that he had guessed right. "The fed and the police have spent three days looking for them," he said. "They're going to find them

258

eventually, but until they do, you're in danger. Do you understand? The sooner Lionel and Dwayne are arrested, the sooner you'll be free."

"Don't you get it?" She bit at her lower lip. "If I snitch, I'm dead."

"You can use a pay phone and give the fed an anonymous tip," he said.

She yanked her arm away and ducked inside the car. He closed the door behind her and stepped back as the engine turned over and the sedan slid forward, then headed across the lot and out onto Seventeen-Mile Road. He watched the red taillights until they dissolved in the darkness.

Vicky came toward him as he started past the vehicles. Another small lone figure, backlit by the glow of light from the hall. Little groups moved in waves around her. She kept the same, steady pace, and even in the dark he could feel her eyes on him.

"Ned's former girlfriend?" she said when he closed the gap between them. "Too bad she was in such a hurry to get away. I wanted to talk to her."

"She was worried that Hawk and Lookingglass might be here." He glanced around at the cars and pickups pulling out of the slots and inching across the lot. There was

259

every possibility the two men had been waiting in a pickup, staring out of the windshield, watching for Roseanne, but he hadn't seen any vehicles pull out behind her sedan. "They followed her today. They want to intimidate her so she won't give up their hiding place."

"She knows where they are?"

"She has a good idea."

"For godssakes, John. She has to tell Gianelli. Marcy's in danger." Vicky drew in a long breath and stared past his shoulder at the vehicles crawling past. The putrid smells of exhaust rolled through the air. "Marcy has cooperated. What about Roseanne Birdwoman? Is she cooperating?" She hurried on before he could say anything. "My guess is that she isn't. She doesn't want to be a snitch — isn't that her excuse? But she's in a position to confirm what Marcy has said and tell Gianelli where the killers are hiding. Doesn't she realize the dangerous game she's playing? If they followed her today, that means they're on the rez. They could figure out that Marcy's at the mission. She shouldn't stay here. She should go back to Oklahoma where her father can protect her."

"Listen, Vicky," Father John said, "Marcy had somewhat of a breakdown this afternoon." He told her about the girl, drunk and wandering down the path to the river, tearing at her clothes and railing against her father. "She's been trying to get away from her father most of her life. She won't go to him."

Vicky gave him a look of incomprehension, as if they were talking about different girls. "Larry Morrison loves his daughter," she said. "He knows she's been under the kind of stress that would buckle people with a lot more experience. So she had a couple drinks? It doesn't mean anything."

"Marcy needs professional therapy," he said.

"What she needs is for Dwayne Hawk and Lionel Lookingglass to be in custody." Vicky started walking in the direction of her Jeep, parked across from the empty slot where Roseanne's car had been, and Father John walked with her. "I know the girl," she said, opening the driver's door and turning toward him. "Talk to Roseanne, John. Convince her to cooperate with Gianelli."

She was about to fold herself behind the wheel when Father John said, "I've been thinking about the burglary ring." The idea of Ned breaking into houses in Lander and Jackson Hole had been free-falling in his mind with no logical stops, no conclusions that made sense, and he realized he had wanted to talk it over with Vicky.

She looked up at him. "What about it?"

"It doesn't make sense," he said. "Donald Little Robe told me that Ned went to Jackson Hole to get away from something, start a new life. But if he had wanted to get out, what made him stay with it?"

"Maybe Jackson Hole had even bigger, richer homes," Vicky said. "Ned and the others had a good thing going."

"He warned Roseanne to stay away from them, that they were no good."

She hadn't taken her eyes from his. Holding on to the edge of the door, her face was half-lit inside the Jeep. "What are you getting at?"

"Ned kept trying to break with the ring. I don't think he was the leader, the guy calling the shots. And I don't think Hawk and Lookingglass could have influenced him to stay in after he got to Jackson Hole. I think somebody else is involved, somebody with a hold over him."

Vicky shook her head. "They had a hold over him," she said. "Do as we say, or you're dead. Ned came back to the rez, started preparing for the Sun Dance, announced he was done with the past. They killed him to keep him from talking. It's as simple as that."

She turned away and ducked inside the Jeep, and he shut her door. He waited until she pulled into the line of vehicles snaking across the lot, then walked toward the Toyota. The hall door was closed, leaving only the stream of headlights bobbing through the darkness and the dim circles of overhead lights. Vicky was probably right, he thought. Ned wanted enough money to buy a ranch, and that was what pulled him back into the burglary ring. Still he couldn't shake the notion that if Ned had thought Hawk and Lookingglass might come after him, he would have been prepared. He would have heard them drive into the yard. He wouldn't have opened the door for a couple of guys who wanted to kill him.

Ned hadn't expected to die that night at the hands of Dwayne Hawk and Lionel Lookingglass.

The sky was filled with stars when Father John turned onto Circle Drive, the cone of headlights sweeping ahead. The streetlamps cast waves of light over the grounds that gave the mission a surreal look. Beyond the lights, the old buildings bunched in the darkness, flat black shadows looming out of the past. He turned off the *Salome* CD and let the nighttime silence drift through the cab. It was easy to imagine the bustle of the mission a century ago, horse-drawn wagons and carts swaying around the drive, Arapaho kids racing about the school yard, the smells of hay in the fields and the neighing of horses in the corrals, the odors of fresh bread wafting from the bakery. Always the past and the present yoked together, he thought, neither able to break free. It was in the silence that he felt connected to something bigger than himself, a whole history that had caught him up with all the old Jesuits — the Black Robes — who had come before him.

He parked at the residence and hurried down the shadowy sidewalk. Light glowed in the living room window, and for a moment, he let himself hope that Bishop Harry might still be up watching TV. He wouldn't mind a little company, another mind to try out his theory that somebody other than Ned and the two men accused of killing him controlled the burglary ring. The minute he let himself inside, he knew by the subdued noises emanating from the living room that Bishop Harry had gone upstairs to bed and left the TV on, a kind of welcome for the pastor, as if someone were here.

Walks-On skidded out of the kitchen and down the hallway sleep dazed, blinking in the light that Father John had snapped on. He patted the dog's head and scratched his ears, then led him back into the kitchen where he shook dried food into the blue enamel bowl and refilled the water bowl. He drained a mug of lukewarm coffee from the container, set the mug in the microwave and watched the oven whir and blink into life. He heard the noise then, the thump and scratch of boots on the back step, followed by the kind of quiet that made him wonder if he had heard anything at all. There hadn't been any engine sounds, and he hadn't seen any parked vehicles outside, but it was always possible that someone had parked in back of the residence. He stopped the microwave and listened. He could feel his neck muscles stiffen with tension. His hands curled into fists. Walks-On had stopped eating and lifted his head. A low growl emerged from his throat. His hair stood up along his spine.

The noise came again, unmistakable this time. A deliberate pressure of human weight on the wooden steps that led to the back porch and the outside door to the kitchen. There was a rhythm in the way the sound came and went as the intruder climbed a step, stopped, then climbed another. Then the rhythm mixed itself up like a jazz riff, point and counter point. There were two intruders.

He realized that the door was unlocked — the little lever turned vertical instead of horizontal. He lunged for the door just as it burst open and two men — Arapahos, black-haired and dark-eyed, the rancid smells of whiskey and vomit pouring off them — threw themselves into the kitchen. He managed to back against the hard edge of the counter as Walks-On jumped on one of the men and sank his teeth in the fleshy, flailing arm.

23

"Call him off! Call him off!" The big man with a black ponytail flailed at the dog with his free arm and jumped about as if he were on hot coals.

Walks-On backed off and, gathering rage-infused momentum, lunged again at the man's arm as a small, black pistol with a muzzle that seemed as big as a cannon rose in the other man's hand.

"Don't shoot!" Father John grabbed the dog's collar and jerked him backward. It took almost all of his strength; the dog was like a mountain lion, throwing himself at the intruder. The gun waved about. "Don't shoot!" he shouted again. He pulled Walks-On in close and moved between him and the gun.

"Jesus! I'm bleeding!" The big man sounded like he might burst into tears, and Father John reached around, grabbed a dish towel off the counter and tossed it to him.

He caught it in mid-air and jammed it against his arm. A thin strand of blood trickled toward his elbow. "Kill that mangy beast," he said.

"There's not going to be any killing here," Father John said, willing his voice to be calm and authoritative. A bit of legerdemain, he thought, as if he were the one in control. Walks-On jumped against his leg. "What do you want," he said.

"You gonna shoot that dog or what?" the big man said, pressing the towel to his arm.

"Shut up, Lionel," the other man said. He kept the gun thrust into the empty space between him and Father John, but he no longer waved it about. Knuckles popped like miniature snow peaks in his brown hand.

"Dwayne Hawk and Lionel Lookingglass," Father John said. He had known who they were the instant they came through the door. "What are you doing here?"

"Where you keeping her?" Dwayne said. He was thin and wiry, a good half foot shorter than his partner, but he looked more menacing, gripping the gun and fixing Father John with narrow, black eyes under the cliff of his forehead. His black hair was cut short, and part of his left ear was missing.

"Who are you talking about?" Keep him

talking, Father John was thinking. Find a place to engage him. The first rule of counseling.

"The bitch that fingered us for Ned's murder."

"Jesus, my arm's hurting like hell," Lionel said. "I need a doctor. That dog got rabies?"

Walks-On growled and snapped, and Father John tightened his grip on his collar. "Take it easy," he said, not sure whether it was meant for the dog or the two men. "He's had his shots. You're not going to get rabies."

"You don't shoot him now, I'm gonna do it, I swear. I'll come back here with a shotgun and blow his brains out."

"I told you, shut up," Dwayne said. He moved forward and pointed the gun at Father John's chest, eyes squeezed into angry slits. Dots of perspiration blossomed on his forehead. "The white girl. Where'd you put her?"

Father John could feel his heart catapult against his ribs. "The fed has her in a safe place," he said.

The Indian was quiet a moment, the slit-eyes looking Father John up and down. "Funny, we heard she's right here at the mission. You been keeping her safe so she can tell her lies and get us locked up for

269

killing Ned. Only we didn't do it, see? It don't matter what she says, we didn't know he was dead 'til we went to pick him up. Figured he'd been stuck with that white girl long enough, needed to get back to his own kind."

"Tell your story to the fed." Father John tried not to look at the gun. "You have a witness."

"Yeah." Dwayne gave a snort. "Roseanne, the snitch. Talking to the fed, connecting us up with Ned. She needs to keep her mouth shut, she knows what's good for her." He shifted his gaze sideways toward Lionel, flopped down on a kitchen chair, clasping the towel against his arm. Beneath his fingers, the towel was turning red.

Father John followed his gaze. "You need ice," he said. Still holding on to the dog's collar, he started for the refrigerator.

"Don't move!" The gun jutted into the center of the kitchen, like a cannon moved into firing position.

"I need to go to the hospital." Lionel was moaning and fidgeting.

"Take it easy." Father John pulled Walks-On closer. "I'm just getting him some ice."

"You wanna die?" The voice was hard-edged, as sharp as steel. The gun was gripped in both of Dwayne's hands, and he had contracted into a shooting position, as if he were on a firing range.

Father John stayed where he was and looked at the man no more than four feet away, and yet a chasm of linoleum and empty fluorescent-lit space opened between them. A thousand half-formed thoughts tumbled through his head. What had happened to Dwayne Hawk? Where had he come from and what had he endured? What was he on? What kind of drug could stifle any sense of empathy or common humanity that might keep him from pulling the trigger. He said, "I'm not moving. You can put the gun down."

"Where is she?" Dwayne hissed the question. Little specks of saliva appeared at the corners of his mouth.

"I told you, the fed . . ."

"Save it," Dwayne said. "Where you keeping her?"

"What are you going to do?" Father John kept his eyes locked on the Indian's and tried to ignore the gun waving between them. "Intimidate her into changing her story? What if she did? The fed will still want to talk to you, get your version. He won't give up until he finds you. You and Lionel can't hide forever."

"Jeez, Dwayne," Lionel said, pushing himself to his feet. "We gotta get outta here. I need help."

The other man shrugged off his partner without glancing at him. He opened his mouth as if he were waiting for the words forming in his throat to push their way out. Before he could say anything, Father John said, "If you didn't kill Ned, who did?"

"What?" Dwayne flinched and blinked a couple of times.

"Why do I get the sense that you know the truth?" Father John said.

"You're smoking, man."

"You and Lionel could take the fall unless you tell Gianelli what you know."

"You think we're stupid?" Dwayne said. Lionel was weaving on his feet behind him, still clasping the towel that had started to turn into quivering red jelly. The towel had started to slip so that blood ran out of the wound. "You think we want to end up like Ned? No way we're going in and snitching."

The kitchen went quiet, except for the sound of Walks-On's nails scraping the floor and Dwayne's quick gulps of air. Father John could hear the sound of a truck on Seventeen-Mile Road. The noise seemed to come from a great distance. He had guessed right, he was thinking. Someone else was in the burglary ring. The general who mapped out the plan of attack. Selected the houses, most likely, checked on security, determined when the owners would be away, then called in the troops — Ned and the two Indians in his kitchen. Whoever it was, this general, the two men were afraid of him. And yet they would be charged with Ned's murder, unless they could get Marcy Morrison to change her story. So they had come out of hiding to find the girl. They had gone after Roseanne, too, wanting to intimidate her, keep her from linking them to the burglary ring and Ned. The minute the link was made, Gianelli would assume that Ned had been holding out. Or maybe Dwayne and Lionel had wanted to keep him from snitching about the burglary ring, after he had decided to turn his life around. Either way, it would look as if they had reason to kill.

But they wouldn't snitch on the general. They didn't want to end up like Ned.

Ned had also been frightened of the general, Father John realized. It explained why he had agreed to rob houses again in Jackson Hole, after moving there to make a new start. It explained why he came back and why he went to Donald Little Robe, searching for the courage to remain firm in his resolve, hoping to find it in the Sun Dance.

"That's it!" Dwayne rammed a fist into the cabinet door. His other hand lowered the gun. "Enough! Where is she? I want the answer now! You got one second, and that stupid dog is dead."

"Shoot him now!" Lionel shouted. "Sonafabitch bit me hard. Jeez, I'm gonna need stitches."

"First the dog," Dwayne said. "Then you, Father. Start with your knees. How'd you like that? Take out one elbow, then the other. Fix you up pretty good, huh? Or you want to start with the elbow first? Where is she?" He grasped the gun with both hands.

"Drop your weapon!" Bishop Harry stood in the doorway, both hands gripping the long-nosed silver Flintlock pistol. Pink, hairy legs — bird legs — hung below the red plaid robe cinched at his waist. The blue collar of his pajamas sprang around his neck. His gray hair was mussed, standing out in thin strands, as if he had stepped on an electric wire.

Dwayne turned his head toward the old man, a startled, bemused look on his face, as if an apparition had materialized out of nowhere. The gun started to move in the old man's direction. "You couldn't shoot a barn with that thing."

"I am aiming at your heart," the bishop said. His voice was like the thud of a bass drum. "Would you like to gamble with your life?"

"The old goat's gonna kill us." Lionel sounded as if he were about to start weeping.

Dwayne's arm started downward in slow motion, reluctant and hesitant, the gun steady in his hand.

"All the way. That's it," the bishop said as Dwayne's hand slid alongside his thigh. "Now let your gun fall to the floor, nice-and-easy-like. There you go." The gun clunked onto the floor. "I suggest you turn around and find your way out of here. The same way you came in, I would suppose."

"Let's go," Lionel said. He had already kicked the door back, and he threw himself out into the little porch off the kitchen. Dwayne was behind him, tossing nervous glances over his shoulder. The bishop stood like a statue, pointing the pistol at the man's back. Dwayne yanked open the outer door, and both men ducked out, knocking against each other in the doorway, then disappearing into the darkness. Boots drummed on the wooden steps. In a minute, an engine fired. There was the noise of gravel scattering beneath tires. A tremor ran along the floor as the vehicle passed by the side of the house, thumped across the field and out onto Circle Drive. Another moment, and the noise was absorbed in the mission quiet.

"I figured the best thing was to get them out of here," the bishop said. "I've encountered men like that. They are frightened and desperate. You never know what they might try."

"You were right," Father John said, still holding Walks-On's collar as he crossed the kitchen and slammed the door, not wanting the dog to bolt after them. He could feel the tension begin to drain out of the dog's muscles, and he let him go. Walks-On jumped up and placed his paws on Father John's chest, doing a little dance on his rear leg. "Good boy," Father John said, patting his head. "You did good."

"I'm going to check on the girl." He took hold of the dog's collar again and guided him downward. Bishop Harry was already in the hall, tapping on the phone, the Flintlock on the table. Father John hurried past, yanked open the door, and headed down the steps. Then he started running. Across Circle Drive and through the field, across the drive again and down the alley between the church and the administration building, dodging in and out of the dim lights flaring from the streetlamps. The thudding sound of his boots filled his ears. The guesthouse was dark. There was no sign of life. He walked past the house, checking for the red pickup. It was gone.

He double-backed to the front and knocked on the door. "Marcy," he shouted, his own voice reverberating out of the vacuum that he knew was inside. He knocked harder, then tried the knob. The door swung into darkness. He reached around and flipped on the switch. The little table lamp next to the sofa cast a faint shield of light across the linoleum floor. "Marcy!" he called again, but she was gone. He crossed the small living room, flipped on the switch in the bedroom that was little more than a back porch and stared at the narrow, empty bed. The tangle of sheets and blankets, the empty whiskey bottle and pop cans on the floor, the only signs the girl had ever been there.

He let himself out and retraced his steps down the shadows in the alley. From somewhere in the distance, beyond the darkness and the black sky ribboned with stars, came the wailing noise of sirens.

24

"You're certain about the intruders." Ted Gianelli planted himself in a triangle formed by his white SUV and two BIA police cars. The light bars flashed red and blue stripes over his face. Tubes of yellow headlights shot across Circle Drive into the field of wild grasses.

"Dwayne Hawk and Lionel Lookingglass," Father John said. Walks-On leaned against his leg.

"Let's go over it again. They burst through the kitchen door. The dog attacked Lionel, and Dwayne pulled a gun and threatened to shoot both you and your dog until Bishop Harry brought out his howitzer. If they show up at the ER, we'll arrest them. They can't be too far away. Every cop in the area is looking for them. What did they want?"

Father John told him they were looking for Marcy Morrison. The front door to the residence stood open, and light spilled out onto the sidewalk. He could see the bishop and the officers in the kitchen, the bishop gesturing and the officers stepping around carefully, as if they were stepping over the traces of Lionel's blood.

"You think they found her?"

Father John shook his head. "She left before they arrived."

Gianelli looked in the direction of the alley blurred in the darkness. "You think she got word?"

"I don't know," Father John said. Then he told the agent that the girl had left the mission earlier today and might have talked to someone. He could hear the false note clanging as he spoke. It was illogical. Marcy Morrison hardly knew anyone on the rez. Who would she have talked to? Who would have warned her that Hawk and Lookingglass would come for her tonight? They had gone after Roseanne this afternoon, but Roseanne hadn't spoken with them. In any case, he doubted that Roseanne knew where Marcy was staying. Nothing was making sense.

"Moccasin telegraph," Gianelli said. "Somebody must have spotted her pickup near the mission. Word got back to Hawk and Lookingglass. They're out there somewhere." He punched a fist toward the darkness on Seventeen-Mile Road. "What else did they say?"

"They said Marcy lied about them killing Ned," Father John told him. "They had nothing to do with it. He was already dead when they stopped by to pick him up. They're desperate to find the girl."

Gianelli interrupted: "And do what? Scare her enough to change her story?"

"What if they're right?" Father John could still see the pinched, frightened look on Dwayne's face, the desperate way his hand gripped the gun.

"If they're innocent, why are they hiding? Why don't they come in and tell their version of what went on?"

"A couple of Indians who probably have records?" Father John said. "Their word against the word of a white girl?"

"What the hell's that supposed to mean?"

"I'm telling you how they're looking at it," Father John said. "They're not thinking straight. They know they're looking at more prison time for burglary and they think they'll be charged for a homicide they claim they knew nothing about. They're scared to death."

"Scared enough to break into your kitchen and hold you at gunpoint? Piling up felonies as high as that roof." Gianelli hitched his thumb toward the residence, then he went quiet, the blue and red lights washing over him. Father John could almost see the thoughts behind his expression. "You believe them, is that right?" he said.

"Marcy's the only one who witnessed what happened," Father John said.

"We've established that. The girl with a bruised face and black eyes, curled in a fetal position, in shock. No weapon, no gun residue on her hands." He paused for a long moment, letting his gaze run over the vehicles and the residence. "Hawk and Lookingglass left a Walther .32 caliber in your kitchen. Not the weapon used on Ned. Forensics says that was a .380 caliber. Why would the girl lie, unless she's protecting someone? What do you have that you're not telling me?"

Father John shrugged. "A theory, that's all."

"Yeah? You and your theories, all logical as hell, I'm sure. Better give it to me."

"I think the burglary gang was bigger than Ned and those two," Father John said, nodding toward the light spilling out of the house, the bishop and the officers still huddled in the kitchen where Dwayne and Lionel had been thirty minutes earlier. "I think somebody else called the shots, some-

281

body with influence over Ned. After he went to Jackson Hole to start over, somebody managed to convince him to break into homes there."

"You're saying this person had something on Ned?"

"Could be," Father John said. He hadn't thought about it like that, but it was possible Ned had more to hide than a series of break-ins. Maybe he was threatened with exposure. And yet that didn't make sense because Ned could have exposed the whole burglary ring. But he didn't, and that was the point. He didn't give up Dwayne or Lionel or anybody else. "I think somebody had an even stronger hold on Ned," he said. "He was struggling to free himself."

"Anybody talk to you about this, mention any names?"

"No."

It was a moment before Gianelli said, "So when Ned moved back to the rez, presumably in an effort to get away from the burglary ring, it was the last straw for this person of influence. He broke into the house and shot Ned to keep him quiet, and Ned's fiancée is protecting the real killer." He made a sucking noise with his breath. "I'm going to talk to Marcy Morrison again. Any idea where she might have gone to?"

"No."

"She could be in more danger than she realizes." Gianelli shook his head, and the colored lights ran together across his face. "Not just from Hawk and Lookingglass, but from whoever she thinks she's protecting."

The brick bungalow that served as Vicky's law office was suffused in the shadows of the evergreens around the yard. The windows were black panes; the night-light hadn't been turned on. Quiet had settled on the whole neighborhood: the other bungalows up and down the street, the cars and pickups at the curbs. Moonlight floated through the trees. Vicky pulled into the driveway and got out. She could barely hear the traffic out on Main, two blocks away. Here, everything seemed on hold until morning.

And something was different about the house. She felt a prickly sense of unease as she walked across the grass, dodging the ponderosa that rose high above the roof. Without the night-light glowing in the windows, the house was like a vacant hull. Not that the light was actually effective in warning away burglars, she supposed, but at least it allowed her to believe it would work. It provided its own peace of mind. It wasn't like Annie to leave for the day without turning on the light.

The outer screened door was ajar. It made a faint creaking noise in the breeze. Vicky started to unlock the main door, then realized that it wasn't locked. She stepped inside, holding her breath. She kept the door open as she ran her other hand along the wall and flipped the switch. In the light that flooded the reception room, she took everything in at once: the opened pizza box on the floor, the slices of pizza spilled onto the carpet with the crumpled paper napkins, the plastic glasses overturned on Annie's desk, the dark liquid puddle at the base of the computer, the papers and folders scattered over the desk.

Vicky stood very still, listening. There were no sounds. "Annie?" she called into the quiet of the interior. "Roger?" Nothing. She waited a moment, then pushed the door back against the wall, allowing the night in, the soft, warm breeze blowing over her arms. She stepped over to the desk, tapped at the keyboard and watched the screen come to life: page 5 of the Martinson contract. She tried to picture what had happened: Annie working late, making a few more corrections Vicky had requested, ordering pizza. Roger had stayed late, too, not wanting to leave her alone — not with a crazed ex-husband with a restraining order against him still in town — so the pizza was giant-sized. There were two Cokes. And then what?

Vicky picked up the phone and tapped the key for Annie's cell. She held her breath, waiting for the buzzing noise, moving around the desk so that she was between the desk and the opened door, unsure of what might be hiding in the shadows. Annie's husband hiding somewhere? In Roger's office, in the hallway, the restroom, the little galley kitchen? The phone rang once, twice. She willed herself to think logically. Annie and Roger had left in a hurry. Run out the front door without locking it. Maybe run out the back door. Run away from Robin.

A third ring, broken off by Annie's voice: "Oh, God, Vicky! Is that you?"

"What happened?" Vicky said. Her own voice sounded shaky and false, the voice of a stranger who had wandered into her office.

"Robin," Annie said. The name came like a sob. "He came to the office. I told him he had to leave, I was calling the cops."

"Annie, listen to me," Vicky said. "Are you all right?"

"He grabbed hold of my arm and yanked

me out of the chair. I was working on the contract. Roger and I had eaten some pizza . . ."

"Are you all right?"

"I'm okay." Annie was crying now, great sobs that burst like static over the line. "Roger's here."

"Where? Where are you?"

"In the ER."

"I'm on the way," Vicky said.

She could see the Lander Valley hospital on the hill when she was still a block away — the bright light over the driveway that curved under the portico, the white ambulance parked to one side, surrounded by the darkness and the wide, black sky. She accelerated into the curve, pulled up next to the ambulance, and ran across the pavement. She pushed past the double-glass doors. Annie was huddled in one of the blue plastic chairs that lined the wall, alone in the waiting room except for the woman behind the counter. Vicky hurried over to her: the black, scared eyes, the red bruise like a birthmark on her cheek.

Vicky sank onto a chair and slipped an arm around Annie's shoulders. She could feel the tremors beneath the thin cotton blouse, the wisps of black hair on her skin.

Annie lifted her hand from the folds of her skirt, and Vicky gasped. A red and purple bruise ran from Annie's wrist, halfway up her arm. "Have you seen a doctor?" she said. "Are you sure you're okay?"

"I'm okay," Annie said, and so much bravery in her tone, such steady determination, that Vicky had to bite her lip to keep from crying. "I've had worse than this," Annie said.

Vicky could feel the truth of it. It was the truth for her once, but that was in a life that had faded away, like the far distances faded into the vastness of the plains and allowed new realities to sweep in between. "What about Roger?"

"He's gonna be okay," Annie said. "A broken rib. Some bruises. Broke his glasses." She gave a forced laugh. "You know how blind he is without his glasses." She shifted around until she was facing Vicky. "He had just gone into his office when Robin burst in. He must've been watching us, waiting for Roger to leave. Roger came flying out. He pulled Robin off me, punched him in the chest, made him let go of my arm. I don't know what would've happened if he hadn't been there," she went on, her voice rising a pitch. "Robin would've forced me to go with him. He could've killed me."

Vicky put both arms around her and hugged her. "You're okay now," she said. She could feel Annie sobbing silently against her shoulder, the moist tears seeping into her blouse.

"Oh, I know," Annie said, pulling away and straightening her skirt over her knees. "Soon's the cops pick him up, he'll go back to prison. I won't have to worry about Robin Bosey for a long time."

"Where's he staying?" Vicky said.

"Who knows?" Annie tried for a shrug. "Probably with his no-good cousin in Ethete. That's what I told the cops."

Vicky sat back, not saying anything. Behind the counter, a short woman with broad shoulders and short, brown hair leafed through a stack of papers; a blonde girl barely out of high school, bent over a computer screen. A practiced air about them of ignoring the waiting room. Robin Bosey could disappear into the emptiness of the reservation, she was thinking, a little house out at the end of a dirt road somewhere, a dilapidated building no one thought about any more, falling back into the earth. Like Dwayne Hawk and Lionel Lookingglass. Everyone looking for them, no one finding them.

A door at the end of the waiting room

swung open and Roger walked out, blinking in the light. There was a naked look about him without the wire-framed glasses. His hair was mussed, a cowlick springing up at the crown of his head. He moved slowly, testing each step, holding one arm against his waist. In his hand was a little piece of paper, a prescription, Vicky guessed. A nurse in green scrubs trailed behind him, keeping a hand on his elbow.

Annie jumped to her feet and ran to him. For a moment, they held each other, Roger pulling her in close against his folded arm. Then Annie stepped back, but he didn't let her go all the way. Instead, he guided her around to his other side as they came across the room.

"Are you a friend?" The nurse brushed past.

Vicky nodded.

"Good," the nurse said. She was tall and severe looking, with blonde hair pulled back and fixed in a bun. "Mr. Hurst should take it easy for a while. He has a prescription that should check the pain," she said. Behind her back, Roger waved the little piece of paper. "We've reported the incident as an assault, but the police had already been brought in."

"Called them on our way to the hospital,"

Roger said. "Any luck, they've got that bastard by now." He leaned down and kissed the top of Annie's head.

"I'll follow you home," Vicky said. The nurse had hurried ahead and was holding open the glass door. The night air was still warm, but the breeze had picked up, sweeping miniature tumbleweeds across the drive. They walked out to the parking lot, and Vicky waited while Roger settled himself into the passenger seat of Annie's car. Annie shut the door, then went around and got in behind the wheel.

"Wait," Vicky said, leaning over the top of the door. "Don't go home. Go to Casper, both of you. Stay with your friend, Annie. Spend time with your kids."

"The office . . ."

"Will get along fine."

"I don't know, Vicky." Roger leaned forward, twisting part way around, and she could see the pain in his face.

"It's my law firm, and I'm telling you I don't want either of you there," Vicky said. "Go to Casper and keep Annie there until it's safe."

Until Robin can't hurt her again, she was thinking. Until he was in custody. Locked away. She closed the door and waited as the car lurched forward, the red taillights blinking faintly and finally dissolving into a single red dot in the darkness down the road. Then she walked back to her Jeep. The ambulance was gone. She started the ignition and was heading around the curve when her cell rang. She fumbled in her black bag on the passenger seat, finally pulling out the thin piece of plastic and flipped it open. John O'Malley's voice on the other end: "Marcy's gone," he said.

25

The cemetery came into view ahead, parched, rolling plains between Seventeen-Mile Road and the mission grounds. A little group huddled around an opened grave, heads bowed, the wind plucking at their clothes. Vicky turned onto the dirt road that circled the cemetery and parked behind the line of cars and pickups. Holding her hair back in the wind, she made her way around the white crosses that jutted out of the earth at the head of mounds of dirt covered with plastic flowers, crumpled and wilted in the sun. So many of the ancestors were buried here. Lone Bear, one of the last chiefs, was here. Her own parents and grandparents, buried in the far corner, the gravesites in the shade of an old cottonwood.

"Grant, we ask you, Almighty God, eternal pardon and rest to Ned Windsong, who has left this life and gone into the everlasting life you have promised the souls of the faithful." Father John's voice drifted out over the graves.

"Amen," someone said, followed by a chorus of amens coughed into the wind.

Vicky stopped a few feet away and listened to the rest of the prayers, her eyes on John O'Malley. He had on a blue shirt and dark trousers. Around his shoulders was the white stole that one of the grandmothers had embroidered in Arapaho symbols for him. He moved around the coffin balanced on leather straps over the grave, dipping a small sprinkler into a pottery dish and sprinkling the holy water. She had attended dozens of funerals, watched the priests go through the same rituals. She accepted the rituals, just as other Arapahos accepted them. Not as their own, but brought to them. A gift, another way of praying. She could almost hear her grandfather's voice. *Pray and pray and pray.*

Marcy Morrison wasn't in the crowd. She had called the girl's cell a dozen times since she had gotten John O'Malley's call last night. She might have been dialing into a void. She stopped by the office this morning and tried Marcy again, then called Larry Morrison and told him his daughter had left the mission and was not returning calls.

The man had remained quiet for so long

293

that she thought his cell must have cut off. "She's very unpredictable," he said finally. "I'm sure she'll show up in her own time."

"Mr. Morrison." Vicky wondered if her tone had betrayed the shock she felt. "Your daughter is in danger. She has witnessed a murder and identified the killers." She told him what John O'Malley had said about Dwayne Hawk and Lionel Lookingglass coming to the mission last night, looking for Marcy. "If they find her, they may kill her."

"I understand," Morrison had said, as if she had just told him that one of his checks had bounced. "But you must understand that my daughter also knows this and is taking evasive action. She is very good at taking care of herself."

"She shouldn't be alone," Vicky said. Then she told him the rest of it: the breakdown yesterday afternoon, Father John's belief that she needed professional care. "He's a pastor, a counselor," she went on. "He's seen people pushed to the end of their ability to cope."

"I see," Larry Morrison said, and for the first time, she had detected a faint note of worry in his voice. "She may have gone back to Jackson. I believe she has a few friends there, an old boyfriend. I can't fly to Wyoming until tomorrow. There's choir practice this evening, and my couples' ministry —"

She cut him off and told him that she would drive up to Jackson Hole, find the girl and make sure she was all right. He told her that Marcy owned a place at Alpine Meadows Condominiums, number 224. She had hung up then, called the cleaning service and arranged to have the mess in the office cleaned up. The office was silent, smelling of pizza, when she let herself out and locked the door. She was at the outskirts of Lander when it occurred to her that Marcy might decide to attend her fiancé's funeral, a last chance to say good-bye. She had turned onto Highway 789 and driven to the reservation through the white sun and the bright, blue sky, the wind banging against the sides of the Jeep.

Vicky could see Ella in front, close to the grave. Marie sat next to her, an arm flung around her sister's shoulders. On the other side, Jerry Adams stood straight-backed and wide-shouldered, holding his cowboy hat to his chest, his bald scalp reddening in the sun. A sense of discomfort, of not belonging, came over Vicky, and she stepped back a little. Ella believed that Marcy Morrison was involved in Ned's death. And here she was, Marcy's attorney, defending the white outsider in the murder of one of her own people.

Jevaneatha yesawathawid hinenida hevedathu. Donald Little Robe had stepped forward, his voice booming over the bowed heads and reverberating around the empty cemetery. John O'Malley was beside him, his own head bowed while the elder prayed.

Ha, hedenieaunin nenetejenuu nau neja vedawune.

Vicky tried to make out the meaning of the words; the rhythm and cadence were like that of a familiar melody. Something about God having breathed a soul into every human. Yes, our bodies will die and return into dust.

Heko, hevedathuwin nenaidenu jethaujene. Hethete hevedathuwin nehathe Ichjevaneatha haeain ichjeva. Our souls will live forever with the Creator in our home on high.

The elder went on for a while, speaking in the formal manner, Vicky knew, the way the chiefs and the holy men had spoken to the people in the Old Time, calling them together. Our People. Saying that Ned had chosen the good Arapaho road, turned his life around, and was working hard to prepare for the Sun Dance. Saying that now the ancestors would escort Ned's spirit into the afterworld and that the people should be at peace and know that Ned was at peace.

Vicky glanced at the men grouped behind the elder. They were also preparing for the Sun Dance, she guessed. Ned would have danced with them. Then she looked out over the cemetery toward the mission, the voice of the elder still rolling over her. Through the cottonwoods, the white steeple swayed against the blue sky, and the roofs of the mission buildings were washed silver in the sunlight. A place of refuge, the mission, for more than a hundred years, she thought. And yet, Marcy Morrison hadn't felt safe. She had fled.

The drums started now, a slow, rhythmic pounding, each thud hanging in the air before giving way to the next. The singers sat around the drum on the far side of the grave, black heads nodding. Slowly the casket began to fall into the earth, the pulley and leather creaking in rhythm with the pounding drums. Then the little crowd formed into a single line and began dropping flowers onto the casket as they moved past: symbols of life and hope.

Vicky stayed where she was as the line moved around the casket. Then people bunched together and started across the cemetery toward the parked vehicles. A space opened between her and the gravesite. Still, she didn't move. John O'Malley clasped Ella's hands and leaned down close, telling her how sorry he was, Vicky knew. She saw the gratitude and even a kind of peace in the woman's expression as Ella turned and started after the other mourners, Marie and Jerry Adams at her side.

She and John O'Malley were the only ones left, and Vicky started over. He glanced around and came to meet her. "Heard from Marcy?" he said.

"I was hoping she might be here."

He shook his head. "I didn't expect her to come."

"You think her breakdown was serious?"

"Any breakdown is serious," he said. "She needs help."

"I've spoken with her father," Vicky said. "He'll be here tomorrow." Then she told him she was going to Jackson to see if Marcy was at her condo. "I'm worried about her," she said. "She's so alone. Her fiancé's dead, her father is . . ." She took in a gulp of air. What is the word she would have used to describe the years she was in Denver going to college and law school while her children were growing up with her parents? "Preoccupied," she finished. "It doesn't help Marcy."

They started walking across the cemetery.

The Toyota pickup and her Jeep were the only parked vehicles, a long, empty gap between them. The other cars and pickups snaked out of the cemetery trailing great puffs of dust. They stopped at the pickup, and Father John said, "Ned's boss in Lander said that he had a contact at Sloan's Electric in Jackson. That's how he got the job. I wonder what he told them when he left to come back to the rez."

"I have to find Marcy," Vicky said. "I was hired to look after her interests, and God knows, she doesn't have anyone else."

Father John held up one hand between them. It was his way, she knew, of letting her know he understood.

The two-lane highway to Jackson Hole was almost empty. A few trucks and RVs, sunlight glinting off the chrome bumpers, crawling south out of Yellowstone Park, an occasional pickup appearing in the rearview mirror, then turning off onto a dirt road, herds of antelope galloping alongside the highway before giving up the chase. Every once in a while, black oil derricks appeared on the horizon, spindly legs and arms moving against the sky. Vicky settled into the rhythm of the tires humming beneath her, the music of George Strait filling the Jeep.

There was a sense of intimacy and seclusion about the vast, open plains that always made her feel at home. This was the country of her ancestors, the place where she belonged. The phone calls still came from time to time: law firms in LA or Denver looking for an Indian lawyer experienced in natural resources law. She wasn't interested. The idea of a city teeming around her, concrete covering the earth and skyscrapers blocking the sun, always left her with a cold, clammy feeling.

She followed the highway northwest past Crowheart and Burris and on through Dubois before turning south and heading through the Grand Tetons toward the valley known as Jackson Hole. Pines and boulders covered the slopes outside the windows, and white pillows of clouds rolled across the sapphire sky. The traffic was getting heavier. More sedans and late-model SUVs gliding around the curves that hugged the mountainside. Log cabins came into view, partially hidden among the trees or tucked away in little canyons.

Finally, the outskirts of the town of Jackson, with more cabins and houses lining the highway. She was deep in the valley now, mountains rising on the west and rolling ranch lands to the east. High on the slopes, she could make out the long, cleared runs of the ski areas and, in the distance, the red cars of a tram skimming over the mountainside. She slowed and followed the traffic toward the town square. She felt as if she had driven into the past, an old Western town with board sidewalks and flat-faced brick buildings and wooden balconies. A stage coach perched on the roof of the corner building with Jackson Hole Museum painted on the front window. There were other signs out of the past painted on some of the buildings: Saloon. Spirits. Billiards. But inside the old buildings were boutiques, galleries, and restaurants. When the traffic stalled, she fished her cell out of her bag and checked the GPS map to Alpine Meadows. Past the square, she turned onto a narrow road that wound upward along the banks of a creek with a thin stream of water falling over the boulders. She imagined Marcy driving up this road, panicky and scared, trying to get away from the men she had seen kill her fiancé. The same men who would kill her.

26

Alpine Meadows was a cluster of cubelike buildings three stories high, with dun-colored siding and long balconies stacked on top of one another. Other condominium clusters huddled among the pines, set back from the road, but Alpine Meadows stood in a field of wild, spiky grasses wilted in the sunshine, with a paved lot at one end. Vicky left the Jeep next to the sign that said Visitors and went in search of unit 224. Brass numbers marked each building. Between the buildings were rolling hillocks of lawn and rose bushes with sprinklers that made a buzzing noise as they shot water into the air. She followed the sidewalk to the second building and took the wooden stairs to the second floor. A moist breeze caught at her blouse as she walked along the balcony. She paused in front of the door with the brass number four and listened for sounds of someone inside, a radio or TV. There was nothing. The building itself had the vacant feeling of mid-day. When she knocked, it was a hollow noise.

Vicky knocked again, then leaned in close. "Marcy," she called. "It's Vicky Holden. Are you there? I'm here to help you." Not the slightest hint of movement or change in the atmosphere to suggest that anyone was inside. "I know you're frightened," she said, feeling a little foolish, talking to a closed door. She was thinking that she could take Marcy to Casper, move her into an apartment where she would be safe. What was clear was that Marcy Morrison would not be safe in her own condo in Jackson. How long before Hawk and Lookingglass figured out she was hiding here?

"Open the door, Marcy," Vicky said. "We can figure things out together."

"She's not there." Vicky started at the voice. There had been no sound of a door opening or closing, no scuff of footsteps. No one else was around, and yet here was a young woman with long brown hair gliding out of the shade farther along the balcony.

"I'm looking for Marcy Morrison," Vicky said. "Do you know where I might find her?"

The girl came closer. Long tan legs above thick-soled white sneakers, blue shorts, and a white tee shirt, a tennis bag slung over one shoulder. She looked as if she had stepped out of an ad for healthy outdoor living, with a spray of freckles across her nose and sunglasses pushed back on her head. "Marcy hasn't been around for a while," she said, turning a thoughtful look toward the closed door. "I heard she moved to the reservation with her fiancé. Ned somebody. Maybe you know him. You from the rez?"

"Vicky Holden," Vicky said. "I'm an attorney."

"Attorney? Is Marcy in some kind of trouble? Wouldn't surprise me, I guess."

"What do you mean?"

"Oh, I don't know." The girl shrugged. She looked as if she had stepped onto a conveyor belt and regretted it. "It's not like we were friends. I saw her around the building. And the courts."

"Marcy played tennis?"

The girl gave a sharp laugh. "I wouldn't call it that! More like, she tried to play. That's when she was engaged to Dave, so she hung around the tennis club all the time. She certainly didn't impress him with her tennis."

"She was engaged to someone named Dave?" Vicky said, fitting this new piece of information into place. This must be the boyfriend that Larry Morrison had mentioned.

"Dave Hudson. Coaches at the club." She tossed her head in the direction of building three and beyond. "Maybe he's seen Marcy around, but I sure haven't."

"I didn't get your name," Vicky said.

The girl shrugged. "Gail," she said. "Like I said, Marcy and I weren't exactly friends. Come to think of it, except for Dave, I don't think she had any friends. Good luck." The girl brushed past and ducked into the stairwell. The tennis shoes thudded on the steps.

Vicky waited a moment before she headed down the stairs. The sidewalks were clear; no sign of Gail anywhere. She had disappeared as quickly as she had appeared. Just past the third building, Vicky spotted the domed roof of a tennis club and the white flash of Gail's tee shirt as she emerged out of the shadows into a column of sunshine, then disappeared past the door to the club.

Vicky hurried along the walkway, aware of the sense of peace that pervaded the complex, the slopes of the Grand Tetons rising like a jagged wall of boulders and pines, and the sky an endless blue sea. The quiet was broken by a chirping bird and the buzzing noise of sprinklers watering the nasturtiums and petunias along the front of the club.

Seated behind the counter just inside the door was a young man who looked about twenty-five, with bleached-looking blond hair, skin tanned the color of bronze, and a name tag that said Kip. He glanced up as Vicky approached, a quizzical look in his blue eyes. "Help you?" he said.

"I'm looking for Dave," she said.

"Yeah?" Kip did a half turn toward the computer screen and tapped at the keys. "Looks like he's got a private over at a client's court." He turned back. "Usually stops in to check messages before he knocks off for the day. Check back in about an hour."

"I'll do that." Vicky pulled the small leather wallet out of her bag and handed her business card across the counter. "Tell him I'd like to talk to him for a few minutes."

"You a lawyer?" Kip said. He held on to a corner of the card, as if it had just caught on fire.

Vicky said she would be back in an hour, then started for the door. She turned back. "Would you happen to know where Sloan's

Electric is located."

"Three or four blocks off the square," he said, still staring at the card. "Turn north when you get back to town. It's on the corner. You can't miss it."

The area was easy to locate, an assortment of warehouses and hardware stores clustered together, a few blocks from the boutiques and restaurants. She spotted the sign painted across the window on the corner shop and pulled into the parking lot. The bell jangled as she pushed open the front door into a small reception area with a polished wood floor that reflected the light from crystal chandeliers dangling overhead. An older woman, heavyset, with curly blue-white hair looked up from a small desk. "Welcome," she said. She had a bright smile that took ten years from her age. "How can we help you?"

"Is the manager in?" Vicky walked over to the desk, conscious of her footsteps tapping the floor.

"Curly?" the woman said. "Who shall I say wants him?"

Vicky gave her name, fished out another business card and handed it to the woman who was half-standing now, gripping the edge of the desk. She studied the card a long moment, something between annoyance and fear moving through her expression, and Vicky looked away. It always surprised her, the way people reacted to the words printed on the card: Attorney-at-Law. Then the woman headed for the door on the side. She was no longer smiling. The door slammed behind her, and Vicky could hear the quick, smothered exchanges. Finally the door opened and the woman stepped out. "Go on in," she said.

"Ms. Holden." The man stood behind the desk, staring down at the card he held in one hand. He was probably in his mid-fifties, with broad shoulders and extra pounds around his middle. His hair had receded into a horseshoe that curled above his ears. "I'm the manager here. Curly Dobbs. Is there some problem?"

"I'd like to ask you a few questions about Ned Windsong." Vicky closed the door behind her. The office was small and cluttered with papers and file folders that spilled over the tops of filing cabinets and piled around the desk.

Curly Dobbs started shaking his head. He dropped with a soft thud into the chair behind him and began rolling it from side to side. "Poor guy," he said, motioning for her to take a side chair. "Bad luck, I'd say.

Run into a couple of crazies on the rez. Should've stayed here. He was doing great right here. They caught them guys yet?"

"Not yet," Vicky said.

"The FBI agent, what's his name . . ."

"Ted Gianelli."

"I've already told him everything I know about Ned. It's not much. He only worked here a couple months. So why are you here? Is there some kind of lawsuit? I did not fire him, if that's what you think. I treat all employees the same. Indian, white, black, Hispanic. Don't make no difference to me, long as they do a good job. Ned was a real good apprentice. No complaints about his work. He left of his own free will, and I was real sorry to see him go."

"Mr. Dobbs," Vicky said. "I represent Ned's fiancée, Marcy Morrison. She witnessed the killing."

He gave a little nod, as if the explanation should make sense. "So what brings you here?"

"Did anything happen that caused Ned to leave?" Vicky said, studying the man's expression for any hint that he knew Ned was involved in a burglary ring.

"Came in one afternoon after work and said, time to head back to the rez. I said, What're you talking about? You need more money? What? Some of the guys harassing you? But he just said it was time to go. Wanted to get back to the Arapaho Way, whatever that means. Said he was gonna go home and prepare for the Sun Dance. Surprised me, 'cause he was doing real good. He was one of my most reliable employees. Soon's he left the office, I called his uncle —"

"His uncle?"

"Old army buddy of mine," the man said. "Jerry Adams. You know him?" He hurried on. "Rode into Kuwait together, Jerry and me, slogging rifles, a hundred and twenty degrees, dusty as hell. It was Jerry that called me and said his nephew was looking for a new job. Did I have any openings? Well, I can always use a good apprentice, so I said send him on up. When I told Jerry his nephew up and quit on me, well, he was as surprised as I was. Said he didn't have any business doing that and he was gonna talk to him. That was the last I heard, until, well . . ." He spread his hands. "I seen in the paper that Ned Windsong got shot and the FBI was looking for two Indians."

"You've been very helpful," Vicky said, getting to her feet. Ned must have confided in his uncle, she was thinking. Told him that he wanted to get away from the reservation, and Jerry Adams had helped him out. Odd, though, that he hadn't told his uncle when he decided to leave Jackson. In any case, Curly Dobbs didn't seem to know about the burglary ring.

She had started for the door when the man said, "That girl came around here a couple times."

Vicky turned back. "Marcy Morrison?"

"Never knew her name." He shrugged. "Blonde and real pretty. High-strung, though. A little crazy, you ask me."

"Why do you say that?"

"Seen her out in the lot." He crooked his thumb toward the rows of trucks outside the window. "Her and Ned got into a big row. She was shouting and screaming. I seen her take her bag and whack him a couple times. It was a real bad scene, and it happened more than once. I told Ned, keep his personal life away from work. I didn't want her around. No telling what somebody like that is gonna do."

"What did Ned say?"

"He'd take care of it." The man gave another shrug. "Wasn't long afterward he came in here and said he's quitting."

Vicky left the man standing behind the desk and walked back through the front office, ignoring the questions on the face of

311

the blue-white-haired woman. The late afternoon sun was beating down hard. She hurried around the building and slid into the Jeep, imaging Marcy Morrison swinging her bag at Ned, shouting, crying. She had a breakdown, John O'Malley had said. The word reverberated in her head: *breakdown, breakdown.* Whatever had happened at the mission, it wasn't the first time Marcy Morrison had lost control.

Vicky drove out of the lot and headed back up the hill toward Alpine Meadows and the tennis club. There were places in the girl, she realized, that she hadn't seen.

27

"Yeah, Dave is here." Kip gestured toward the hallway that ran into the back of the building. "Go on out to the courts. You'll see his office on the left."

Vicky followed the directions down the hallway and through the glass door onto a platform with rows of chairs that faced two courts. Several spectators occupied the chairs, intent on the balls thumping back and forth. Women's doubles on one court, men's singles on the other. Gasps went up, followed by low sucking sounds, as if the spectators were trying to get their collective breath. The air was dry and stale.

She walked behind the chairs and knocked on the door with Dave Hudson in black letters on the pebbled-glass window.

"Come on in." The voice sounded muffled, low-pitched and a little on edge.

Vicky stepped into an airy room that overlooked the outdoor courts. Gail was playing singles, her white tee shirt, blue shorts, and long legs flashing on the court. Across the room was a desk with a large polished surface that looked unused, and next to the desk, a tall young man with muscle-knotted arms and short-cut brown hair was bent toward a metal machine, stringing a tennis racket.

"You the lawyer wants to see me?" He gave her the sideways grin of a man accustomed to holding a woman's attention with minimum effort. "What can I do for you? Nobody's suing me, I hope. No players upset because they didn't make Wimbledon." He gave a snort of laughter at the little joke.

"I represent your former fiancée, Marcy Morrison."

Dave Hudson brought a handle down hard and swung around, leaving the tennis racket balancing on the machine. The joking mood had passed, and in its place was the hardness of steel. He had blue eyes, so pale they were almost white. "What's her beef? Breach of promise or some weird thing like that?" He took a moment, staring straight ahead, as if a new idea had materialized across the room. "Jesus, don't tell me she's pregnant. What is this? A paternity thing?"

"It's nothing like that," Vicky said. She could sense the tension melting out of him. Still the hardness remained in the set of his jaw. "I'm trying to find her. I hoped you might have seen her recently, or heard from her."

Dave dropped into the chair behind the desk and ran a hand over the top of his stubbly hair. "You telling me she's back," he said finally.

"I take it that means you haven't heard from her." Vicky perched on an upholstered bench pushed beneath the windows.

"I don't want to hear from Marcy Morrison," he said. "Ever. Is that clear? You're her lawyer, you give her the message. Better yet, don't mention my name and remind her. I can only hope she's forgotten me. Out of sight, out of mind, you know what I mean? So if that's why you came around, to see if I know where she is, the answer is, I don't. And I don't want to know. End of discussion."

He started to get to his feet, and Vicky said, "Marcy could be in danger. She witnessed a murder."

"Murder?" He flopped back into the chair. "She saw somebody get murdered?"

"Her fiancé, Ned Windsong. Maybe you knew him?"

"That Indian she took up with? He got murdered? And she says she saw it?" He lifted both hands as if he wanted to stop an oncoming truck. "You believe that?"

"The FBI believes her. Why wouldn't I?"

"Oh, let's see." He flattened both hands on top of the desk and leaned forward. "Maybe because she's psycho and a pathological liar. She lives in Marcy world. You ever go there, you'll get as crazy as she is."

"But you were engaged to her," Vicky said. In her mind was the blonde girl, pressed in the corner of the sofa at the mission guesthouse, huddled into herself with fear. "You must have seen some good in her."

"Let's get something real straight," Dave said. "I don't know what was going on in Marcy world, but in the real world, we were never engaged." He pushed away from the desk, got to his feet, and started walking back and forth, elbows crooked, hands jammed against his waist. Finally he stopped and faced Vicky. "You want the truth? I met her in Denver. I was coaching at a club, and she came in for lessons. She was lousy at tennis, two left feet, stumbling all over the court, couldn't connect with the ball. But I admit, she was pretty good-looking, so I bought her a drink and we went out a few times. That was it. The extent of my engagement, 'cause that was all it took to see that she was nuts. So I quit calling, and that's when all hell broke loose."

He was nodding, as if the rest of the story were self-explanatory. "What happened?" Vicky said.

"What happened?" He shouted. "What happened? She kept coming to the club, hanging around outside my apartment. I'd come out of the dry cleaners, and she'd be waiting on the sidewalk. Everywhere I went, she stalked me. Begging me to take her back, saying we belonged together, nobody ever loved her except me and a lot of crap like that. She was a bloodsucker, and I couldn't get her off me. A friend of mine owns this place, so I quit the club in Denver and moved up here, thinking I'd ditched her. Two weeks later, she showed up. Same thing started up all over again. I was about to take a job in Arizona when she met that Indian. That was my lucky day, 'cause she laid off me and went after him. So the poor bastard's dead! What'd he do? Try to break up with her?"

"Two men broke into the house, beat up Marcy and shot Ned," Vicky said. "There's no evidence she had anything to do with it." Except, she was thinking, there could have been a motive if Ned had wanted to break things off with her. She pushed the thought away. "There was no weapon in the house, and no evidence that Marcy had fired a gun," she said, wanting to convince herself, she supposed. God, Marcy, who are you?

She stood up, went over to the desk and set her card down. "If you should hear from Marcy," she said, "I'd appreciate it if you would give me a call." Then she left Dave Hudson stationed beside the desk, like a statue, the tennis racket still balanced on top of the stringing machine.

The sun had dropped behind the mountain peaks by the time Vicky drove toward the town square, fit the Jeep into a vacant slot and walked to a little shop with black metal tables and chairs out on the sidewalk. She ordered a sandwich and soda, sat at one of the tables and tried to form a picture of Marcy Morrison from all the different pieces that the girl seemed to have broken into. Marcy Morrison, twenty-three years old, blonde hair and beautiful despite the bruised cheek and blackened eyes. Then a slow fade backward — seventeen, twelve, nine, six, until finally she was a little girl, barely a bump under the covers of her bed, crying in the night for her mother. That was the needy, frightened little girl that Dave

Hudson had described.

Vicky finished the soda, crumbled the sandwich wrapper, and stuffed the trash into the metal container. Then she walked back to the Jeep and drove out of town. The air had turned cool; blue shadows rolled off the mountain slopes. She fumbled with the radio, finally tuning in a Western music station. She felt as if a hot iron had been set on her chest. Was that how it had been with her own children while she was in Denver going to school? She hadn't known. She hadn't known.

The white light of the TV blinked in the darkness of the living room, couples in tuxedos and long gowns dancing across the screen. The gray head of Bishop Harry poked over the back of the sofa. A bowl of popcorn sat in his lap. Father John leaned around the jamb. "I'm off to the social committee meeting," he said.

The old man held up a fist full of popcorn and waved. "Do enjoy yourself." He sounded as if his mouth were stuffed with cotton.

Father John hurried outside, down the steps and out to Circle Drive. Pickups and sedans were pulling into the mission, headlights flickering through the cottonwoods.

Three pickups stood in front of the church. The air was cool, the breeze rustling the grasses, moving through the branches. He crossed the field, his mind on Vicky, wondering if she had located the girl, knowing that, if Marcy had gone to Jackson, Vicky would find her. This morning, at the feast at Eagle Hall after the funeral, Ella had told him she'd seen Vicky at the cemetery. What was she doing there? Ella had wanted to know. Why did she come? Couldn't she see that the white girl had something to do with Ned's murder? He had tried to tell her that Gianelli would sort it out and if the girl was involved . . . He had stopped at the shuttered look in her eyes, the implacable set of her chin.

He picked up his pace and darted through the headlights of a pickup. He was halfway down the alley, the lights of Eagle Hall streaming over the gravel, when he heard the footsteps pounding behind him. "Father! Father!"

He turned around and waited for James White Eagle to catch up. "Heard the news?" the man called, thick arms pumping at his side. He limped from one bowed leg to the other, as if he had just gotten off a horse and wasn't used to the hard earth under his feet.

"What news?" Father John said.

James waited until he was close before he said. "Them two Indians the fed's been looking for."

"What about them?"

"Shot to death out in an old barn on North Fork Road. My nephew's one of the officers out there right now."

Father John nodded. It was the way the moccasin telegraph worked. "Are you sure it's Hawk and Lookingglass?"

"Oh, it's them, all right. Buddy, that's my nephew, says there's no doubt. Guess they won't be shooting any more Arapahos."

Father John set a hand on the man's shoulder. "Can you handle the meeting tonight? Betsy Burton will help. She knows who's been taken to the hospital or needs food."

The Indian nodded. "You gonna go out there and pray over them?" he said. "Seems to me that type don't need prayers."

"We all need prayers," Father John said.

28

The barn stood at the end of a dirt track, the kind of abandoned building people had forgotten was still there, leaning sideways from the wind and snow that had pummeled it for decades. The old Toyota bounced over the ruts, fighting the wind that swept across the flat, open ground and whistled through the cracks around the doors. Father John had gone a half mile down the track before the glow of police lights materialized in the darkness. He followed the lights around a curve and across the bare dirt yard. He parked behind the coroner's van.

Officers stood in little groups, heads bent together. The subdued buzz of conversation filled the air like the noise of cicadas. Light glowed in the opened doors to the barn. Inside officers in gray uniforms milled about, snapping photographs, stooping to scrape something off the dirt floor and slipping it inside plastic bags. Gianelli came through the whirl of blue and red lights. "You made record time," he said. "I just asked an officer to call the mission."

"Moccasin telegraph," Father John said. One way or the other, the news of homicides and sudden deaths, accidents, suicides, made its way to the mission. "Hawk and Lookingglass?"

"Officially, we don't have the IDs yet. Unofficially" — the fed drew in a deep breath — "shot in the back of the head, execution-style. The killer wanted to make sure they were dead. See for yourself." He nodded toward the barn.

Father John made his way around the vehicles and two uniformed officers who stepped aside. Straight-faced, eyes shielded, they gave him a perfunctory nod, as if he were part of the crime scene, one of the regulars who could be counted on to show up, like the coroner. Inside the barn, past the uniforms, the two bodies sprawled facedown on the dirt floor, legs askew, arms flung outward, as if some memory lodged in their muscles had sought to run before the bullets tore off the back of their heads.

He went down on one knee beside the bodies. My God! The thick-set neck and narrow shoulders of Dwayne Hawk, part of

323

his left ear missing. The long, muscular torso of Lionel Lookingglass, the dirt-smudged bandage on his arm, the black ponytail splayed on the dirt. They were wearing the same clothes they had worn last night, the plaid shirts and grubby blue jeans, when Dwayne had turned the gun on Walks-On and threatened to take out Father John's knees and elbows. Which did he prefer to begin with? The sole of Hawk's left boot had a hole the size of a quarter, and Father John could see a piece of gray flesh. Surely there must have been someone who loved them. They must have families somewhere in Colorado or Oklahoma. Gianelli would notify the families; the coroner would arrange to send the bodies home for burial.

"Dear God, whatever these men may have done," he said out loud, realizing that the officers gathered around had been waiting for him to say something. "Have mercy on their souls. You alone are the final judge. You alone know the secrets of our hearts and the brokenness and the pain of our lives. You alone can forgive our sins. We beg your mercy on Dwayne and Lionel who stand before you, because your mercy is all we can trust in."

"Amen," voices said around him as Father

John got to his feet. Next to the rear wall, he could see the imprint of boxes or cartons that had been heavy enough to dig into the dirt floor. So this was where the burglary ring had stored the stolen items. An empty, forgotten barn. He wondered how long the items were kept before they were moved. Who made the arrangements to sell the stolen merchandise? Who had those kinds of contacts? Ned? Hawk or Lookingglass? Three Arapahos on a reservation? There was someone else, he was sure of it.

The officers kept their places as he walked back across the barn and out into the black night air that had turned cooler, with the wind picking up. The light bars on the police vehicles had been turned off, leaving only headlights shooting over the ground. The driver's door on one of the police cars stood open, and an officer straddled the edge of the seat, one boot planted on the dirt. A radio crackled and buzzed. Through the shadows and dim light, Father John spotted Gianelli huddled with a couple of men by the coroner's van. He waited. There was something he wanted to ask him, although the fed wasn't good at giving answers. Asking questions was what he did.

Out on the road he spotted a single beam of light that gradually separated into two headlights. He waited as the headlights turned onto the track and juddered toward the barn. It was Vicky's Jeep, but he had known that, he realized, when the vehicle was still on the road, as if he had sensed that she would be on the way. He walked over and opened her door as she pulled to a stop.

"How did you hear the news?" he said. She slid off the seat, looking tired and a little defeated, not like herself. Even in the dim light, he could make out the shadows under her eyes.

"The radio said the police had been called to a barn on North Fork Road where two men were reportedly shot to death. I had a feeling . . ." She broke off, then began again. "Hawk and Lookingglass?"

He nodded, then told her they had been shot in the back of the head. Executed, it looked like. Then he blurted out what he'd been thinking: Ned had also been executed, even though he'd been shot in the chest.

"The same weapon?"

That was the question he wanted to ask Gianelli. "I don't know yet," he said.

Vicky crossed her arms and hugged herself, as if she were freezing. The black bag she always carried hung off one shoulder. She looked small and vulnerable: such brave determination about her. "Marcy didn't go to Jackson," she said. "Have you heard from her?"

"No," he said, looking back. The girl had wandered through his mind all day: at the get-together in Eagle Hall after the funeral, during the afternoon meetings, the counseling sessions with parishioners. He had found himself looking around at the sound of an engine, half-expecting the red pickup to appear on Circle Drive, the girl herself walk into his office or head for the guesthouse. But she hadn't come.

He realized Vicky was saying something about the girl's former fiancé, and he pushed back his own thoughts. "His name is Dave Hudson," Vicky said. "Coaches tennis. He and Marcy met in Denver, and when he moved to Jackson, she followed him."

"Followed him?" Father John said. Another image of the girl worked its way into his head. The wind moving in her blonde hair, the long, tanned legs, and the lost look about her. "Where can I find Ned Windsong?" she had wanted to know the day she came to the mission. The fiancé who had left without a forwarding address. "The way she followed Ned here?"

Vicky was quiet, glancing around the

vehicles, the uniformed officers moving about, the coroner and his assistant disappearing inside the barn. "She's my client," she said finally. "I'm here to protect her interests, not make judgments."

But she had already made them, he knew. He could see the worry behind the confident stare she gave him. "I talked to his boss in Jackson," she was saying. "You were right about Ned moving there to start over. The manager said he'd gotten a call from Ned's uncle, Jerry Adams. Turns out, they were old army buddies. Jerry said his nephew was looking for a job, and the manager agreed to take him on." She stopped, not taking her eyes from his.

"Adams got him the job in Lander, too," he said. "Maybe it doesn't mean anything."

"Except that he was looking after his wife's nephew. Marie and Ella probably nagged him about helping Ned. Anyway," she said, hurrying on, "Ned was a good employee. The boss was sorry to see him leave. He has no idea of what Ned and the others were up to. Ned told him he was moving back to the rez to start over. I think he did intend to make a fresh start. Leave the past behind." She took a moment before she said, "I've wondered if he would have confessed."

She wasn't talking about the confessional, Father John knew. "I don't think he would have gone to Gianelli and implicated the others," he said. "But I think he was wrestling with it. It was one thing to implicate himself, it would have been something else to send others to prison."

"But they couldn't be sure he wouldn't snitch," Vicky said, half to herself. "So Hawk and Lookingglass killed him, and now they're dead. Maybe for the same reason, to keep them quiet."

"Vicky, I'm glad you showed up."

Father John wasn't sure when Gianelli had walked over, but the fed was standing beside them, a bulky shadow backlit by the headlights. "I want to set up an interview with your client," he said. "Tomorrow, first thing. My office or yours, either way."

Vicky did a half turn toward the agent. "Surely you don't believe Marcy Morrison had anything to do with this," she said, nodding toward the barn.

"Everything's still on the table," Gianelli said. "Coroner's best estimate is that the two men in there have been dead for about twenty-four hours. Marcy Morrison left the mission yesterday evening. Where did she go? How did she spend her time? Simple questions that I'm sure your client won't mind answering. She's still the only witness to Ned Windsong's murder, and she identified Hawk and Lookingglass as his killers. They came to the mission last night looking for her. Maybe she decided to take matters into her own hands and go looking for them."

"That's ridiculous," Vicky said. "She didn't know where they were hiding. Had she known, she would have said so. She wanted them arrested."

"Somebody knew," Gianelli said, and Father John saw the way he focused in on Vicky, slipping into another mode. This was what the man was trained for, interrogating people, gauging responses, reading the meaning behind the words. "Somebody with a disguised voice made an anonymous phone call from the Ethete convenience store a couple of hours ago and suggested I go looking for Hawk and Lookingglass at the abandoned barn on North Fork Road."

"My client has nothing to hide," Vicky said. Father John caught a faint flicker of worry in her eyes. "She wanted nothing more than for Ned's killers to be brought to justice." She stopped, and in the way that she turned toward the barn, he understood the rest of her thought: *now that has happened.* "As soon as I contact her, we can arrange the interview," she said, turning back. "Tomorrow."

"She's scared. She thinks they're still after her, and she's gone to a safe place. When she hears the news, she'll call me."

Gianelli nodded, but there was skepticism in his narrowed eyes. He did a slow turn and was about to start walking away when Father John said, "Was the same weapon used to kill Ned?"

The fed looked back and drew in a long breath. "No casings anywhere. Whoever did this was careful to pick them up. Ned was shot with a .380 caliber. I suspect those two in there" — he nodded toward the barn — "had a whole arsenal. We might find the .380 around here someplace." He shrugged, then headed across the dirt yard toward the barn.

"What difference does the weapon make?" Vicky said. "Hawk and Lookingglass killed Ned. I take it they didn't kill themselves, which means someone else is responsible." She halted again, as if she kept coming upon arroyos that were too wide and deep to cross. No matter which way she turned, another arroyo opened up. Marcy Morrison had disappeared last night and the girl had a motive to kill the two men sprawled on the floor in the barn.

"It's possible that whoever else was in the burglary ring killed Hawk and Lookingglass," Father John said, wanting to ease the worry in her eyes. But he couldn't shake his own uneasy feeling about the girl. What might she have decided to do to save herself? What was she capable of?

"Marcy's sure to call tomorrow," Vicky said, as if she were trying to convince herself. "If she happens to call you . . ."

"I'll tell her you're waiting to hear from her."

She nodded, and even in the shadows, he could see the mixture of apprehension and concern working through her features.

He waited until she had gotten into the Jeep, backed up and turned down the track, headlights flashing, red taillights flickering. Then he got into the Toyota and fished his cell out of the glove box. In the faint light spilling out of the box, he checked his watch. Ten minutes to eleven. He gripped the cell and thought about Roseanne, hiding out in a house that she hoped Hawk and Lookingglass would never stumble onto. She could have heard the news on the radio and figured out that two men shot to death in an old barn had to be Hawk and Lookingglass. She could be asleep by now.

He started to put the cell back in the box,

a different picture forming in his mind. Roseanne, sitting up half the night, dozing a little, jumping at any nighttime noise — the sound of a rabbit skittering outside, the far-off howling of a coyote. He punched in the number of her cell and started the pickup while he waited the couple of seconds for the connection. Then the buzzing noise of the ringing phone, followed by her voice saying: "I'm not available. You know the drill."

He set the cell back in the glove box, closed the door and eased the pickup down the track, over the hard ridges and out onto the road. In the side mirror, he watched the dark shadows of the official vehicles and milling figures recede in the diminishing glow of light.

29

Father John slowed past the pastel-colored houses that rose like specters in the night. It had been a while since he had visited Betty Mock's house. Her daughter had gotten married in California, and he had stopped by to tell Betty he wished them a lifetime of happiness. A few months ago, he heard the couple had gotten a divorce and Betty had gone to California to help with the new baby.

He spotted the house with the rectangular flower box next to the stoop and thought of the petunias overflowing the box and how Betty had followed him outside and dumped a glass of water on the flowers. He parked close to the stoop and got out. The house was dark and vacant-looking. A few dried stalks poked out of the flower box. He waited a moment, giving Roseanne a chance to peek past the curtains and see who had driven up. The sound of the pickup pulling

334

into the dirt yard had probably frightened her. Perhaps she wasn't inside, and the thought gave him an uneasy feeling. He stood absolutely still, waiting, unsure what he was waiting for. A dog yelped in the distance, or perhaps a wolf. The other houses down the road were dark and quiet. He might have been the only man on the reservation.

Still no sign of Roseanne.

He walked up the steps, knocked hard on the door and called out, "It's Father John! Don't be scared!" Dear Lord, the whole neighborhood had probably heard him. He leaned in close and said, "I have some news."

The door opened about an inch. A tiny voice came through the dark crack.

"I came to tell you that Hawk and Lookingglass are dead," he said.

The door swung open, a lamp switched on inside, and Roseanne stood in the opening, light flowing around her. She had on jeans and a rumpled white blouse, and she gripped a large, overstuffed pack against her chest so hard that he could see the knuckles popping in her hands, as if the pack contained everything she had in the world. "Dead?" she said, backing up. Her bare feet stumbled on the linoleum floor before she sank against the wooden armrest of a sofa. "How did it happen?"

He remained on the stoop a moment, then stepped inside, keeping the door open. The house was stuffy, closed up. The breeze moving through the door ruffled the pages of a magazine on the little table in front of the sofa.

"They were found shot to death in the barn," he said.

"You saw them? I mean, how can you be sure?"

"I saw their bodies."

"Oh God. Oh God." She jammed a fist against her mouth and leaned onto the pack. For a moment, he thought she might slide onto the floor. "I did what you said." She was shaking, and rocking back and forth, like someone in shock. "The fed will blame me. He'll think I killed them."

"Why would he think that?" Father John said, but he saw her point. She had made the anonymous call from Ethete, just as he had suggested. Whoever had killed Hawk and Lookingglass had known where to find them. If Gianelli knew she was the caller, he could suspect her of having something to do with the murders.

"I didn't know they'd be dead," she said. "It'll look like I did it 'cause they were chasing me, threatening me. They said they'd kill me if I snitched to the fed." She gulped in some air and stared up at him with wide, pleading eyes. "Oh God. You told him?"

"I didn't tell him, Roseanne."

"He doesn't know they were after me?"

"Not unless you've told someone else who might have told him."

She dropped her forehead onto the pack and grabbed at her hair with both hands. "I don't know anymore. I don't know who I've told stuff to. I can't remember what I might've said at Ella's or Berta's. My whole life's in the gutter. I don't know what I'm doing. I don't know who I am." She was crying now, her shoulders shaking. "I just miss Ned so much. Why did this have to happen? I was too scared to go his funeral this morning. I was so scared Dwayne and Lionel would be looking for me."

"Listen to me, Roseanne." Father John pulled over a metal folding chair and sat down. "Hawk and Lookingglass are the only ones who threatened you. They're both dead." He stopped himself from saying she needn't be afraid anymore. He wasn't sure it was the truth. "You should still be careful," he said, "until Gianelli arrests the killer."

"She did it, the white girl." Roseanne

lifted her head and stared at him with tear-bleared eyes. "She killed all of them. Ned, Dwayne, and Lionel."

"What makes you so sure?" he said.

"I been thinking a lot," she said. "All I do all day and night is think about the night we went to Ned's house, Dwayne and Lionel and me. They were gonna talk him into going to the party. He used to like parties, 'til he got back from Jackson Hole and started down a new road. Dwayne and Lionel figured he wasn't serious. I just wanted him to come along, you know, so maybe him and me could talk and maybe it could be like old times. I was hoping the white girl was gone, 'cause he'd told me he was gonna make some changes. So I went along with Dwayne and Lionel. God, I seen their faces when they come out of Ned's place. They looked like they'd seen a ghost, and I knew something bad had happened. They never would have gone back to that house if they knew Ned was there, dead. They didn't know the white girl was gonna say they killed him."

Father John didn't say anything for a moment, giving the girl a little time and space in which to gather herself. She was in shock, she was grieving. He couldn't shake the feeling that it kept coming down to Marcy

Morrison as the outsider, the one who was different, the one it was easy to blame. Ella blamed her, and Marie and Jerry Adams probably blamed her. For all he knew, every Arapaho on the reservation blamed her. But the evidence suggested she was as much a victim as Ned. She had been attacked, pushed against the wall. She had a bruised cheek and black eyes. But, unlike Ned, she was alive.

And she was gone. Running, hiding, scared. He tried to hold on to that image of Marcy Morrison, small blue veins rippling through her pale skin, not much more than a child, lost and alone, but another image kept coming through: Marcy Morrison screaming and tearing her clothes by the Little Wind River, out of control, a mad child. Who could predict what a mad child might do? He wondered if Gianelli had somehow glimpsed that part of her. Was that why he wanted to interview her about the murders of Hawk and Lookingglass?

He pushed the idea away. Still it lingered in his mind like a shadow. "Maybe you should stay here awhile longer," he said.

"You said they're dead."

"Whoever killed them is still around."

"She killed them, I told you. I'm not afraid of her." Roseanne patted the top of her pack, and for the first time, he made out the sharp edges of a gun protruding through the blue canvas.

He started to suggest that she might want to talk to Gianelli, tell him everything she knew about the burglary ring. He stopped himself. It was ridiculous. Roseanne would never talk to the fed willingly. She was scared of being implicated in the murders, the burglaries, the whole ugly mess.

She sat very still, gripping the backpack, lost in some new idea. He watched the comprehension creep across her face as if she had read his mind. She would stay here, he realized, hiding. Not from Marcy Morrison, but from Gianelli.

He left her at the house; dawn began to glow in the sky and a weariness stalked his movements as he started the pickup and backed out of the yard. A killer was out there somewhere, walking around, laughing at the way Gianelli and a lot of uniformed officers were chasing themselves in circles.

It was later in the morning than she had intended when Vicky let herself into the office. She hadn't expected to get any sleep last night, thoughts of the missing girl tumbling in her head — the imaginary fiancé she had stalked the way she had stalked Ned, the other members of the burglary ring murdered, Gianelli insisting upon interviewing Marcy first thing in the morning. And she had no idea where the girl was. Instead of lying awake, she had crawled into bed and dropped into a black hole of exhaustion. She had a faint memory of reaching for the ringing alarm and retreating back into the hole when the noise stopped. The sun splinted the drapes when she finally awakened. She had bounded out of bed, showered, thrown on a blue sleeveless dress and sandals and run out of the apartment and down the stairs to the parking lot, her bag slung over her shoulder, her briefcase in one hand and, in the other, a stale bagel she had found in the kitchen.

The office was quiet, but it was the kind of quiet that settles in after the phone has stopped ringing. She had the sinking feeling that the best part of the morning had slipped past, and that she had missed something important. Marcy would have heard the news by now. She might have been trying to call her. Vicky could almost hear the relief in the girl's voice. *They're not after me anymore. They can't hurt me.*

Vicky was about to shut the door behind her when the sound of a roaring engine stopped her. She swung around, conscious of the icy feeling that gripped her. The tan pickup squealed around the corner on two wheels, shifted into low and growled past. She peered hard out the door trying to get an imprint of the driver in her mind, but he sat low, sunk into a dark jacket, staring past the steering wheel. The pickup shot past and she shifted her eyes to the license plate. The numbers blurred into one another.

She closed the door and leaned against it a moment. Robin Bosey drove a tan pickup; hundreds of people around here drove tan pickups. How could she be sure that it was Robin? He could be in custody by now. She stared at Annie's desk, the surface clear and shiny, as if Annie had never sat there, answered the phone, greeted clients, typed and printed out and collated a thousand documents. God. Nothing was the same; everything had changed. The work was still there. She could imagine it swelling inside the computer. A couple of corrections to the contract that the timber company insisted upon and she had agreed to; they wouldn't change anything, but the section had to be retyped and proofed and sent to the tribal officials for approval.

She bolted the door before she went into her office and dropped her bag and briefcase on the table behind her desk. Then she picked up the phone and dialed the house in Casper where Annie and her kids and Roger were staying. Hiding out from a crazy man who may have just driven down the street. The ringing seemed to go on forever. Just when she was about to hang up, Annie's voice said, "Vicky? Everything okay?"

"Is everything okay with you?" Vicky said.

"The same. The police haven't found him yet."

Vicky could feel the icy claws moving over her. Robin was in the pickup, she was sure of it. Looking for Annie, watching the office. Wanting her to know that he could come for her whenever he wanted.

"Maybe he's left the county," Annie said, "and that's why the police haven't picked him up. I keep thinking about the office and the work needing to be done. Roger's been working on his laptop, but it's not the same as being in the office. I think we should come back."

"That's not a good idea."

"If Robin's still around, he'll show up soon as he knows I'm back and the police'll pick him up. I can draw him out of whatever hole he's hiding in."

"Give it another day, please, Annie." Across the office, past the front window, Vicky could see the large, dark figures of two men coming up the walk. She walked through the reception room and peered past the edge of the window, half-listening to Annie saying that Roger couldn't stand another day of sitting around the house. Outside on the porch, wearing jeans and dark shirts and cowboy hats, were Larry Morrison and his bodyguard, the man called Angelo Crispie. "Hang on," Vicky said, fumbling with the bolt. She pulled the door open, beckoned the men inside and, tipping her head toward the phone, said, "I'll be with you in just a minute." Then she went back to her own office, aware of the men shuffling across the reception room, breathing hard as if they had just climbed a mountain, finally dropping onto the side chairs. She closed the beveled-glass doors. "Larry Morrison's here," she told Annie. "I'll have to call you back."

"Everything all right with his daughter?" Annie said, and in her voice Vicky could hear the hunger of someone who knew that food was spread on the table, but she no longer had a chair.

"I'll fill you in later." Nothing was right, Vicky was thinking. She hit the end key.

The noise sounded as if a truck had crashed through the front door, sudden and sharp, reverberating through the floorboards, rattling the blinds at the window. Vicky stared through the beveled-glass doors at the blurred figure of Robin Bosey, the clublike arms, the clenched fists, the murderous rage in the way he stomped toward her office. She dropped the phone. She had the sense that she should be moving, flinging open the doors and shouting at him to get out, but her feet were frozen to the floor, her legs numb as if they belonged to someone else.

Then, on the other side of the beveled glass, Larry Morrison and the man called Angelo, burly with broad shoulders, loomed like a wall in front of Robin Bosey. "What do you want here!" Morrison shouted, his voice hard and full of authority. "Who are you?" The bodyguard moved in closer, and Vicky watched the blurred shape of Robin Bosey swing about and dart out the door, head thrust forward as if he were running a race.

Vicky found her breath, picked up the phone again, and tapped out 911. Pressing the phone against her ear, she opened the doors, ran past the two men, and looked outside. The tan pickup jolted away from the curb out into the lane and shot around the corner.

"What is your emergency," a woman's

voice said in her ear.

Vicky gave her name and said that Robin Bosey had just broken into her office. "He's looking for his ex-wife, my secretary," she said. "There's a restraining order against him. He had no right to come here. He's heading toward Main right now. For godssakes, stop him. Stop him before he kills someone."

There was more information the operator required: make of vehicle, license number. What was his name again? You say there's a restraining order. "He's on Main Street by now," Vicky shouted. "Please, send some cars."

She pressed the off key and sank against the hard edge of Annie's uncluttered, vacant desk, aware of the weakness crawling over her and the two men still stationed in the middle of the reception area, the beveled-glass doors open behind them.

"Client of yours?" Morrison said.

30

"The Lord has blessed us with love, the most powerful force in the world." Larry Morrison planted himself in the corner of Vicky's private office, hands clasped in front as if he were delivering a sermon to millions seated in front of their TVs. Vicky had dropped onto the edge of her chair. Through the closed beveled-glass doors, she could see the bodyguard stationed in the center of the reception area, facing the front door. "Love can cause us to act at our most unselfish best," Morrison droned on. "Through the love the Lord God has placed in our hearts, we are able to share in his power to create miracles." He paused, giving Vicky a profile view of the serene and wise expression on his face. "Unfortunately," he said, reluctance in his voice now as he seemed to contemplate truths too painful to express, "love can be perverted into anger, hate, and lust for revenge. Ugly emotions that dishonor us and destroy all the good we may have done."

He faced the desk and locked eyes with Vicky. "Will you pray with me?"

"What are we praying for?" she said.

"The man who burst into your office. You said he was looking for his ex-wife. We must assume he once loved her, but now, in the anger that consumes him, we see the perversion of that love. Lord God Almighty," he said, bowing his head, fingertips pressed together in a little tipi, "we ask you to remove the perversion from this man's heart and restore the calm beauty of love. Amen."

"Amen," Vicky heard herself say. Robin Bosey could be on the reservation by now. The man was uncanny, a chameleon melting into the vast, impenetrable landscape of the plains. He could hide for weeks, crashing with a cousin or a cousin of a cousin, or some other distant relative, fitting in with everyone else.

"We have to talk about your daughter," she said, forcing her thoughts back to the reason the man was standing in her office, hands still pitched in prayer, after spending half the night negotiating airports and flying here from Oklahoma.

"Oh, yes. Marcy." Morrison sat down on the side chair that rolled back a half foot with his weight.

"She's still missing," Vicky said. "She didn't return to Jackson. Last night, the men she accused of murdering Ned were found shot to death. They had been dead almost twenty-four hours, from about the time Marcy left the mission. Agent Gianelli wants to talk to her in connection with the murders. I can't arrange for the interview because I have no idea where she is." She studied the man across from her. Nothing she said had changed the calm, fixed expression on his face. Not the murders or the implication that his daughter was a suspect. She wondered if he had heard anything.

Finally Morrison drew in a breath and held on to it for a couple of seconds before he exhaled. "I'm afraid Marcy may be an example of the perversion I've mentioned," he said. "She's capable of great love, but such people can also be capable of great hatred. Two sides of the same large coin."

Vicky clasped her hands on top of the desk and leaned forward. "I'm not sure you understand," she said. "Marcy is under suspicion in a double homicide."

The man slapped his hands on the armrests, bolted out of the chair, and started striding about, head thrust forward. "She is a troubled girl," he said. "I'm sure you've recognized that by now. She spent several years in treatment."

"Why didn't you tell me?"

"Because I believed the Lord had blessed her by returning her to herself. She was a sweet, wonderful girl until that terrible time . . ."

"When her mother left."

He stood still. "As God is my witness, I share the blame. It was not her mother's fault that she could no longer cope. Now I realize she was a delicate human being, fragile, like our daughter. So much happened so fast in our lives. The congregation doubled, redoubled, tripled. We couldn't keep up." He lifted both hands overhead. "I have asked the Lord God to forgive me and not burden the child with the consequences of her parents' sins." Lowering his hands at his side, he swung toward Vicky. "The Lord has blessed us with prosperity, a sign of his forgiveness, you see. Naturally, I believed Marcy would no longer be troubled, but I see now that I was lying to myself. It is a deadly sin to lie to oneself. When she left —"

Vicky interrupted. "When she left Oklahoma?" The girl seemed always to be leaving someplace.

"We had a terrible argument. She had

been home from the clinic less than a month. She and my wife, LuAnn, began arguing over something so trivial, so meaningless that it makes me cringe to think about it. Whether Marcy had put her laundry away! What difference did it make? We have servants to handle such matters, but LuAnn believes children should be responsible for chores. The next morning, Marcy was gone. Her bed was made, the room tidied up. It looked as if she had never been there, except for the clothes she left in the closet and bureau. She just drove away in the pickup that our landscaper used."

Morrison sank back into the chair. "Do you have any idea what it is to lose your child?" He hesitated. "And not regret it? You see, there was peace in our home again, like the peace we had enjoyed while she was in the clinic."

"But you found her, didn't you?"

"She was still my child. I had to make sure she was all right. I hired the best detectives. But she had made her escape very well. She finally called me. She was in Denver, living on the streets. She had to beg coins for the phone. Naturally I flew there immediately, bought a condominium and got her settled. I set up a bank account and credit cards so that she would have the money she needs. I could not have my daughter living on the streets."

Vicky took a moment before she said, "Perhaps she needs more treatment."

Morrison didn't say anything, and Vicky pushed on. "What are we dealing with here? Is it possible Marcy could have shot those two men?"

"She never forgave me for putting her in the psychiatric hospital. When she came home, her love had turned to hatred. I saw it in her eyes. She wanted revenge, wanted to hurt me — destroy me — the way she felt I had hurt and destroyed her. She deliberately picked fights with me and Lu-Ann. She tried to pit us against each other. She was always looking for sympathy — she would hurt herself, bang her head against the wall. Knocked herself unconscious once. But things were going well at the ministry, so well that I made myself look away from the discord Marcy was sowing. Surely our prosperity was a sign of God's grace, that all was well. When Marcy left, I told myself it was God's will. I felt relieved. About a week later, I discovered, quite by accident, that the pistol I kept in my closet for security . . ." He let the thought trail off and tilted his head toward the bodyguard on the other side of the beveled-glass doors.

"Angelo can't be around every minute, and sometimes folks become very angry when God has not blessed them immediately with prosperity. Anyway, the pistol was missing. It had been a while since I had checked on it. I wasn't sure how long it had been missing. I suspected Marcy, I admit. LuAnn went through her room, the bureau, the closets, all her things. There was no gun. Later we found where she had hidden it. She's a clever girl. She knew we would search her things, so she had taken precautions. A tile behind the toilet in her bathroom fell out while the maid was cleaning. Marcy had carved out the wallboard behind the tile. The box in which I had kept the gun was still inside the wall, but the gun was gone. I knew the truth then. It was as though the Lord God had spoken to my heart. If Marcy had stayed, she would have killed LuAnn and me."

"Are you saying she might have taken revenge on Hawk and Lookingglass for killing Ned?"

"I believe she loved that young man and that love could have turned to hatred toward the men who took him from her."

Vicky leaned into the back of the chair. She had agreed to take on a client, a white girl, traumatized by the murder of her fiancé. She had agreed to look out for her interests, make certain blame for the murder didn't shift to her client, the outsider. And now she could be defending a murderer.

"What kind of gun?" Vicky said.

"SIG P232. A .380 caliber."

Vicky had to look away. Ned had been shot with a .380, but the gun hadn't been found. It wasn't in the house. The words drummed in her ears. *It wasn't in the house.* "We have to find Marcy," she said, turning back to Morrison. She could sense that the man had never taken his eyes from her. "Where would she go?"

"My daughter will find me," he said. "It is only a question of time. The minute I cancel her credit cards and close the bank account, she will call. You see, Marcy has a great love for prosperity and comfort and a great hatred for life on the streets. She will not return to that. She will call me." He stood up. "As to where she has gone, I don't know. Frankly, I'm surprised she wasn't in Jackson. Marcy likes the familiar. She settles in, you see. The familiar is her true love, and when that is yanked from under her, the hatred takes over. Should you hear anything, you can reach me on my cell" — he had turned part way around and was moving toward the beveled-glass doors — "I'll be at a house outside Lander until tomorrow. Members of my ministry were kind enough to make it available."

Morrison flung open the doors, and the bodyguard stepped to the side, giving the pastor a clear shot to the front door. "I suggest you lock up behind us," Morrison said, glancing back.

Berta's house looked the same as the night of the party, Roseanne thought. The dirt yard still littered. All that was missing was the loud thump of music and the shadowy figures moving through the dark night. Mervin was at the side of the house, bent under the opened hood of a green pickup. She recognized the skinny stovepipe legs inside the blue jeans, the sweat-smeared back of his shirt.

Roseanne pulled in behind the truck, got out, and slammed the door. Out of the corner of her eye, she saw Mervin bolt upright and bang his head against the edge of the hood. "Berta around?" she called.

"Whered'ya get off, sneaking up like that," Mervin said, shuffling toward her, rubbing his head.

"I'm here to see Berta. You got a problem?"

He shook his head and started backing

up. "Inside," he said. "Look out somebody don't shoot you, sneaking up like that."

"Berta?" Roseanne said, yanking open the door and stepping inside the dim, cluttered living room. "Where are you?"

A scraping noise came from somewhere in the house. There was the slightest movement through the shadows at the end of the hallway, and then Berta emerged into the living room as if she were sleepwalking, her white tee shirt and blue jeans as rumpled as pajamas. "Where you been?" she said. "I went over to the house and Martha said she didn't know where you were."

"Nowhere," Roseanne said. "I've got to talk to you. I've got to find the girl."

Berta sank onto the sofa. "I pulled the late shift at the nursing home last night. Didn't get home 'til five this morning. I need some sleep. Who are you talking about?"

"The white girl. Marcy Morrison. She killed Ned and now she's killed Hawk and Lookingglass. She's just gonna keep on killing 'til she's found."

"You know that for sure?"

"She's the only one could've done it." The words hung in the air, and Roseanne could hear the doubt running through them. She dropped onto the wobbly seat of a side chair. "Who else would've done it?" she said, feeling the helplessness rising inside her.

"The fed came around yesterday," Berta said. "Asking questions about the burglary ring. Who was in it, that kind of thing. Wanted to know if Mervin was part of it."

"What a load of crap." Mervin stood in the doorway, and Roseanne wondered how long he had been there. "No way is the fed gonna lay that on me. I never had nothing to do with stealing."

"Then why'd he come here, Mervin?" Berta's voice was like a long wail. "You promised me you wouldn't have nothing to do with Dwayne and Lionel. You knew they were trouble. Then you went and told 'em about the party."

"I told you the same as I told the fed," Mervin said, running a black-smudged cloth over his hands, "Dwayne asked me if I wanted in on a good deal. He could fix it."

"Fix it with who?" Roseanne said. She could almost hear Father John's voice. Who else is mixed up in the ring? Who's in charge? Who's calling the shots? Now the fed was looking for the same answers.

"I don't know and I don't care. I figured anything them guys was mixed up in was gonna mean a one-way ticket to prison for me, just like Ned told me. So I told Dwayne to forget it."

"Why'd they come to the party?" Berta said.

Mervin shrugged. "It was just a stupid party. They was always looking for parties, but Dwayne was acting crazier than usual that night. After I heard the white girl said him and Lionel was the ones that shot Ned, I believed it. They probably got into some beef over the stolen stuff. It wouldn't surprise me none if she was the one that killed them 'cause she was so mad." He took a moment. "Berta! You listening to me?" he shouted.

Roseanne flinched and shifted sideways to look up into his face. "I was never mixed up with any of that stuff. The burglary ring, none of it!"

It was true, Roseanne thought. She could hear the truth in what Mervin said. And that meant the rest of what he said could also be true, that Dwayne and Lionel had killed Ned, just like the white girl said, and that she had killed them because they took Ned away from her. The white girl would come after her next — the thought gripped her like a vise. The last time she had seen Ned, he had told her things were gonna be different. If the white girl thought Ned wanted to leave her, she would blame

Roseanne. Oh, yes, Marcy Morrison would come after her next. But who would believe that? Not the fed. No matter what she tried to tell him, the fed believed that she was involved in the burglary ring, that she had gone to the barn and shot Hawk and Lookingglass. She had to stay hidden, locked up in the secret house.

Roseanne got to her feet and brushed past Mervin, hooking her backpack over her shoulder. She stopped at the door and looked back. "If the fed comes around again, you haven't seen me, right?"

"Why's he looking for you?"

"He's not, okay? Just keep quiet."

Berta started toward her, one arm outstretched. "You in trouble?" she said. "You should stay here with us."

Roseanne swung herself about so fast that the backpack slammed against the doorjamb, knocking her off balance. She lurched outside and ran for the car. In five minutes, she was speeding down the dirt road, glancing every few seconds into the rearview mirror, half-expecting the fed's white SUV to appear.

31

"You okay, my boy?"

Father John glanced up from the stacks of phone messages and bills he'd been staring at on his desk, unable to start through them. He wondered how long the bishop had been standing in the doorway. He didn't say anything, and the old man headed into the office and took one of the hard-backed chairs.

"Heard you up last night," the bishop said. "The two men who paid us a visit were murdered." He was shaking his head. "Doesn't lend itself to sweet dreams."

"Nothing makes sense," Father John said. He had spent most the night wandering between the kitchen and his study, brewing pots of coffee and trying to put pieces of information together. He hadn't been able to shake the sense that something was eluding him, dancing in front of him, then behind him, like a shadow, always out of reach. "The only conclusions I can come up with are illogical."

"Ah." The bishop sat quietly a long moment, as if he had run into such problems in the past, and they were meant to be contemplated with single-minded attention. "In the words of St. Paul," he said, "we see through a glass, darkly. We are often blinded by our own suppositions."

Father John stared at the old man. He felt a coldness moving through him, a certainty taking hold. Roseanne Birdwoman was in great danger. Whether she realized it or not, she knew who had killed Hawk and Look-ingglass. The killer was probably looking for her now. He stood up and crossed the office. "I'm going out for a while," he said. He could hear the bishop rising out of the chair as he headed into the corridor.

"Do be careful," the bishop called.

In the pickup, he called Roseanne's cell, then made a U-turn on Circle Drive and sped toward Seventeen-Mile Road, listening to the tinny ringing noise, followed by Roseanne's voice saying that she wasn't available and he knew the drill.

Roseanne left the car a quarter mile away in a stand of cottonwoods and hurried toward the house, running, walking, gasping for

361

breath. The backpack banged against her shoulder blades. At one point her cell started ringing in the backpack. She had ignored it and kept going. She glanced back as she cut across the sagebrush fields. The fed's white SUV wasn't anywhere in sight, but it could show up at any moment. He could take her in for questioning, turn everything she said against her, arrest her for murdering Dwayne and Lionel. Who else knew where to find them? No one, no one. She shouldn't have gone to Berta's; it was too risky. She cursed under her breath. She had to think straighter, stay strong, if she was going to stay alive and out of prison.

She swung around the rear of a house where the door banged in the wind and kept going, darting through another cluster of cottonwoods and coming out behind Betty's house. It looked vacant, the way she had left it. Curtains pulled in the bedroom windows, shade pulled halfway in the kitchen window.

She stopped in the trees and checked all around. No traffic on the road, no tire prints in the dirt yard. No one had been here. She sprinted for the back door, let herself in with the flimsy key, and closed the door softly behind her. A kind of relief swept over her, the relief of the prisoner back in her familiar cell. The phone rang again. "Shut up!" she screamed. "Shut up!" She couldn't talk to anyone. She couldn't take the chance of anyone guessing where she was hiding.

She dropped the backpack on the table, then turned on the faucet and waited until the cell stopped ringing and the water ran cold. She filled a glass and drank until it was empty. She was about to refill the glass when the thumping noise started at the front of the house. She turned off the faucet and listened. The noise came again. She could feel her heart fluttering, a bird trying to get out of her chest. She made herself walk past the table and the two chairs pushed in at the ends to the doorway into the living room. She had a clear view of the front door with the window curtain pulled back a little way. Someone was outside on the stoop.

The figure moved toward the window, like a shadow on the other side of the curtain. Roseanne backed into the kitchen. The edge of the table bit into her hip. She kept her eyes on the doorway, reached for the backpack, and fumbled with the zipper until she had jerked it open. Her fingers closed over the cool metal of the Colt.

"Roseanne! You in there? Open up." It was Aunt Martha's voice, as real and familiar as

Roseanne's own breath, hot and tight and painful.

Roseanne jammed the pistol into the backpack and crossed the living room. She cracked open the door and stepped back, her voice stopped in her throat. Aunt Martha lurched inside and kicked the door shut. "I been calling your cell, leaving messages," she said. "You never call back. I was worried you were dead or something."

"How did you find me?"

"I went to Berta's and seen you driving off. I followed you, 'til you took off on foot. I guessed you might be hiding out at Betty's house, since she's in California."

"You shouldn't have come here." Roseanne moved sideways and glanced around the edge of the curtain, forcing herself to stay calm. She tried to block the images in her head. The fed could have been watching Aunt Martha's house. He could have followed her to Berta's and seen Roseanne's car. He could show up *here.* And the white girl. She could be out there somewhere, watching.

She faced the woman: pale and drawn, eyes circled with black shadows, a look of terror shining out of her black pupils. She wasn't sure whether Aunt Martha was drunk or just hungover. Usually it was easy

to determine which point on a long con-
tinuum from sobriety to dead drunkenness
Aunt Martha had landed on, but now
Roseanne wasn't sure. She was losing the
sure-fire touch acquired from living with an
alcoholic.

"I'm not drunk, if that's what you're
thinking," Aunt Martha said, looking at her
out of the corners of her eyes, and it struck
Roseanne as the truth. "I been real worried
about you. Agent Gianelli come by early
this morning, got me out of bed. Wanted to
talk to you. I said I didn't know where you
were. I said you was ungrateful for all I done
for you, and you just took off, not even telling me good-bye. Oh, I was real good,
Roseanne. You would've been proud. He
thinks I don't know where you went."

Roseanne tilted her head back and closed
her eyes. Now the fed would be convinced
she had something to run from, something
other than fear for her own safety. She
wondered if he suspected anyone else of
shooting Dwayne and Lionel, or if she was
the only one he was looking for. And what
about the white girl? She was the one he
should look for.

"Okay," Roseanne heard herself saying.
"Okay, okay. You have to leave now."

"Something else." Roseanne waited. It was

365

a long moment before Aunt Martha went on. "I seen that same man outside last night, parked across the road, watching the house."

"Who is he?" Roseanne had thought Dwayne was the man, but last night . . . Last night, Dwayne and Lionel were dead.

"I don't know. He's in a dark truck, and he stays slumped down, keeps his cowboy hat low."

"You gotta go," Roseanne said. "Don't come back, okay?"

"How am I gonna know if you're all right if you don't answer your phone?"

"I promise to call. Just stay at the house. Soon's this is all over . . ."

"When's that gonna be, Roseanne?" Aunt Martha's eyes were filling up, little black pools of water. "First Ned, then those killers get shot to death. Who's gonna be next? I'm real worried about you. What've you got to do with all this?"

"Nothing, Aunt Martha. I swear to you."

"Then why are you hiding?"

The knocking on the door sounded as if someone had started beating a drum, loud and insistent and angry. Roseanne saw the way Aunt Martha's expression froze, the way she seemed to turn into stone, and she felt the same thing happening to herself. She was like a statue, unable to move, barely able to glance sideways at the opening in the curtain. She tried to take in the front of the dark truck jutting past Aunt Martha's pickup. When had it rolled into the yard? She hadn't heard anything past the sound of Aunt Martha's voice, the arguments and panic erupting in her own head, and the dim noise of the ringing cell.

The knocking came again, followed by a man shouting, "Open up! I know you're there. Open up before I bust the door down."

"Don't go to the door," Roseanne started to say, but the sound of a boot crashing against wood filled the air and the door burst open. She recognized the man looming in the opening — the sunburned face, the permanent squint in the blue eyes, the black cowboy hat and starched pink shirt and pressed blue jeans. Someone was screaming, and she wasn't sure whether it was Aunt Martha or herself, her whole attention focused now on the black pistol in Jerry Adams's hand.

"Answer your cell!" Father John shouted into the sound of the wind crashing through the cab. He tossed his own cell onto the passenger seat and pressed down harder on the accelerator. The pickup bucked and

367

shimmied. As soon as he had gotten past his own supposition — that Jerry Adams had looked out for Ned, found him jobs because his wife and her sister had asked him — the pieces had fallen into place. Jerry Adams, the man who had hired Hawk and Lookingglass on his ranch last summer, had placed his nephew in jobs that gave him access to houses where he could check the security systems and figure out how to dismantle them. Jerry Adams, an ex-army man with connections, the kind of connections who would know how to move stolen jewelry, cameras, TVs, computers — whatever Ned and Dwayne and Lionel took from the houses. A man who wouldn't have tolerated anyone cheating on him. A man who would know how to kill.

He thought of what Roseanne had told him, that she couldn't remember what she might have said at Berta's or Ella's. She could have mentioned the barn when she was at Ella's, and Jerry Adams could have heard her and figured out where the two members of his burglary ring were hiding. It was Roseanne who could connect him to the barn.

But Roseanne didn't know any of it. She would trust Jerry Adams. She could let him in.

■ ■ ■ ■

Jerry Adams moved into the living room, caught the edge of the door with his boot, and slammed it behind him. "Shut up," he said, swiveling toward Aunt Martha. Then he looked at Roseanne. "You can't hide from me, no more than your friends could hide."

Roseanne could feel her tongue moving, the muscles in her throat twitching. Words bunched in her head, but no sound came. She swallowed hard and forced herself to lift her eyes from the gun. "What do you want?" she managed.

"I want what belongs to me," he said.

Aunt Martha let out a high-pitched scream, as if she had been struck by a hot poker.

"Shut up, you crazy old woman." Adams pointed the pistol at her, and for a moment, Roseanne thought Aunt Martha would drop to the floor. Instead she pressed both fists against her mouth. Her eyes had gone round with a mixture of fear and disbelief.

"I don't know what you're talking about," Roseanne said, but she was beginning to understand, little pieces fitting themselves together in her head, a picture taking shape.

The man was a killer. He had killed Hawk and Lookingglass, and she . . .

She felt sick to her stomach, the taste of acid in her mouth. Oh God, she was the one who had told Jerry Adams about the barn.

"I want the stuff that belongs to me," Adams said again, turning the gun on her. "You're gonna tell me where your friends stashed it."

"They weren't my friends."

"Don't lie to me!" he shouted, and Aunt Martha let out another squealing noise, muffled by her fists. "Don't make the mistake of thinking you can outsmart me. You showed up at Berta's party with Dwayne and Lionel after they killed Ned. I knew what they were up to the minute I heard they shot him. They found out he was holding out on them, stashing stuff for himself. Ned was like that, eager to get money for a ranch. Held out on all of us, and them two got wise. I figure Ned told 'em where he hid the stuff just before they shot him. That way, all the stuff was theirs, and they were dumb enough to think I'd never figure it out. Kept it in the barn for a while, then moved it someplace else. Now you're gonna tell me, Roseanne, where did they move it?"

"You killed them," Roseanne said. The

words had burst out on their own. Acid burned in her throat. Aunt Martha was whimpering, slump-shouldered, fists still pressed into her mouth. "You went to the barn and shot them."

"Where did they hide the stuff?" he said, his voice steady, the pistol an extension of his hand. "It won't do you any good." He gave a little laugh. "Where you gonna sell TVs and DVD players and cameras and jewelry? That's the same mistake Dwayne and Lionel made. What did they know about unloading that stuff? Ned, now, he was different. Smart, Ned was. He could figure it out. I almost admired him, challenging me that way, pretending he didn't want anything more to do with the burglary ring, saying he was gonna dance at the Sun Dance, become a good Arapaho, when all the time he was muscling me out. My buyers in Denver called me. They told me they got shorted. Dwayne and Lionel thought they could do the same. After all I did for them stupid cowpokes." He started shaking his head, a look of bemused grievance moving through his expression. "Hired 'em on the ranch, taught 'em everything they knew about ranching, gave 'em a chance to make some real money out of the big houses outside Lander and up in Jackson Hole, taking stuff people don't even remember they got. All they had to do was what I said. I handled the rest of it."

"I swear to you," Roseanne said, "I don't know anything. I wasn't even with Ned anymore. He was with that white girl."

"Don't lie!" he shouted. "You were with him for a long time. He told me he was trying to break up with that white girl. He never told her about the business. You're the only one that knew."

Roseanne stared at the man; she couldn't take her eyes away. He was going to shoot them both, and he would get away with it, just like he'd gotten away with killing Dwayne and Lionel. No one knew he was the leader of the burglary ring. An idea started to form in her mind, as flimsy as air. She struggled to grab hold of it, force it to make sense. She could pretend to take him to a hiding place, and then what? When there was nothing there, no TVs and cameras and jewels, he would shoot her. But she could gain time; there was always the chance that someone . . .

Aunt Martha let out a wild, piercing scream and darted for the door, like a bobcat desperate to get out of a trap, and in that instant, as Jerry Adams swung around, grabbed her and flung her against the wall,

Roseanne darted for the kitchen. She found herself crouched on the far side of the table, unaware of how she had gotten there or how the Colt came to be in her hands, steadied on top of the hard wooden seat of the chair, pointed toward the doorway. Her heart pounded in her ears. Aunt Martha was no longer wailing, and for an instant the quiet was like the quiet in a dark cave.

"Bitch!" Adams shouted. He was still in the living room, but she could hear him moving toward the doorway, coming closer. She gripped the pistol hard, her finger on the trigger. Then he filled up the doorway, waving the black gun into the kitchen.

The sound of a gunshot splintered the air as Father John drove over the dirt yard. He braked hard behind the dark truck and the pickup and got out. His heart was hammering. He was too late. Too late. And inside was a man with a gun.

He crouched down alongside the front of the house and ran for the corner. Then he made his way down the side, trying to see through the curtains in the windows. In the back, he worked toward the door and peered past the half-drawn shade into the kitchen. It took a moment before his eyes adjusted to the dim light inside and he could see beyond his own fear and dread. A man lay on his back in the doorway between the kitchen and the front of the house, a dark puddle of blood growing on his light-colored shirt. In the center of the kitchen, behind a kitchen chair, down on one knee, was Roseanne, both hands extended onto the chair seat, gripping a pistol.

He moved to the side of the door and knocked. "It's Father John," he called. He could hear the tightness in his voice. Dear Lord, the girl would be in shock. She could swing around and pull the trigger. "It's Father John," he said again. "Put the gun down, Roseanne. No one is going to hurt you. You're okay now." He waited a moment before he looked through the glass pane. The girl had set the gun on the table and was slumped on the floor. He reached for the knob, stepped into the kitchen. Crouching down beside her, he set a hand on her shoulder. He could feel the tremors coming from somewhere deep inside. "You're okay," he said again.

32

"It's over now." Elena stood guard in front of the stove, the coffeepot hoisted in one hand.

Father John pushed his mug across the table. The bishop had said Mass this morning and eaten breakfast before Father John had gotten downstairs. "I'll be praying for all of them," he'd told Father John last night. The old man had already gone to the office.

Father John watched the stream of black liquid spill out of the glass container. The coffee was hot, pungent and strong, the way he needed coffee this morning. He felt as if he hadn't slept at all, although he suspected he had probably dozed off in between getting up and looking out the window at the moonlight flooding the mission grounds and the wide strip of the Milky Way arching across the black sky. A noise had pulled him from bed, but there hadn't been anything unusual outside. He had crawled back into bed, tossed about in the tangle of sheets, and dozed, most likely. Then the noise had sounded again.

He had imagined it, he thought now. He must have been dreaming, a whole night of disjointed dreams that he couldn't remember.

"Outsiders, all of them." Glass clanked against plastic as Elena set the coffee pot in place. "That white man, Adams. Who invited him here, anyway? Them two Arapahos from Oklahoma. Why didn't they just stay home?"

Father John stirred some milk into the coffee and took a long sip. He waited for her to mention the white girl, but she seemed to have reached the end of her list of outsiders.

"Would've saved all of us trouble," she said. "Saved themselves, too. Now they're all dead, and we gotta go on and try to remember Ned the way he used to be, before he got mixed up with that crowd."

"It was the way he wanted to be again," Father John said. He finished the coffee, his thoughts on Ned. "Talk to me," he had said the last time Ned came to the mission, but Ned had turned away, and Father John knew that he would always carry that picture of Ned turning away and would always regret not having tried harder.

He finished the coffee, got to his feet and winked at Elena. A five-star breakfast, he told her. She rolled her eyes and shook her head. Walks-On was already at the front door as Father John walked down the hall, and he wondered how long the dog had been waiting. They went outside together. The morning air was already hot, filled with the smells of sage and moist grasses and wild roses. By the time he got to Circle Drive, Walks-On had found the Frisbee, trotted over and dropped it in front of him. Father John sent it sailing back across the field.

He watched the dog bound after the red disc, nose it out of a clump of tall grass, and head back. He tossed the Frisbee again, sending it farther this time. He tried to shake the uneasy feeling that had clamped itself onto him and refused to let go. "Come on, buddy," he called, as if the sound of his own voice, might push the feeling away. Then he hurried along the drive toward the administration building. The sky was a perfect blue, unmarred by any disturbance, and yet something was off. Two days ago he had found Elena mopping the linoleum in the guesthouse, the windows and doors thrown open. "Getting rid of the whiskey smell," she said, and he had taken her at her word, but now he wondered what other disquieting thing she had been trying to dispel.

The odd sense of unease seemed to back off a bit in the familiarity of the old building, the sun dancing on the stucco walls and the photos of past Jesuits lining the corridor. He could hear the tapping noise of computer keys, and he headed for the rear office.

He stopped in the doorway and waited. "Preparing Sunday's homily," the bishop said, looking up. "I intend to speak on the power of forgiveness, the way in which forgiveness frees us, while the lack of forgiveness holds us in bondage. Will that meet with your approval?" He motioned Father John toward the folding chair by the window.

"Whatever you wish to say would meet with my approval," Father John said. He was grateful the old man was here. He had so much experience; he understood so much.

"How is the girl?" the bishop said.

For an instant, Father John thought he was referring to Marcy Morrison. Then he realized he was inquiring about Roseanne.

"She's pretty shaken," he said.

"As well she should be. It means she's human," he said. His voice had gone quiet and reflective, and Father John wondered what the old man was looking back upon. "It is unnatural to kill another human being," the bishop said, "even when that person intends to kill you. It remains a haunting experience. I hope that in time, she will learn to forgive herself for what circumstances had forced her to do."

"She and her aunt have gone to Denver to stay with relatives for a while. It wouldn't surprise me if they decided to stay and make a new start."

"Good. Good." Sunlight shimmered in the old man's white hair. "It will call her back to herself, being with her own family."

"She's still grieving for Ned."

"When would you expect that to end?" The bishop gave a slow, inward smile. "She will eventually grow accustomed to the burden of her loss so that it will feel lighter." He took a moment, then said, "Unable to sleep again last night?"

"Thought I heard noises," Father John said. "It wasn't anything."

"You're thinking about her?"

Father John tried to keep his expression still. How much had the old man read in his mind, seen in his heart? He had been so careful. He had walled off the truth, kept it from everyone, even himself, most of the time.

"I'm not referring to *her*," the bishop said, "although she has reminded me of my friend in India. I still think of her. It was always platonic." He waved a hand between them, and Father John wondered if there was a hint of regret in the wave. "I pray for her every day, and I thank God for the time she was part of my life. Love is always a blessing, you know."

Father John kept his eyes on the bishop's for a moment, then looked away. He had an image of the years stretching ahead, like the calendar pages flipping in old movies, and every day he would pray for Vicky, wonder how she was, where she was, and he, an old man, sitting in an office somewhere, would tell some young priest that love was always a blessing. Not mentioning the pain.

"I haven't heard anything about Marcy Morrison," Father John said, carrying on as if they hadn't opened the cover of a book and glimpsed the meaning of the story inside. "I can't shake the feeling she's still around," he went on, struck by the illogical path he had headed down. It was the red pickup he had expected to see last night, curving around Circle Drive, heading toward the guesthouse. "People here still blame her somehow," he went on. "They think she brought trouble to the rez."

The bishop waited a moment before he said, "What do you think?"

"There's no evidence to tie her to Ned's murder."

"That wasn't my question."

"I'm not sure what to think," Father John said. "She was a chameleon. A different person at different times, a very good actress."

"Why did she leave the mission so abruptly?"

"She had a breakdown," Father John said, the image of the girl flailing about in front of him. "I tried to calm her. I told her that I thought she needed help."

The bishop nodded. "You had seen into the core of her, the part she was hiding. Naturally she wanted to get away. We always want to escape the prying eyes of those who see into our most secret places against our wishes. But as you say, there's no evidence to link her to a crime. This has been a trying time. So many senseless deaths, but death is always senseless. It casts a pale over everything, puts people off balance. No wonder you're tossing about at night, imagining all sorts of things. The girl has her own psychological problems, but that doesn't mean she will ever return to the mission. I suspect she is trying to run away from the sadness and loss she has experienced. She will find that is impossible, of course, but she's probably miles away."

"You're right," Father John said, getting to his feet. Marcy Morrison had run away. He stood in the doorway and went over the next couple of days' schedule with the bishop — the educational committee's elections for a new chairperson, the social committee meeting to discuss a possible fundraiser to purchase supplies for the kids before school started in the fall. Then he walked down the corridor to his own office, trying to convince himself of the logic in what the bishop had said. The Sun Dance would take place next week. The people would come together and pray, and things would begin to return to normal. Still, the uneasy feeling followed him, like the bespectacled eyes in the portraits along the walls.

The yellow police tape flapped in front of the small yellow house. Vicky stepped over the tape and tried the front door. Locked. She followed the tape around to the back door, and this time the knob turned in her hand. The door creaked into the dingy kitchen with cabinet doors hanging open and plates, cereal cartons, and newspapers scattered over the counters. She made her way into the living room. The sofa cushions had been upended, the drawers in the cabinet and tables were open, crumbled sheets of paper poking over the tops. A couple of chairs lay on their sides.

She headed down the hallway, stopping to peer into the two bedrooms. Mattresses pulled off the beds, linens tossed about, drawers open, and clothes and towels on the floor. A dark blackish stain spread over the center of one mattress. "Everything's on the table," Gianelli had said. She could hear his voice in her head, see the way he had watched Marcy Morrison while he interviewed her. He had always suspected her, she realized. And he and the Wind River Police had done a thorough job of searching the house for the murder weapon, but they hadn't known where to look.

She crossed the hall into the small bathroom with the yellow shower curtain tossed in the tub. On a ledge above the sink was an electric shaver, a bottle of aftershave, and a black comb that had probably belonged to Ned. She opened the cabinet and stared at the shelves, empty except for a bottle of aspirin. There was no hint of

Marcy Morrison, no feminine combs or brushes or lipsticks. She got down on one knee and studied the wall behind the pipes that jutted from the toilet. Nothing but the sameness of the white wall. She felt a sense of relief. She had taken a chance, crossing the police tape, walking through a crime scene, suspecting that her own client had hidden the murder weapon. And she was wrong.

Then she spotted the thin lines in the wallboard on the far side of the toilet, as faint as a spiderweb. She had to get on both knees to reach around the toilet and push on the wallboard within the lines. The piece broke free and fell forward. Inside the wall, was a small space big enough to hide a gun, but there was nothing there.

33

The Sun Dance grounds spread below, a field of white tipis shimmering in the sun. From the rise, Vicky could make out the brush shades scattered among the tipis with cottonwood saplings piled up the walls and over the roofs. There were corridors of shade on the grounds, a hum of activity. She could hear a baby crying. This was how it was in the Old Time, she thought. Villages scattered about the vastness of the plains, and where the plains buckled and lifted themselves, a warrior would stand guard. She knew the stories. They ran in her blood.

She followed the road downhill and left the Jeep at the far edge of the parking area. Thursday evening, the beginning of the Sun Dance, and people stirring about, little groups flowing around the tipis toward the center of the grounds. She hurried along with the others. The lodge poles that would be pushed up to the center pole lay in a circle around it, the bark and branches stripped, the cream-colored meat exposed. A line had started to form, and people had begun moving toward the poles. Everyone carried strips of fabric — reds, blues, yellows, greens, whites — and one by one, they leaned over and tied the fabric around one of the lodge poles. Each piece was a prayer flag, a sign of the prayers that would be offered during the Sun Dance.

She had brought her favorite scarf, red with a blue, green and yellow design, the colors of her people. She shook out the folds as she approached a lodge pole, then stooped over and tied on the scarf. *Take care of Ned Windsong. Let him be with the ancestors.*

She stepped back and watched the line dipping and swaying until each pole was nearly obscured by the thick, colorful prayer flags. Annie was near the end of the line, pushing her two children ahead. She leaned back to reassure Roger who stayed close behind her, looking awkward with a piece of fabric in oranges and violets draped over his hands. They had been back in the office two days now, and everything had returned to normal, all the office rhythms restored, as if a man named Robin Bosey had never appeared. The Lander Police had arrested Robin before he'd gotten to the boundary of the reservation the morning he had burst into the office. An hour later, Annie had gotten the news and packed the kids. She and Roger were home by mid-afternoon. Robin was still in the Fremont County Jail awaiting transportation to the prison in Rawlins, but someday he would be free, Vicky knew. Annie knew it, too, she realized, watching Annie bend over to tie her fabric and help the children tie on theirs. Annie looked up and gave Vicky a little wave.

A hand brushed her shoulder, and she knew from the touch that John O'Malley had come up behind her even before she heard him say, "How are you?"

She turned and faced him. "I'm okay." She smiled up at the handsome, sunburned face, the blue eyes, and crinkly laugh lines under the rim of his tan cowboy hat. "You were right, you know."

"Not about everything," he said.

"I haven't seen Roseanne. How is she doing?"

"She and her aunt Martha went to Denver to stay with relatives." He nodded toward an area across the grounds where, Vicky knew, the Birdwoman family had camped for years. It was a small, vacant space. "The

Sun Dance would have been hard without Ned," he said. "Maybe she'll find peace being with family." He took a moment before he went on. "I've talked to Gianelli. Roseanne won't be charged. She shot Adams in self-defense, and her aunt witnessed the whole thing. Adams would have killed them both. He was carrying the 9mm Beretta that he used to kill Hawk and Lookingglass."

"Well, you were certainly right about the mastermind in the burglary ring." Vicky gave him a smile. "Adams was close to bankruptcy a year ago, at least that's what the moccasin telegraph says. He must have gotten the idea to save his ranch by robbing empty houses. Hawk and Lookingglass were working on the ranch, so he brought them in. Trouble was, they ran into alarm systems."

"And his wife's nephew was an electrician who knew how to circumvent alarm systems." Father John shook his head. "Ned wanted his own ranch more than anything else. The thing is, he didn't like burglarizing houses. It put him out of balance."

He glanced in the direction of the center pole, and Vicky followed his gaze. At least two dozen men were lifting the pole upright. They hoisted it across the ground a few feet, dropped the end into a hole, and braced the pole in place. They would construct the Sun Dance Lodge now by building the side walls and pushing up the poles covered with prayer flags to the center pole, like the rafters of an open-air roof. "Ned should have been here," he said.

Vicky waited, and after a moment, he went on. "Gianelli thinks that after they broke into a number of houses around Lander, Adams decided to move the operation to Jackson Hole, where he could make bigger hauls by breaking into fewer homes. So he talked Ned into moving there and used an old army connection to get him a job that would get him inside the houses."

She started walking, and Father John stayed beside her. Other people trailed past, heading for the camps. He said, "I think Ned wanted out before he went to Jackson Hole. It's possible Adams let him think he could make a clean start there."

"Then drew him back in?" Vicky said. Ned was a good electrician, she was thinking. He could have kept the job in Jackson as long as he wanted. Eventually he might have saved enough money for a down payment on a ranch.

"Adams knew how to play him." Out of the corner of her eye, she could see John O'Malley shaking his head. "A few more break-ins, some expensive items, and Ned could get his ranch. He wouldn't have to wait any longer. According to Gianelli, Adams had connections in Denver where he sold the stolen goods. Every month, Hawk and Lookingglass drove a ranch truck loaded with stolen goods to a warehouse. There was every opportunity to hold out on him, and Adams knew it." He waited a moment before he went on, "A falling out of thieves, Gianelli called it. Hawk and Lookingglass shot Ned, and Adams shot them."

Vicky kept to the side of the road, John O'Malley in step beside her. Ella's camp was ahead. She could see the woman's head bobbing about the brush shade, Ned's relatives and friends gathered around. "They think I took the part of the outsider," she said, nodding in the direction of the camp.

"You tried to protect your client's rights," John O'Malley said. "Everyone here would expect you to do the same for them. Ella knows that. She asked me to invite you to supper."

"Does she still believe Marcy was involved in Ned's murder?"

It was a moment before John O'Malley answered. She could sense the thoughts turning in his head. "Maybe she'll always think so," he said. "She called Marcy 'Niatha' and said she was as clever as a spider. Have you heard from her?"

Vicky shook her head. "Even her father has no idea of where she is. But he can find her, he told me. All he has to do is cut off her credit cards and close the bank account, and she'll call him." She walked on for a moment, then turned toward him again. "As long as there isn't a scandal that would affect the Glory and Success Ministry, and Marcy stays out of trouble, I doubt he'll do anything."

The sun had started to drop, an orange ball flaring over the mountains and bathing the peaks in orange light. The western sky was a tapestry of oranges, reds, and magentas that reflected in the white tipis. Now, Vicky knew, after months of preparing the dancers, the Sun Dance grandfathers would begin feeding their Sun Dance grandsons and their families. When they had eaten, the dancers would gather their bedrolls and line up outside the lodge. They would enter the lodge as their names were called. It would take a while, she knew. She remembered Sun Dances when the last dancer wasn't placed inside the lodge until after midnight. Then the drums and singers would start. And every morning for the next three days, the dancers would line up at their places inside the lodge, face the opening to the east, and dance as the sun rose. People would come from across the camp and stand outside the lodge. At first there would be the complete silence of the plains, but the moment the sun had fully risen, the women would begin to tremolo. Then the people would return to their camps. And on Sunday evening, the dancers would face the West as they waited for the evening star. Then they would dance out of the lodge.

Most of the crowd was back in the camps now, getting ready for the evening meal, Vicky knew. She was quiet, conscious of John O'Malley beside her. She wondered what he thought, this white man from another place, another past. "I think Ella's right," she said finally. Then she told him what Larry Morrison had said. How Marcy had taken his .380-caliber SIG P232 and hidden it inside the bathroom wall, how he had found the hiding place after she left for Denver, and how the pistol was gone.

"But there isn't any evidence she was involved," he said. "Gianelli is convinced that either Hawk or Lookingglass got rid of the pistol after Ned was shot."

Vicky took a moment before she told him about going to Ned's house yesterday. "I found the place in the bathroom where

Marcy cut out a small piece of wallboard. The space behind it was big enough to hold a gun."

"What are you saying?"

"She hid the pistol along with the latex gloves she must have used. I think Ned had wanted to break up with her. I think he must have told her she had to leave. She lives for revenge, her father said. He feared she had intended to kill him and his wife." Vicky glanced over at one of the camps, the people milling about, children running around. "He told me she used to hurt herself," she went on. "Bang her head against the wall, knock herself unconscious. She knew how to do it."

John O'Malley stepped away, then turned back, eyes narrowed in comprehension. "She could have gone to Ned's house for the gun and the gloves the night she left the mission," he said. "She was probably worried that sooner or later Gianelli would find them. She's destroyed them by now. There won't be any evidence to link her to Ned's murder." He paused, keeping his gaze on her. "The case is closed, Vicky."

"She left the mission because of you," Vicky said. The ground seemed to shift under her feet, and an icy feeling cut through her. "She knew you would put things together. If you heard that she had stolen her father's pistol, you would inform Gianelli. You were the one who saw into her, John. She knows that you know what she's capable of." She put a hand on his forearm. Beneath the thin cotton of his sleeve, she could feel the knots of his muscles. She could not imagine what she would do if anything were to happen to him.

"Are you certain she hasn't come back to the mission?" She caught the way he hesitated, and she pushed on. "She has, hasn't she? She's still out there," she said, her voice barely a whisper. "She's somewhere, and she knows that you know her. She knows that sooner or later you'll know what she did."

John O'Malley was quiet a long moment. Finally he placed his hand over hers and held it, as if it wanted to reassure her. "Ella's waiting on supper," he said.

ABOUT THE AUTHOR

Margaret Coel is the *New York Times* bestselling, award-winning author of the acclaimed novels featuring Father John O'Malley and Vicky Holden, as well as several works of nonfiction. Originally a historian by trade, she is considered an expert on the Arapaho Indians. A native of Colorado, she resides in Boulder. Her website address is www.margaretcoel.com.

We hope you have enjoyed this Large Print book. Other Thorndike, Wheeler, Kennebec, and Chivers Press Large Print books are available at your library or directly from the publishers.

For information about current and upcoming titles, please call or write, without obligation, to:

Publisher
Thorndike Press
295 Kennedy Memorial Drive
Waterville, ME 04901
Tel. (800) 223-1244

or visit our Web site at:

http://gale.cengage.com/thorndike

OR

Chivers Large Print
published by AudioGO Ltd
St James House, The Square
Lower Bristol Road
Bath BA2 3SB
England
Tel. +44(0) 800 136919
www.audiogo.co.uk

All our Large Print titles are designed for easy reading, and all our books are made to last.